CHASTITY HOAR: MY LIFE

CHASTITY HOAR: MY LIFE

George Evans

*To Nancy – many
thanks for your support.*

George

iUniverse, Inc.
New York Lincoln Shanghai

Chastity Hoar: My Life

iUniverse books may be ordered through booksellers or by contacting:

iUniverse
2021 Pine Lake Road, Suite 100
Lincoln, NE 68512
www.iuniverse.com
1-800-Authors (1-800-288-4677)

This is a work of fiction. All of the characters, names, incidents, organizations and dialogue in this novel are either the products of the author's imagination or are used fictitiously.

ISBN-13: 978-0-595-40303-5 (pbk)
ISBN-13: 978-0-595-84679-5 (ebk)
ISBN-10: 0-595-40303-4 (pbk)
ISBN-10: 0-595-84679-3 (ebk)

Printed in the United States of America

For Marion K. Stocking
wonderful teacher
who, 50 years ago,
pointed me to
the road here taken

CHAPTER 1

It all started over forty years ago, in the New World, with my name. Mother had the bad fortune to marry in haste, for she was well along with me. It was either marry in haste or tarry at the whipping post, the penalty for fornication. Unfortunately, the man she was lying with was better at loving than he was at naming. His name was Leonard Hoar, and when my mother married him, barely saving herself from twenty lashes at the post, she became Mary Hoar.

The magistrates, who were always curious about early births, summoned her to court, wondering at the closeness of her marriage and my birth. They addressed her first as Mary Hoar. When there was snickering in the court, they realized what they had said, and corrected themselves, now calling her Goodwife Hoar. This was little better than Mary Hoar, so they simply called her "woman." "Woman, you've been summoned." Or, "Woman, how is it that your child so quickly sprang from you, fully formed?" "I have a name," Mother replied; "I know not this woman you address."

The magistrates knew that it was customary to name the person summoned, that it was highly irregular at the court to address the man or woman as "Man" or Woman," and were afraid to be called on their breaching the rules. Besides, they had a more serious case of hog stealing in which the hog stealer claimed that the man he stole from had called his wife "a lewd drab" and "a pernicious trull," and losing his hogs was a fair punishment for the slander of his wife. The other man claimed that every man in the neighborhood had lain with her, so it was no false name she was called.

The magistrates, eager for the next case and tired of wondering how to call my mother, set her free, demanding only that she post a bond for her good behavior in the future. Mother refused to pay it, and the magistrates summoned her again, but this time they had further charges.

That was my first acquaintance with the court. "Woman," they said, "we have heard you do mock this court and your husband."

"I have never done so," she replied.

Mother told me later that she sought only to overturn my father. Or rather, to overturn his name, which was now hers.

"Your husband has opposed the name you chose for the child, and he is master of the family," they said.

Apparently Father wanted to call me Rachel, after his dead mother.

But Mother had other ideas. She named me Chastity, so I become Chastity Hoar. She thought a good first name would outweigh a bad last one, as a hog outweighs a chicken. Unfortunately, she never asked my opinion, for I'm neither hog nor chicken.

I preferred Rachel.

"Her name will draw men as mice to tallow," Father said.

"Nonsense," Mother said. "It will send them away as well as your musket."

Father did use his musket, but not on the boys. Instead, he used it on wild turkeys on the way to the Boston meeting house on Corn Hill Road and King Street several blocks away. "Wait, daughter," Father would cry. Then he'd shoot a wild turkey and on his return retrieve it, if it hadn't already been retrieved by a fox or a hungry hawk. The ministers would have preferred he shoot wild savages, as they called the Indians, but Father shot only the birds.

It was at the meeting house where I first met the Reverend John Wilson, pastor at the church. He would fill the air with dead words that stretched to the horizon and back, or, rather, to the bottom of the hourglass and back, as he turned it over. In those days I prayed for deliverance from that hourglass, wishing it to fall and be broken forever.

It was also at the meeting house where I first met Mistress Anne and her young friend. I was dreaming, as I often did in those days, of running free in the fields around our house. Suddenly, I heard a commotion, such as I had never heard before in the meeting house. I turned my head and saw a woman stand on the woman's side and shout at the preacher. "You speak not the truth," she cried. "I will not listen to these Popish lies."

The Reverend Wilson stopped and stared at her. Who is this woman, I thought, that has saved us from the preacher? I would like to meet her. The woman turned her back on the preacher. Then other women along the wall followed her example, all of them facing the door, their backs to Reverend Wilson. Their husbands, on the other side, only scowled. What was possessing their wives?

When the reverend began speaking again, pretending as if nothing had happened, the woman walked out of the meeting house. Another woman, much younger, joined her, and then several others followed outside, passing by the stocks and pillory as they did. I feared for the women because I already knew that turning your back or speaking hard words to a man, especially a preacher, was a terrible sin. Of course, Mother would often do that to Father when she was angry with him, but that was another matter.

I turned to look at Mother, wondering what she was thinking. She was not standing with the other women, but I thought she wanted to. Perhaps she was protecting me, thinking that a Mary Hoar turning her back on the preacher and then walking out on him would bring grief to both of us. It didn't matter, though. We both found grief enough even though we remained until the last grain of sand had fallen through the hourglass neck, shortly before the last of the congregation had dropped to the dirt floor, exhausted from two hours of hellfire and damnation.

"Who was the woman?" I asked Mother after the service ended.

Mother looked around, afraid she'd be overheard. Father walked ahead, more interested in finding a wild turkey.

"I'd rather not say."

Of course telling me that made me more curious and determined.

"If you don't tell me, I'll ask her myself."

She looked at me, frowning at my threat. "All right. But promise you'll say nothing."

I thought the woman must have been a witch and to say her name would mean that Mother was a witch and then I'd be one too. I should have been worried, but I wasn't.

Mother sighed and finally gave in. "Her name is…Mistress Anne Hutchinson."

Mother took my arm and squeezed it. "There, I've told you. Now hear me, child. Do not ask more about her."

I walked along the road, stepping in the puddles from yesterday's rain and considering her request. Finally, I asked, "Who was the young woman who followed her? She seemed little older than me."

"Your curiosity, child, will bring you pain. Ask no more."

I was still young, though, and thought her silence foolishness. "I'll ask her myself then," I threatened.

"All right, all right. You pester like the mosquitoes. I believe it was Mistress Mary Dyer. Now, I've said all I'm going to say."

"Is one of them a witch, then?" I asked, much too loudly.

Mother gasped and pulled me to her, holding me by the shoulders and speaking as sharply as she could. "Do not say that ever, child! Women have been hanged for less, much less. Do you understand me? Never. Never speak that word against women. Promise me."

She frightened me she was so intense. "All right, I promise, Mother."

She relaxed her grip and we resumed walking, but I knew she was troubled. "Our name," she said, "which your Father unwisely gave to us, is quite enough of a problem." She said that loud enough that Father, still searching for his turkey, could have heard her. If he did, he didn't pay any attention. Turkeys were more important to him than names.

I thought about what she said. "You didn't have to take the name. You didn't have to marry him."

"Silly child. And where would you be if I hadn't married him?"

I didn't have an answer for that. But it didn't make me any less curious.

I wanted to meet that woman—and the younger one who followed her. I wanted to meet all of them. What could have driven them to turn their backs on the minister and walk out of the church?

It was then I noticed a strange thing. Mother had had enough of my questions and didn't want to attend afternoon services, but I reminded her we would be missed and charged with the absence. So she relented, and we walked the path again to the meeting house. This time Father stayed home, saying he had quite enough piety for one day. He had better ways to spend his time.

It was a different minister who spoke at the afternoon services. His name was Reverend John Cotton, and though he spoke at length, I liked his voice and his manner. He was a pleasant man to look at.

But this is what was strange. Mistress Anne and Mistress Mary were sitting on the same bench as we were, not far away. I watched them out of the corner of my eye, making sure that Mother was looking the other way, and both of them never moved. They didn't stand up, they didn't say anything, they just sat there, listening to every word he spoke, as if they were sipping the sweetest of wines.

After the service, not far from the door, I moved closer to the women. Standing near the scaffold and the pillory, I heard the older one, Mistress Anne, say to her friend, "His words touch the heart. They fill me with a tender joy." "Aye," her friend said, "for me as well." Then they moved away, joined by other women, and I watched them, arm in arm, walk toward their homes. If they are witches, I thought, they are happy witches. I wanted to be like them.

A few days later in the marketplace I encountered a friendly-looking older woman, her head covered in a dark hood.

"Ma'am?"

"Yes, child."

"Would you know where Mistress Hutchinson lives?"

She frowned at me. "Why do you ask that, child?"

"I wish to speak with her."

She looked me over carefully. "Are you troubled?" she asked, looking curiously at my body.

"Oh, no, ma'am."

"You're sure?"

"Yes, ma'am." Of course I had troubles like everyone else, but I didn't think she meant that.

"Why do you seek her then?"

I began to wonder if this woman was a secret witch and testing me. I didn't dare say that though.

"I saw her at the meeting house last Sabbath. She seemed...a fine woman. I only wish to speak with her."

The woman didn't say anything. She seemed to be considering whether to tell me more. Why was everyone so careful in speaking of the bold woman in the church? The secrecy made me more curious. I knew I had to find her, whatever the danger.

"Do you know where she lives?" I asked again.

Again the woman said nothing for the longest time. "Are you sure you have no hidden reasons for seeking her?"

"Yes, ma'am, I'm sure." Of course, I wasn't sure of anything except I wanted to see her.

"Well, you seem an honest girl. I'll tell you then. She lives across the street from me."

"Where is that, ma'am?"

"On School Street. Near Corn Hill. You pass by daily, girl, if you come from the south."

"Isn't that where the governor lives?"

"Across the street."

"But you said you live across the street."

"Yes. I do."

"You're a servant, then?"

"Sometimes I think so," she laughed. She saw the puzzlement on my face. "I'm Margaret Winthrop," she said, touching my hand.

"Oh, my." I was speaking to the governor's wife. Mother had warned me about her, and also about the governor. She said he was a harsh man, whose rules were passed down from Heaven. At least that's what everyone thought. And this woman was his wife, so she would be much like him.

She must have seen the concern on my face. "Don't worry, child, I'm only his wife. That means little these days." She turned away when she said that, as if she didn't mean to and wanted to swallow the words before they reached my ears.

But they did reach my ears. I've never forgotten them.

"If you wish to see Mistress Hutchinson at this time of day, you will probably find her at the spring."

"At the spring? Thank you, ma'am. I'm obliged."

I left the governor's wife and walked quickly to the spring, which was not far from the marketplace.

There I saw her, watching as several other women were dipping their pails into the gushing water. One of them was the younger woman, Mistress Mary Dyer, who had followed Mistress Anne out of the meeting house. They were engaged in lively talk.

I approached them slowly, not knowing what to say or do. After all, they could be witches, meeting to plan someone's terrible affliction.

I stood there watching them as they filled their buckets with water and their ears with joyful talk. Mistress Hutchinson laughed often, and the others laughed at her words.

Then one of the women saw me standing there, mute as if I had no tongue. "Look, Anne," one of them said. "We have a visitor."

Mistress Anne turned to me. "Hello, child," she said. "I see no pails. Have you come for more than water?"

I said nothing, not knowing what to say.

One of the older women, wearing a blue cape, approached me, frowning. "One of Winthrop's spies," she grumbled. "They're getting desperate."

"Is that true, child?" Mistress Anne asked. "You spy for the governor?" She tried to look stern, but she couldn't suppress a smile.

I was beginning to think they *were* witches, and I shouldn't be meddling in such business.

"They seek us out wherever we go," the blue-caped woman said. "Is it not enough they send spies to your house, Anne? Truly, they mean us harm."

I could see I wasn't wanted and was about to leave when Mistress Anne touched me on the shoulder. "I don't believe it," she said. "Child, tell us the governor hasn't sent you."

"But he did," I said without thinking.

The women were suddenly quiet.

"Is this true?" she wondered.

"Well, his wife did. I mean, she directed me to find you here."

Mistress Anne smiled. "Well, that is an entirely different matter. Margaret is a good woman who would join us if she weren't married to that man who rules us like a king. He imprisons her in an iron cage that our men seem to think appropriate for their women."

"Not my husband," the young woman, Mary Dyer, protested. "William's a good man who grants me much freedom."

"Aye, my William as well," Mistress Anne said, reaching out to her friend. "I speak more of the magistrates and governor. And that black-hearted Wilson, who tries my patience each Sabbath."

She turned to me again. "Well, our young friend, if you don't come here for the pure water, sweet as the finest honey, do you come for pure thoughts?"

"No ma'am."

"No?" She seemed amused. "Impure thoughts, then?"

"Oh, no, not those either."

"Because if you did, you need go no farther than some of the houses where a woman's time has come. The women's words will make you blush. On the other hand, if you want pure thoughts of God's gift of Grace, you should visit some of us when we discuss the sermon of the week. Not John Wilson's you may be sure. But John Cotton's, the good Lord's gift to us. Which is it, child?"

I didn't know what to say. She talked so fast, gesturing with her hands as if she were leading a choir, that the words flew off like birds in the treetops. I couldn't catch them and had no net to slow them down.

"Confused, are you?" she asked. "Well, that's no worse than some of us are these days. Why don't you do both? I'm taking this water to Goody Johnson's house shortly. Would you care to join me?"

"Yes, ma'am."

"I should warn you, though. Midwives are thought to be the Devil's disciples, stealing the baby for his secret rites. Are you of stout heart?"

"Yes, ma'am."

That's what I said, but that's not what I thought. I should have said that my heart was more like a soft pumpkin left too long in the autumn fields.

"Good...good. Now, tell us your name. I believe I've seen you and your mother at the meeting house."

"Yes, ma'am. Mother thinks it best we go, though Father is often disposed to do other things. He's not inclined to have the magistrates meddling in his life, he says. Let them tend their cattle, and he'll tend his."

"Ah, yes," she said, amused at this admission. "Some of us would agree with your father."

"Yes, ma'am. I noted that last Sabbath."

"I trust the Reverend Wilson also took note."

"He did, ma'am. But he continued on until our stomachs complained they were abused."

"Error knows no limits," she said, looking at her friends. "We learned that in the old world and we learn it anew in this one." She looked sad at that. But the sadness passed quickly. "I don't believe you've told us your name yet," she said, lightly touching my shoulder.

"No ma'am. It's Rachel. Rachel Brewer."

"Rachel Brewer is it? Well, I'm pleased to meet you, Rachel Brewer. I don't recognize the name." She held out her hand, and I took it.

The older woman spoke up. "Your name is not your mother's then?"

"Yes, ma'am," I lied. But I knew it was no use. I had not yet learned the useful art of lying.

I was terribly sorry to have lied to these friendly women. They all were watching me, wondering if the lie would stick on my tongue. It did.

"Rachel's not my real name," I blurted out. "My name...is Chastity."

"Chastity what?" one of them asked.

"Chastity...Hoar," I swallowed.

Seeing my discomfort, Mistress Anne took me by the shoulder and looked deeply in my eyes. "Never be ashamed of your name, Chastity. A name is merely an adornment; it is no measure of the person who carries it."

"Yes, ma'am. Thank you."

"But if you prefer, those of us here will call you Rachel."

"I'd appreciate that, ma'am."

"All right, then. For today, you're Rachel. A strong Biblical name," she smiled. "And how old are you, Rachel?"

"I'm sixteen, ma'am."

"Ah, a good age. I have a daughter myself, Bridget, about your age. She watches the younger ones when I'm busy with the women in their travail." She paused and closed her eyes. "Another one, Elizabeth, would be about your age. Sweet child, she lies in England, abandoned by her parents, God help us." She turned away when she said that, and was comforted by her friends. None of them said anything for several minutes, and I felt uncomfortable, not knowing what to say or do.

Finally, Mistress Anne turned back to me. Her friends stood next to her, waiting for her words. She shook her head and spoke softly. "We were told it was the parents' sin that the child died young. 'Look to yourselves to find that sin and root it out,' they said. So they still preach, the Reverend Wilson and the others. I know not what that sin was. The word rolls easily off the lips of these men who don't know the pain that comes with losing a child before its time."

Suddenly, she shook off the dark thoughts and was herself again. "Well, enough of that. We have work to do. Will you accompany me to Goody Johnson's, child? We can begin instruction in helping women during their travail."

"I will, ma'am." I would have accompanied her to hell itself if she had asked me, such was her power over me.

Just then one of the women whispered, "Quiet. He's lurking."

We looked up and saw, standing next to a small tree, the Reverend Wilson, dressed in a flowing black robe. None of us had seen him approaching.

Mistress Anne drew herself up like a cat facing a menacing dog, "Can we not draw water without your everlasting spying?"

"If your thoughts are pure as the water, you have nothing to fear by my presence," he said. "But I suspect they're not."

Mistress Anne approached the minister, anger flashing from her eyes. "Those with impure thoughts think to find them in others. Examine the mote in your own eye, Reverend Wilson, before you find the specks in ours."

"You quote Scripture to your own purposes, Mistress Hutchinson. I'm told you do that frequently in the secret meetings at your house."

"We seek merely to understand the texts given us each Sabbath."

I was amazed to see her confronting the Reverend Wilson as if he were another woman, as if he weren't an important man in the colony whose voice was listened to by the magistrates.

"I'm told you seek more than that," he said, not turning away from her.

Both of them stood their ground, the small cat, its back and fur raised, and the menacing black dog, towering over the little cat, making as if it would swallow it in a single gulp.

"I seek only the truth. That it make us free."

"Free, is it? Yes, free to sow the seeds of dissension throughout the colony. Before you came among us three years ago, there was peace in the colony. Now there is disharmony at every meeting. You turn your back on God's word in the meeting house and seduce others to follow you. Mistress Hutchinson, I speak for many of us."

"You speak for no one but yourself," she fired at him.

"I speak for the governor himself. I speak for the magistrates. I speak for the church. Mistress Hutchinson, I warn you. We are of one mind on this. You have planted disorder's seed, and it grows unchecked. Disorder is the Devil's seed, and those who reap it will reap the whirlwind."

She still didn't back down. I had never seen a woman attack a man in this way, not even my mother when she was angry with my father, as she often was.

"If there is a whirlwind, it is you who have brought it on us. You preach your own laws, not God's. You preach the letter, not the spirit. You cannot feel the spirit because your heart is frozen in the laws. Mind you, John Wilson, you bring God's wrath upon us all with your teaching!"

"You speak as a woman," the reverend replied as if he were speaking to a child.

"Indeed," Mistress said. "I'm amazed one so blind should see what is so plainly obvious to everyone."

Reverend Wilson was getting red in the face, and it was not from the hot sun burning down on us. "It was Woman who fell to the snares of Satan," he snarled, "and for that weakness we've all been punished. It is not meet you should expound on Scriptures or turn your back on God's word."

At that, she turned her back on John Wilson and returned to us. "Let us not waste our day with him," she said. "We will spend our time with the women who need us, their men being too busy with other matters to hear their cries."

Reverend Wilson heard her and responded quickly. "Those other matters you speak of, Mistress Hutchinson, have found you derelict of duty."

"And what are they?" she responded, turning back to him.

"You know well what they are. Every family was required to send one of its own to protect the colony from the savages who kill us at every opportunity. I have just returned myself as chaplain to our brave men. The cowards from your family were nowhere to be seen."

Anne was furious, so angry I thought she'd strike him. "I'll send none of my children to murder the innocent in the name of God. You shame us in using God's name for such unspeakable acts of cruelty."

"It was your duty as citizen of this colony."

"Don't speak of duty to me, John Wilson! You sugar the word to hide the blood you have spilled. These men and women were guilty of no more than worshipping a different God. May the good Lord forgive you for their murder. Because I will never forgive you."

She was about to move away, but in her anger she didn't see the buckets of water at her feet. She kicked one over, and the water seeped into the earth. She tripped and fell to her knees, crying softly.

"Even the water rejects you," the minister said, pleased that he now had the advantage.

Mistress Anne had slightly hurt herself in falling. But as the minister was turning away in triumph, from her knees she spoke to him again. "Even your wife rejected you," she said. "For five long years. You had to drag her from England against her will."

Those words struck him dumb, and he turned away quickly and left us, mumbling something we couldn't hear.

"That man will bring us grief, Anne," the young woman, Mary Dyer, said.

"Aye, he will do his best," Anne said, rising to her feet. "That is the only road he knows. He will walk it whatever pain it brings."

She turned to me. "Let us wash ourselves of that man's stench by bringing some relief to Goody Johnson." She looked at me closely because I had backed away from her fury. She spoke more quietly now. "You see what we face each day, child. We bear the travails of our children…and our men. It is much to bear, like this hot sun." Then she smiled. "Do you weaken in your desire to follow me?"

"No, ma'am," I said. "I will follow you."

And so I did. That's when it really started.

CHAPTER 2

I was alone with Anne, for so she begged me call her, as we walked to Goody Johnson's house somewhat south of the Common and close to Fox Hill and the marsh, which was noted for its mosquitoes. The bay was close by, its waters calm in the summer heat. Not so my new friend, who stirred whatever waters she touched.

We walked briskly, killing mosquitoes as we went.

"Surely these pests have mistaken us for the Reverend Wilson," she said, swatting one on her face. "I cannot think the good Lord meant to torment us in this way."

"Perhaps the good Lord is like my father," I said. "He seldom sees what I'm doing."

"Hmm. Perhaps I should raise the question next Sabbath day, and let the good Reverend Wilson wrestle with the matter. Does the Lord watch all his creatures, big or small? And if he is so pleased with this city upon the hill, as the authorities tell us, how is it the mosquitoes plague us day and night?"

I thought about that. Did God watch every mosquito, swarming about us in greater numbers than stars in the heavens? If he did, what meaning did he send with each one? But if he didn't watch them all, then perhaps he didn't watch everything we did. It was a great puzzlement.

"I hope we're in time," Anne said, touching a pocket she had tied to her waist.

"Before the baby—"

"Before the old women work on her. They mean well, but they are more trouble than the mosquitoes."

"Mosquitoes bring only pain."

"Just so their remedies. One of the women told me once that to relieve labor pain, one should remove a lock of a virgin's hair, the virgin being half the age of the woman in labor, then cut it into small pieces, mix in twelve ants' eggs dried in an oven, and feed it to the woman with a quarter of a pint of red cow's milk or strong ale wort. Lord, Lord, the remedy is worse than the pain."

I grimaced at the thought. I didn't like the ants that were everywhere in our kitchen, and I certainly wouldn't eat their eggs. What if they hatched in my stomach and ants were crawling inside of me? And if they needed air, they might start crawling out my nose or ears or mouth, and what would boys think, seeing the ants crawling on my lips?

Anne looked at me and laughed. "The thought doesn't appeal to you? You may be sure that when your time comes, I'll have better remedies."

"What is it you would use?" I wondered, expecting something like what was inflicted on my mother when she had me. Mother said an old woman filled an iron pot with toads, heated them over a fire, and then ground them into a fine powder which she administered to her in a tankard of beer. Ever since I've hated toads, thinking they were somehow a part of me. The beer was another matter though.

"I have them in my pocket here," Anne said. "Pennyroyal, basil, mint-flavored dittany, a good quantity of saffron, burdock, fennel, dill, and many more. All flavored, of course, with a strong dose of love for those whose hard lives are so bereft of any softness."

Just ahead we saw Goody Johnson's house, which was much like our own and not more than ten minutes from where Mother was probably wondering where I was.

As we approached the house, a man stood in the door. It was Goodman Johnson, her husband. He seemed worried—and not from the biting pests. Something else was eating him.

"Her labor begins," he said. "I didn't know what to do."

"Are the women here?" Anne asked.

"Yes, ma'am. But they wait for you."

"Good, then be on your way. You'll not be needed."

The man was gone before we were in the door, thinking to be as far away as he could safely manage. This was a woman's business, and he wanted no part of it. He had already done his part in bringing his woman to bed.

Inside, several women greeted us. Some of them I had seen in the marketplace but not at Sabbath services. Goody Johnson was in bed in a small, dark room at the back.

I sat on the floor while the other women sat on blocks of wood.

Anne put the water over a small fire in the fireplace and then went to help Goody Johnson, who was quietly moaning.

The women instructed me as if I were to be next in labor.

"Take care, girl," a large woman said, "that you not raise your arms over your head. Not even to hang clothes or daub clay on your walls."

"Why is that?" I wondered.

"The cord will be twisted, and so will the child if it grows."

Later I thought about that advice. Perhaps it explained why my life was so twisted and full of punishment.

"And never let the cord touch the floor," a withered woman said. "If it does, the child will be unable to hold its water."

That was no concern of mine. I could hold water the entire day, and then some. Mother often worried that something was wrong with me. Perhaps there was, but it wasn't because I could hold water so long.

The women went on and on with their stories, as if Goody Johnson were not in the next room hearing them. A thin woman, much like one of our chickens, clucked that if it were a boy, to be sure the midwife not cut the cord too short. They all laughed heartily.

"Why is that?" I asked.

"Because, child, when the boy becomes a man he will be short and unable to do his duty in the bed." They laughed again, pleased, I suppose, their own men had no such problems.

We sat for the longest time, as Mistress Anne went in and out, sometimes asking one of the women to help her.

Finally, the large woman bent over and said to her neighbor, loud enough for everyone, even Goody Johnson, to hear, "It's said that Sam Johnson's was cut too short."

"Aye, I've heard that," the thin one said.

"What's more," the large woman continued, "it's said that Richard Morgan down the road was called in to remedy the situation."

"Is that the truth?" She seemed pleased with the new knowledge. "Well, it's good to put the saddle on the right horse," she said. "But if the magistrates hear of it, there'll be a whipping at the post."

"Or a rope around the neck," the old woman said. "Like that one over in Plymouth."

"Aye," they all agreed. "That one."

"But whose neck will it be?" one of them said. "The man's or the woman's?"

They didn't answer the question. They already knew the answer and didn't wish to dwell on it.

The silence was broken by a scream from the other room. We all rushed in to see Mistress Anne bring another child into the world, into that dark room along the marsh.

More food for the mosquitoes, it seemed to me, as I swatted one on each arm. As if there weren't enough blood for them already.

I killed another on my neck.

Better a mosquito than a rope, I thought.

In the months that followed, I met Mistress Anne, sometimes joined by Mary Dyer, at the spring to talk about our lives. Several times I even went to meetings at Anne's house, where she was joined by many women of the town and even a few men. They talked much about Grace and Works and other matters, but I understood little of what they said. I did understand, though, when she said one Sabbath evening that men and women were equal in the eyes of God and that women should have the same rights as men. "God must surely frown on this colony," she said, "that my young son can vote, and I, nor any of our women, can neither vote nor serve on the court that makes the rules." She stamped her foot and walked among her listeners. "Do not the same rules apply to all of us, men and women? How is it, then, that only men can make those rules?"

All of the listeners spoke with great passion about the rules and their lives in this new land. This was strange to me because Mother and Father said little to each other, and the silence dropped on our lives like a heavy cloak on a hot summer's day.

Mother discovered that I was meeting with the women on my journeys to the market, and spoke sharply to me. "Chastity, I'm told you see those women," she said.

"I meet with many women," I said, which was true enough.

"Mistress Hutchinson and Mistress Dyer are not many women," she replied. "Nor are they common women."

"I know that, Mother."

"You know very little, daughter. You are headstrong and foolish. I know what you do, and I know what they do. The paths they walk are no paths for you. Take care, child. They mean you no harm, I'm sure, but harm will come nonetheless if you're thought to agree with them."

"They're good women, Mother."

"I have no doubt they're good women. They are also wealthy women. That is what protects them. But neither their husbands nor their friends will shield them if the magistrates and ministers decide to attack them, as they already have."

"Mother…"

"Of course you don't listen. As I didn't when I was your age."

"What was that, Mother?"

"Never mind. Nothing would be served by telling you."

I wondered what she had done, but she wouldn't tell me. And I didn't tell her that two days before when I was returning from the market, I passed Governor Winthrop and Reverend Wilson and another man I didn't know standing in front of the governor's house. They were all frowning and talking among themselves. As I passed near them, one of them, I think it was Reverend Wilson, said, "The matter is urgent. We must act now before the infection spreads." "That's so," the other man agreed. "We hear discontent in all the towns."

Just then the governor looked up and saw me. I smiled at him, not knowing what else to do, but he merely frowned. The other men looked my way, and they, too, frowned. I couldn't hear what they said, but I thought it was my name. Not Chastity, but my surname, Hoar.

As the weather cooled with the coming of autumn, our lives became warmer, as if a fire were burning under the entire city. I had noticed at the spring that Anne and Mary were troubled by the growing dissension around them. But they also seemed excited by it. Anne continued to speak harshly to Reverend Wilson and turn her back on him at the meeting house. Mary was more reserved, perhaps because she was with child and not feeling well. She often looked into the distance, as if searching for the path she was to take.

I think we all found that path, or its beginning, a few days later. Mary was not at the spring, as she always was, and we didn't know why. "I feel something is wrong," Anne said.

Something *was* wrong. Just then another woman came running to the spring. "Anne…Anne…come quickly. Her labor begins."

"Oh, Lord, it's two months early!" Anne said and swept me up with her. "Come…"

The three of us ran to Mary's house, speaking to no one on the way.

Mary's husband, William, showed us in. "She's there," he said, pointing to a curtained bed behind the fireplace.

I was told to sit on a bench in the front room while the two women worked on Mary. She called out to each of them, "Anne…Jane…help me. Oh, my God, help me."

Her husband paced the floor, looking in at his wife crying out in terrible pain. There was nothing he could do. There was nothing I could do. It was like facing a bitter cold wind in winter, alone on a vacant plain. What can you do? You bend your head and move ahead, come what may.

Then there was a terrible silence, as if the storm had blown over and a peace had settled on the land.

But there was no peace in that house. Not then. Not ever again.

Anne brought the child, wrapped in a blanket, into the front room. She had covered its head.

"William, I'm sorry. It was a stillbirth."

He walked over to see his child.

"William…I think you should not look."

"It's my child," he said with some anger.

"William, please. It's…it's deformed…a monster."

"God help us."

Then he remembered the silence in the house.

"Mary…?"

"Unconscious. Such pain I've never seen."

"I must see the child."

Anne uncovered its head, and I could just make it out. But I couldn't look long. The child had a face but no forehead, no skull. It seemed hardly human.

He turned away, and Anne covered the head again.

"What do we do?" he asked.

"We must bury it in secret. There is no other choice."

"The law forbids it," the other woman said.

"Aye, it does," Anne agreed. "But if the magistrates discover a monster, Mary will be blamed. And you, as well, William."

"Aye, all of us who have opposed them," he said.

"Jane is already thought a witch," Anne said, touching her friend's arm. "That will be all the evidence they need."

"I need to stay with Mary," William said.

"We'll do it," Anne offered. "God help us to see the way."

So it was that the three of us, Anne, Jane, and I, left the house in the cool autumn darkness and walked toward the small church burying ground.

"We need a shovel…and advice," Anne said. "Let us stop here, at John Cotton's house."

John Cotton, I thought, John Cotton. He's the preacher at the church. This is the end of us. We'll all be condemned for breaking the law and sent to prison, if not worse.

But John Cotton was not John Wilson, not yet anyway. He came out of his house with Anne still carrying the baby, and found a shovel in a shed behind the house. "Come," he said. "Quietly now. No one must see us."

It was the blackest of nights, with no moon to lighten our path, just a small lantern which Jane carried. I walked behind, carrying nothing but my fear for what we were set to do.

I should have listened to my mother. Here we were on this dark and cold night, burying a monster child in secret, for which there would be a terrible punishment if we were caught. Two of us were midwives, which was bad enough; one of them, even worse, was thought to be a witch, and a black-coated minister was helping us for reasons I couldn't understand.

And finally there was me, a girl, a willful, disobedient girl my mother called me, following them in the blackness to the graveyard. If God were watching, as he watched each mosquito, what was he thinking? Would he slap us dead and flick us to the ground? I shivered to think of it.

The reverend dug quietly, pausing from time to time to look around to see if we were observed. But there was no one, no noise except a dog barking mournfully in the distance.

The rest of us watched each clump of dirt fall from the shovel onto a small mound. Anne held the child to her and watched the deepening hole, dark shadows from the lantern flickering over it. I remembered that Anne had once mentioned she, too, had lost a child. I went to her and put my arm around her. She smiled sadly at me. I think she was also remembering the child she had left across the sea in the old country.

"It's deep enough," the reverend said. He took the child wrapped in its blanket, and placed it softly in the grave. "No beast will touch it," he said, replacing the dirt.

When he was finished we all knelt by the grave. "Bless this child," the minister said. "And bless its mother that she be restored to health and life."

He paused for a minute. Then he said, "You test us each day in this new land, oh Lord, and we know not your purpose in these matters. You have taken this child to be with you, and we give thanks it has an eternal home. We open our hearts to your everlasting Grace as it shines upon us and lights our way in the darkness of this troubled land."

He bowed his head.

"Amen," we said. "Amen."

Anne and Jane were crying softly now, but no tears came to my eyes. I was wondering why God saw fit to make that child a monster and then take it away, as if he had made a mistake and didn't want anyone to see it. I could give no thanks for such a cruelty, for that's what it was. I thought of Mary, unconscious from the pain, and she hadn't learned yet what had happened to her child.

Something was wrong with God's plan for us.

On top of that, the minister had said no beast would disturb the child. That was true in part because no beast did find the child. But it was disturbed nonetheless. And, as always, it was the men who were the disturbers.

I didn't fully understand what happened next, and I understand it no better now, so many years later.

Anne and Mary were summoned by the magistrates to a hearing in Newtown, across the river. I didn't go with them, as it was a bitter cold day, and the river was frozen solid with layers of ice and snow several feet deep. The wind was blowing first one way, then another, and one could hardly see any distance ahead. I wanted to go with them, but Mother needed me at home. I think it was more that she didn't want me with them, but I heeded her and remained at home.

My friends were never the same again. When they returned, they told me they and their families had been banished from Boston, banished from the colony, and Anne would be imprisoned some miles from us, in Roxbury to the south.

"What have you done?" I asked when I saw her after her return, surrounded by two men who watched her every move. She looked very tired, as I had never seen her before. But she tried to smile.

"What have I done? Nothing but what I've always done. Spoken the truth as I've been commanded by the good Lord above. Told the magistrates they were not fit to rule the colony and that God will judge them harshly. As he will…as he will."

The two men moved to take her away.

"Is that all?" I asked. "That is nothing."

"What disturbed them most, I believe, was to find the accuser a woman."

At that, the men took her by the arms and led her off.

"Will I not see you again?" I called to her.

She partly turned to me and spoke into the wind so that I could barely hear her. "You will see me again, I promise."

Then she was gone. I wrapped my wool scarf around my face and headed home in the driving wind to meet my mother, who would say, "I told you so." Or so I thought. I was surprised. When I told her what had happened, she only said, "Poor woman…poor woman."

It was a long and bitterly cold winter. The wind blew the cold and snow through the cracks and chinks in our walls, cracks which Father was supposed to have patched but had not found the time to do so when it was warm enough to work with the clay. Now it was too cold and too late. Mother was angry with him, and he was angry with himself because he could find little work in the cold. He was a carpenter, a good one, but had to confine himself to smaller indoor projects for men who were busy in town with their trades. For one woman he built a cradle, but it made me sad to see it. I thought of Mary's child we had buried in the churchyard; it would have no cradle, no warm bed by the fire to rest its head.

I did see Anne again, just as she promised. But it was worse than before, much worse.

I had heard from talk in the marketplace there was to be another trial. It seems that one trial was not enough for such a woman. One lady told me when I asked, "The first was to let the magistrates at her; now the ministers want their chance."

It was in March, when there was often hope of spring, but there was no hope in that month as the cold winds blew through the cracks in the mud-plastered walls. Hopes and dreams died in that terrible building, which I hoped never to enter again.

Mistress Anne was forced to stand in front the ministers, maybe forty or more of them. They looked like hideous bats or crows as they sat in their comfortable seats, ready to feast on their victim's tender flesh. She had to stand and face them all.

Anne was not the same woman I had seen just a few months before. She was quiet now and her bulging coat revealed that she was again with child. What did it matter to the men, though? They had never carried children and cared little about this woman's weakness.

One by one the ministers took their turns pecking at her. For speaking against the ministers. For holding meetings in her house. For teaching men and women when only the ministers were fit for that. For holding foul and gross opinions that they claimed would lead to the promiscuous and filthy coming together of men and women.

Finally, though, the Reverend Cotton, who had helped us bury Mary's child, stood up in her hour of need. He was a strong and good man, well respected, so I knew he would defend her.

I could not believe what I heard. He turned on Anne, his friend, and told us all that we should vomit up her opinions, which would poison us and the entire colony. He continued on, but I felt sick at heart. I wanted to vomit his opinions, and vowed that I would not listen to him or his kind again.

They were not finished, not those black-coated men. It was finally that monster Wilson's turn to speak. He stood there, like the fat little toad he was, and said that Anne was Satan's disciple and had come among us to destroy God's kingdom. Suddenly, there was silence in the meeting house. Outside, the wind gusted around the building, as if God himself was listening and not pleased.

John Wilson paraded in front of us, puffed up, and spitting his venom. His eyes shining, he stood there, waiting for the right time to unloose his venom. Then he spoke: "In the name of the church I do not only pronounce you worthy to be cast out, but I do cast you out and deliver you up to Satan that you may learn no more to blaspheme, to seduce and to lie." Then he turned and raised his arm, bringing it down slowly, and pointed at her. "Therefore, I command you in the name of this church as a leper to withdraw yourself out of the congregation."

The men, as usual, had the last word. Or thought they did.

Anne pulled her coat about her and moved to the door. And when a woman standing at the door said, "The Lord sanctify this unto you," Anne turned and said, "The Lord judgeth not as man judgeth."

Mary followed her out of the building, and I followed close behind. Others watched me scornfully as I pushed through the crowd.

At the door I heard a woman ask, "Who is that woman who follows the condemned one?" "That is Mary Dyer," another said. "The one who bore a monster."

There was a gasp from the people and then silence. Several of the ministers had heard the secret, and I knew even then, as young as I was, that the consequences would be serious, but I couldn't have imagined the poison these men were capable of.

It didn't matter to the men that Anne and Mary had left the colony. They dug up Mary's monster child and examined it and then proudly told the colony of its features, hideous as they were. I think they enjoyed that even more than they enjoyed observing the whippings outside the meeting house on lecture day afternoon.

I didn't go to the Sabbath or lecture services again, but friends told me that the ministers, and the governor himself, said that the deformed child was proof that those who held monstrous opinions would also bear monstrous children; that God had demonstrated once again that he smiled on his ministers and their people and punished those who followed Satan and wrote their names in his book.

I didn't see Anne again but learned later she was killed by Indians. That was also part of God's plan, we were told by the men. I remembered it was our men, with Reverend Wilson as their chaplain, who massacred the Indians, every man, woman and child they could find. They returned home singing and drinking and celebrating their victories. But it was Anne who refused to send her sons to kill the Indians.

If it was God's plan, it was a strange plan, and I wanted no part of it. I told Mother that I was going to Sabbath services, and when John Wilson spoke, I would stand up and tell him that God's plan was evil if it meant rejoicing in women's pain and killing Indians.

Mother didn't say anything, but it was not long after that we moved farther south, so that it was too far to walk to John Wilson's meeting house.

We never moved far enough away, though, to escape John Wilson and the other black coats. Maybe that was part of God's plan, I don't know. Wasn't God too busy, with earthquakes and plagues and killing Indians, to be following us everywhere we went?

CHAPTER 3

The gentleman, his legs opened to display his fine blue breeches to best advantage, rubbed my arm slightly as I placed the tankard of ale on the board in front of him. "Bend your head, girl," he said, "so that I might admire your marble neck."

"Aye, marble neck," I said. "Cold and hard."

"Warm and hard," he said, bringing his legs together and smiling at me.

So began my real troubles, as numerous as the wolves howling about our house each night.

We had moved south, just far enough to be at some distance from the Boston meetinghouse and John Wilson. We didn't move farther because Father suddenly found his place in the world. It was in Roxbury, just south of the Neck and near the mosquito marshes. Father announced that he was tired of working for others, building houses and cradles and other things for those too busy and rich to build them for themselves, so now he would build for himself alone.

Mother and I looked at each other, wondering what madness he had settled on now. A few weeks before he had journeyed north to Salem in hopes of finding his place there, but he had returned with the news that his place in the world would be a long distance from the lunatics who lived in Salem. When we looked at each other, shaking our heads, he said, "You don't believe me? Listen to this. I'm walking past a farm house, just outside of town, enjoying the weather, and I see these people gathered in a circle, shouting at each other. Well, I think, maybe they'll be needing me to help them finish that keg of beer. Course I didn't see no keg of beer. I just figured what else could they be disputing on such a fine day. Well, weren't no beer they was screeching about. You know what it was?"

We shook our heads. "Well, it wasn't no beer but a well they was standing around. One of 'em says, 'We can't do. Sabbath comin' on.' And another one says, 'Boy drowns if we don't. You want the boy to drown?' First one says, 'Preacher says no work on the Sabbath, or God'll strike us dead. You want that, Jeb? All of us struck dead?' Another one says, 'Bowels of hell, thas where he's at. Satan down there, just waitin' for one of us. Already took the boy.'"

Mother and I looked at each other again, not knowing whether to believe him or not. But he went on, not minding either of us. "I'm hearin' all this, not knowin' what's happening, so I go up to the well and look down. Sure enough, there's a boy down there, crying his little heart out. And those folks, even his ma, want to leave him there because the preacher told them not to work on the Sabbath. Well, I didn't care two figs about Sabbath comin' on. I cared about that boy gettin' out. So I take this rope one of 'em's hanging onto like she didn't want to shake it for fear of God strikin' her dead, and I lower it to the boy. 'Come on, lad, hang on. I'm pullin' you up.' I takes him out, wipes a bit of the water off his face, and directs him to his ma. 'Here's your boy,' I says. 'You wantin' him, or should I just take him with me 'cause I only got me a girl, could use a boy helping me,' and she grabs the boy and boxes his ears for fallin' in the well and causing all that trouble. 'Jesus, Lord,' I says to them people, 'if he's takin' to leaving boys in wells to drown, I don't want no part of him. No sir. You can just have that Lord of yours, and I'll be on my way.' People look at me like I'm the Devil's familiar. 'The Lord strike you down for that kind of talk,' one of them says. 'I'm reportin' you to the preacher.' I didn't say a word more. I just turned around and came back, fast as I could."

So we didn't go north. We didn't go south very far either, because Father stopped on the way and planted himself like a tree. Not a step farther would he move. "There it is," he said.

"What is?" Mother wondered.

"Where I'm buildin'."

"What're you building?" she asked, not really believing that he was interested in a plan that could remotely be called sensible.

"Our house. I'm building our house. Big one. We live upstairs, other folks down. That's where the money is, sweetheart," he says, doing a little jig around a puddle in the road. "It's what they call an inn. Tavern in the front, quench a man's thirst, and sleepin' in the back room and around the fireplace. Top of it all, on the second floor, we'll watch our investment, snug as bugs in a rug. So, what'd you think, Mary, Mary, my sweet little canary?"

"Doesn't matter what I think, does it?" she said. "You ride your own horse no matter what we say."

It didn't matter what we thought, just like Mother said. Father found a partner with money to spend on whatever foolishness came his way, and Father's plan for an inn just happened to come his way when he was itching to part with it. Father was able to get a license, too, though he'd never tell us how. I think he promised free beer and food to one of the magistrates. Maybe he promised other things as well, I didn't know then.

It wasn't hard to find men to help him build the house, especially when they were paid each day with all the beer they could drink and food they could eat. We found a lady close by who agreed to bake fruit pies to bring over at the end of the day. They were almost as good as the beer.

Father would stand outside our new house each morning and watch it, expecting the walls to tell him something, I suppose. Something about the house didn't quite meet the picture in his head. But then one morning he had a vision, and he seized it like he'd found a wild turkey having breakfast in our kitchen. "That's it!" he shouted, "I've got it!" He went to work like a man possessed. There was a gully running along in front of the house, which had filled to a small stream several times after a heavy rain. So Father built a drawbridge over the gully, which could be raised or lowered by pulleys and a wheel that someone could turn in front of the house. That's when he thought of the name, which he etched in a big wooden sign hanging next to the door: A MAN'S CASTLE. On the sign he carved a picture of a castle with a moat and drawbridge.

That was the name of our house. A MAN'S CASTLE. When Father finally got around to asking what we thought of it, Mother shook her head. "A little late to be asking that, wouldn't you say?"

Mother and I were expected to be maids, as well as cooks, while Father greeted travelers at the door to make them welcome. He also posted the news of the day on the wall near the big wooden door, but generally he liked to save visitors the trouble of reading the posters. So he'd announce the news himself in a loud voice that rang through the front room where the tavern was. Some visitors received the news four or five times, whether they were interested or not. "Francis Ward lost three pigs," he'd shout. "Reward of four shillings offered." Or, "Whipping next Lecture Day, Jane Stout for lascivious carriage."

Father came to know more of what was happening in Roxbury and Boston than the tithing man and the constables, which was sometimes a good thing.

The name of our house met with general approval from the men travelers who came through, but one ugly man with flesh rolls like one of our pigs proposed another name. "Why, man," he roared at the serving board when he learned my father's name, "you couldn't do better than THE HOAR HOUSE for a name." At that he laughed until he nearly fell off his bench. He spilled his tankard of beer, and Father made me offer him another free of charge.

Father was indignant at first, but said nothing. I think that's when he began hatching new plans for the inn, because when one of the neighbor men suggested his daughters could use gainful employment, Father agreed, even though we didn't yet need any more help. Of course, he didn't tell Mother and me about it until it was too late.

The neighbor man had a large family, mostly girls he didn't know what to do with. "Always underfoot," he complained. "Bunch of grasshoppers for all they're worth." He had different feelings about his sons, who as far as I could see did little more work than their lazy father.

One afternoon when the man was talking with Father, the two of them drinking their beer as if it didn't cost us anything, I heard Father ask his name. "Roger," he said. "Roger Clap."

Oh, Lord, I thought when I saw Father's eyes light up. "What are your daughter's names, then?" "Gave them good Christian names," Roger said. "Experience is the oldest. Then there's Wait and Unite and Supply. The youngest we named Desire."

Desire Clap, that was her name. It was worse than mine, bad as it was.

Father wasn't at all troubled by the name. He saw it as an opportunity. "I can't pay much," he said, "but one of them can live with us. You won't be stepping on her then. She can sleep with my girl, serve tables, work in the kitchen." He smiled thinking about it. "I'll take Desire," he said, "if you can part with her."

Mister Clap agreed to the proposition immediately, and the two men hoisted another tankard and drank to their agreement.

Father must have thought it was funny, that it would bring business to the inn. I didn't think it was funny at all. I thought of two girls serving all these men, one of them Chastity Hoar and the other one Desire Clap.

Mother was furious when he told her about Desire Clap working for us and sleeping in my room upstairs. She threatened to leave my father, taking me with her, but she relented when she met Desire, who turned out to be much nicer than her father and a good worker to boot.

There was nothing Desire and I could do about our surnames. They were like the brands that the men later began burning into the skin of those who disobeyed the rules or believed in a different God. Once you were branded you were branded for life. It didn't occur to us at first that we could change our surnames by marrying, but when it did occur to us, we weren't sure that any man or marriage was worth the trouble. Besides, other names weren't much better. Not far from us was a Hope Crackbone and her husband, Jack Crackbone. Why would Hope ever want to marry a man with such a name? It didn't seem sensible. On the other side of Muddy River was a woman named Patience who had married Ezekiel Shatswell and became Patience Shatswell. She named their son Ernest Shatswell. Mistress Anne had told me once that a person shouldn't mind his name, that the inner person was more important than a name, but I notice she didn't marry a Hoar or Crackbone or Shatswell.

Anyway, Desire and I served the beer and the ale, which were legal with the license Father received from the colony. But though he had a license to open an ordinary and sell drinks, he had to sell with one hand tied behind his back. He was watched by all the authorities—the magistrates and ministers and the tithing man, all of them determined to take whatever joy might be had from the drinks they had licensed him to sell.

With one hand they gave, with the other they took away—and found great pleasure in doing so. I decided in those days I would give with both hands and take away with neither. It was the only way I could be happy among people so determined to be unhappy themselves and so devoted to making everyone else as unhappy as they were.

When Father tried to sell an ale-quart of beer for more than a penny, he was fined six shillings and told he would lose his license if he did it again. When he celebrated the opening of his inn, Father and his guests were drinking toasts around the room, each drinker more boisterous than the last, the magistrates found out from the tithing man, and he was fined ten shillings for wasting good beer and encouraging drunkenness.

"Damn those busybodies!" he would cry. "Didn't the good Lord himself lift a glass or two, and who fined him ten shillings?" Unfortunately, he said that once too often, and a minister passing through heard him and reported him to the magistrates. So he was fined another twenty shillings, ten for encouraging drunkenness and ten for blasphemy. One magistrate thought he also deserved twenty lashes at the whipping post, but the others didn't listen. I think they might have liked father—or at least his beer and ale. Or perhaps he had a few shillings in the hand tied behind his back.

I enjoyed the cooking early in the morning as much as serving the beer and ale, and sometimes, when the authorities were busy with more important matters of the colony, I prepared the special cider Father concocted in his cooking room, as he called it.

For several of our guests, Mother taught me how to make a boiled eel dish fit for a king—or a magistrate whose ear one of the ministers had found and whispered into. We would stuff the eels with nutmeg and cloves, cook them in wine, and serve them on a chafing dish garnished with lemons. One magistrate, a frequent visitor, would taste a bite, wink at Father, and tell him it was a good thing he obeyed the law and wasn't overcharging for his meals, which meant that Father would charge him nothing for the eel, knowing that the magistrate would overlook the evidence Father had been selling more than beer and ale and charging more than the established limits for his foods.

The man with the blue breeches who admired my neck came in every day about four in the afternoon. After reading the postings on the wall, to learn of ships coming in or new scandals in the colony, he looked over the inn, searching for either Desire or me. We would both hide in the kitchen until Father sought us out, but not before we could hear Mister Pigghogg bellowing to all within hearing, "Where's that wench Desire? I'm hungry for Desire." Another man would shout out, "Is it Clap you desire, then?" "Not if I can help it," he'd shout back, and all the men would roar with delight at their wit.

If Desire found herself busy with the eel or hasty pudding, then fat Pigghogg would call for me. "Where's my Chastity?" he'd call. "Is that the Hoar wench you desire?" another would call back. "I know nothing of the Hoar," he'd shout, smiling broadly. "It's Chastity I desire." That would bring more howls of laughter from whatever men were drinking and eating.

Father was not so pleased when he witnessed the consequences of his plans to have Desire and me serve the customers, especially when his own name was the object of derision. But that's the way Father was. Other men as well, I came to find out. They would walk straight into a swamp or off a dock if the swamp or dock happened to be two steps or three steps ahead. They delighted only in the next step and whatever pleasure it would bring them. Sufficient unto the first step were the delights thereof. Tomorrow they would consider the next step—from the swamp or the sea.

Mother, of course, was furious. Desire and I could hear the two of them through the walls at night. "So you've become pimp to your daughter and her friend?" she shouted one night. "It's disgusting. I should leave you and take them with me." Father wouldn't say anything. What could he say? We already had our names and would have them forever, even if we married and changed them. And where could Mother go? Unmarried women were a danger to themselves and their children because the magistrates and ministers would watch everything they did. They didn't think to watch Mister Pigghogg or the other men who thought we couldn't live without them.

One evening Father summoned me to his room. Mother was still in the kitchen cleaning up after a gathering of men who were making plans to invite more wealthy shippers to the colony. There was one chair in the room and he bade me sit on it while he stood at the door, as if he wanted to escape quickly after he told me his news.

"Daughter," he said, looking uncomfortable. "Daughter, I've something to tell you."

I knew it would not be good. He never announced he was going to tell me anything. He just told me and went about his business, assuming I would do what he asked.

"Let me guess," I said. "You've tired of serving bodies and decided to serve souls instead. You're becoming a minister."

"It's no time for jesting," he said. "I have a serious proposal."

"What could be more serious than serving our souls?"

"Marriage," he said.

"Marriage? You already have one wife. There's penalties for more than one."

"But you have no husband," he said.

I was so surprised I didn't know what to say. Marriage. Who was thinking of marriage? It's true many girls my age were married, some having two or three children already, but I had not ever thought of it. Besides, the men I knew were either married or no more appealing than the mangy dogs lying in the roads, deserted by their masters.

"I need no husband."

"But your husband needs you," he said.

"Not if I don't have one."

"When you have one, he will need you. He needs you already."

I could tell now that Father, not having learned anything from the innkeeping business, had already hatched another scheme. "Did you have someone in mind?" I asked. I should have just run from the room to find Mother.

"I do. A very desirable choice if I do say so."

"And who might that be?"

"You already know him."

"I don't know any men," I said with some truth. "Not any that I'd want to marry."

"Well, he has a great deal of money. He's a partner in this inn. An elder in the church. A respected man."

I still didn't know what he was talking about. Maybe that's because I didn't want to know what he was talking about.

"Mister Pigghogg is sound as gold."

"Mister Pigghogg? Father…"

I nearly fainted when I heard the name. I couldn't believe Father was serious. I knew from the way he grimaced when the man entered the inn he didn't like him any more than I did. He tolerated him because he was a partner and a customer.

"He carries great weight in the colony."

"Aye, he does. Several hundred pounds."

"Weight lifts many obstacles, my girl."

Crushes them too, I thought.

Then I remembered. Father was only joking. "He's married already," I laughed.

"Now he is. He won't be shortly."

I couldn't imagine what he was talking about. You couldn't just leave your wife because you were tired of her. Or your husband either for that matter, else Mother might have left years ago.

"Is his wife thinking of leaving him?" I joked. "I wouldn't blame her."

"She is," he said, not smiling. "She's dying."

"Dying? What…?"

"That's what he told me. Hasn't been herself for a long spell. He's had her coffin already made. Munning did it down at his shop. I coulda done it myself, but Pigghogg didn't think it would look good being as how you…well, you know…"

"It wouldn't look good? So how does it look he's preparing for a new wife and his old one's still living with him, probably making his food and caring for the house, sick as she is? If she's dying, she's dying from being worked to death."

And that was the truth. Women and children were always dying faster than the men. Ten, twelve children and our bodies gave out, just stopped working—like a corn mill or cider press, worn out. And there wasn't any fixing of women's bodies when they gave out. The men didn't even try, not that the magistrates would let them get close enough to find out the problems. The doctors couldn't even touch a woman's body, that was the law. But the men, all of them, did their share of lying on the women, even unmarried women, and the law was blind to that.

As it usually was when it came to women.

So what did the men do when they found their wives, their cider presses, wearing out? They found themselves another cider press if they couldn't fix the old one. Got themselves a new wife to provide for them—except they usually waited until the old one gave out. Fat Pigghogg couldn't wait that long. He wanted a new one before the old one was gone.

"So what do you say, daughter?"

"About what?"

"About Mister Pigghogg. He'll make you the best of husbands."

"No he won't. I wouldn't marry him if he gave me all the ships that come to Boston harbor."

Father looked around, fearing someone had overheard me. I was hoping they had.

"Daughter," he said quietly, "I need you to marry him. You will marry him."

"Not in this world I won't."

Father looked hurt and then angry. "If you offend Pigghogg in any way, he'll take his money out of the inn. You want that? You want us out in the streets?"

"I'd rather be in the streets than under him."

That shocked Father. He had been thinking only of losing the inn. But imagining me, his only daughter, crushed under that pig of a man was another matter, especially since he didn't like the man.

He loved me, and he loved his inn. He had to choose, and he never liked hard choices.

But watching him standing in the doorway, not knowing what to do or say, I suddenly realized that I had to choose as well. I had to choose my family—or Pigghogg.

"Father," I finally said. "Do you want me to be Chastity Pigghogg? What kind of name is that?"

"No worse than what it is," he said. "You think about it. Pigghogg expects to hear from us tomorrow." He turned and angrily left the room.

That much was true. My name wouldn't be any worse than it was. Chastity Hoar. Men should be flogged or jailed for giving women such names.

Later that evening I found Mother in the kitchen, working by candlelight to increase our supply of metheglin, which was illegal to sell, but which Father was allowed to provide to several men of influence in the colony.

"Fetch me the rosemary," Mother said. "Over there with the angelica and wild thyme. We need to get them boiled tonight." She looked up at me. I couldn't hide my fears.

"What ails you?" she asked. "You look like you need a dose of snail pottage. Or you've already had it, one or the other."

"What ails me no snail pottage or any other medicine will cure," I said, thinking of the times when I was younger she had given me the snail water to cure my fevers.

I gave her the herbs and stood next to her. I wanted her to hold me as she did when I was a young girl.

She stopped her work. "So what is it...oh my God! You're not with child? Lord save us, daughter, it's not that, is it?"

I was surprised she would even think such a thing. I had seen several men who were agreeable to my eye, but they were either married or more fond of touching me than axes or shovels in decent work. I wanted no one touching me until I was ready to be touched.

Besides, what man wants to be seen with a Chastity Hoar?

"Have I given you reason to think that, Mother?"

"Not you. But the men you serve give me much reason. They seem to think you and Desire are beaver pelts, so much they stroke you."

"I care nothing for these men—or any men."

"So what ails you then?"

"A man."

"What man?"

"Father."

"Father, is it?" she laughed. "Well, he ails me as well." She went back to her work. "So what has your mad father done now to make you look so sick?"

"He wants me to marry."

"Marry? Well, there are worse punishments in the colony."

"I would rather suffer at the whipping post than marry."

She paused again, holding up the pestle she was grinding the herbs with. "No you wouldn't, Chastity. That's foolish talk."

"No whipping could be worse."

"Speak with one who's been whipped and you'll hear another story. It's a terrible pain. The medicines will heal the body in time, but there is no medicine to cure the mind of the humiliation. That's what Sarah told me, and she should know. She suffered twenty for speaking her mind about the ministers."

"Pigghogg is worse."

"Pigghogg? What about him?"

"Father wants me to marry him."

She stopped her work again and searched my eyes. "Pigghogg? Father wants you to marry Pigghogg? Be serious now, Chastity. What did he say?"

"He said I must marry Pigghogg or he'll take his money out of the inn and we'll be in the streets."

"God help us." At first she was stunned with the news.

"What should I do, Mother?"

"He's married. Does Father know that?"

"His wife's leaving him. She's dying, so he needs a replacement."

"Replacement? Replacement?" She was like a clubbed wolf. If you didn't kill them with the first stunning blow, they would furiously turn on their attacker. "As God is my witness," she shouted for everyone to hear, "you'll be no replacement for Pigghogg's wife."

She took my hand and found father, laughing with one of the guests. "Upstairs," she said to him. "Now!"

She turned and marched to our quarters upstairs with Father following behind.

We were not going to be snug as bugs in a rug as he had dreamed.

CHAPTER 4

Father should have known better than to make Mother angry. She wouldn't give him a moment's peace. She would snap and bite like a goose before we covered its head to render it harmless before the plucking.

But Mother should have known that Father could be like the brick wall near the springs in Boston, where I met Anne and Mary to draw water and discuss women's lives. All the geese and animals in the colony couldn't change its hard, cold face. It paid no attention to the boys who would scratch their names in it nor to any others who would mar its surface. It stood strong and hard, changing for no man or beast.

Just so with Father when he determined the path he would take. He had decided to build his inn near the marshes in Roxbury and had named it, not listening to us nor to any who thought him mad. The inn had become successful just as he had predicted it would, and he had made sacrifices to ensure that it was. He had put his heart and soul into building the inn, and he took great pride in its success. He once told us he could finally stand tall, bowing his head to no man—except one, of course, that he had not mentioned until just now.

He would not easily give up his inn.

When we reached their room upstairs, furnished with the bed and chair he had carefully made himself, Mother turned on him, snarling and biting. "Mister Pigghogg, is it?" she cried, taking his arm and squeezing it hard. "You think that beast of a man is good enough for us?"

"His money is," Father replied calmly.

"Pfsst!" she snarled. "I spit on him and his money."

Father remained calm, despite her anger. "Spit all you want. His money feeds us and keeps us off the streets."

"I'd rather beg on the streets," she said, not releasing her hold on his arm.

"I reckon you'd whistle another tune when they whipped you for begging," he said, pleased now that he had the advantage.

"Better whipping than Pigghogg," she said, forgetting in her anger what she had just told me about whipping. She let go of his arm and walked to the window, as if to look out at the streets she'd trade for my freedom.

"It's not decent," she said. "He's already married."

"Not for long," Father replied, pressing his advantage.

"You want Hannah dead, then?" Mother said, turning to him angrily. "You want her dead so he can marry our Chastity?"

"I want no one dead. But dead is what we'll be one day or the next."

"God grant her a long life, then," Mother said.

I don't think Mother realized what she was saying in wishing Hannah Pigghogg a long life, for that meant a long life with Mister Pigghogg, since leaving your husband was unheard of, no matter the need. It was permissible to leave your husband only by dying.

"I won't have it," Mother said.

"You won't have her dying?" Father said, relishing his position.

"God will do what he will with poor Hannah. I won't have our Chastity marrying that man."

"I'm master of the house," Father said simply. "She will marry him if I order her to."

Mother didn't say anything. She knew that Father was right, that he was master of the house, of the castle he had built with his own hands, and that the authorities would investigate any house where the woman tried to rule her husband. It might even bring charges of witchcraft, especially to people of our station. Witchcraft charges might mean beating at the post or even hanging. Several women in the colony had already been investigated and charged.

Mother and Father had both heard at Sabbath services that the man was master of the house as Christ was master of his followers. That was the law which ruled us, and Mother knew it well. She might have thought it as foolish as charging witchcraft because a woman's cheese curdled or a cow stopped giving milk, but she had to obey the law. None of us wanted John Wilson or the magistrates investigating us.

What's more, Pigghogg was a magistrate. It didn't matter that no one liked him. What does it matter to a giant tree that the squirrels and rabbits playing underneath don't like the moss on its trunk? They have no power to show their displeasure. They must either live with the moss or find another tree more to their liking.

We couldn't find another tree—or rather didn't think we could. Father was the tree and we would have to live with him or risk punishment.

I looked at Mother and saw in her eyes and body that she was broken, defeated, like most of our women were. Like Anne and Mary and others that I knew. Perhaps there were other ways of winning, but I didn't know them then. I only knew that in that upstairs room he had built for us, Father had mastered Mother, and we all knew it. It made me very sad, as much for Mother as for myself. At the time, though, I didn't know what it would mean for me.

Pigghogg was what it would mean, unless I discovered a way to make his wife immortal or myself invisible. But even if I did become invisible, by disappearing from the colony, I would be sought out and punished for not obeying my father. And if I found medicines to help Hannah Pigghogg live longer, I would be suspected of witchcraft, of signing the Devil's book and receiving special powers that he reserved for those who sold their souls and followed him.

What could I do? What could any woman do? We were like the crabs being slowly boiled in one of our large kitchen pots. If we tried to climb out of the pot, we would fall into the fire stoked by the colony's men. But if we stayed in the pot, in the gradually warming water, pulling and crawling over each other, we would still die, only more slowly. Those in the colony who later climbed out of the pot died quickly on the gallows, their ears cut off, their tongues bored though with a hot iron. Those who stayed in died like Hannah Pigghogg was dying. And, though I didn't think of it at the time, like Anne and Mary and even my mother.

As Father said, dead is what we would be one day or the next. I elected for it to be the next day. I would stay in the pot and not flee. That meant Pigghogg—and trusting that his wife's desire to live was stronger than her husband's desire that she die.

Unfortunately, Hannah Pigghogg had no desire to live, not with her husband, not in this colony where the men would either burn you in their fires or boil you in the steaming waters. Within a month of Pigghogg's telling my father he wanted me for his wife, we were informed that Hannah was failing.

Mother announced to Father we were leaving.

"Leaving?" he roared. "Who said you could leave? The travelers are hungry."

"Feed them, then," she said, tightlipped.

"What? Feed them? That's not my responsibility."

"Today it is. Let's go, Chastity."

Father stood in the doorway, hoping to prevent us from leaving. Several of the travelers waiting for their breakfast watched the proceedings, enjoying the spectacle of a man asserting his authority to no effect.

"I say you're not leaving."

"And I say we are," Mother said, pushing him aside.

"You'll go to the kitchen like I commanded," he said, looking for approval from the guests.

Just then Desire appeared in the kitchen door, wondering what all the commotion was. Father saw her and shouted, "Get back to your work, girl! It's none of your business."

That was all Mother needed. She decided it *was* her business and motioned to her. "Come here, Desire. We're needed elsewhere."

Desire started toward us and then stopped, unsure of what to do. It was her duty to obey Father in all that he asked of her, but she loved Mother, as she loved her own mother. She was torn between duty and love.

"What is it, ma'am?" she cried.

"Duty," Mother said. "A woman's dying."

I don't know if Desire thought it was her own mother or if her love of Mother was stronger than her fear of Father, but she walked slowly to us. "Yes, ma'am," she said timidly, afraid to look at Father.

"You're not leaving," Father repeated, his arms flung out.

"Aye, tell 'em who runs the place," one of the guests said, finding the spectacle a reward for missing his breakfast. "Give these women an inch and they'll hop in bed with the next man parading through."

"Good riddance, I say," another one spoke up. "Let 'em go. There's better fish in the sea."

I don't know if Father was more angry at us or at the men, but he started shouting. "I'll not have it. Not in my castle. Leave and you're gone. That's my word. The magistrates will support me, they'll listen to no women. The pillory, stocks, branding iron, ducking chair, that's what's outside the door. You set one foot by me, and the constable will have your necks faster than I can nail a board."

Father was flinging his arms in every direction as he made his speech, so the guests thought he might have been referring to them. They sputtered and snorted and swore at Father, who picked up a tankard and threw it across the room, just missing a little rodent man sitting in the corner. He left for the back, shouting that he would be calling the magistrates.

Mother put her arm around Desire and me and led us to the door. Father saw her and leapt back to guard the door, seizing Mother by the arm.

"Don't touch me," she said, throwing his hand off as if she'd found a cockroach crawling on her. "You're not fit to tell us anything."

The guests roared in derision. "Softer than a rabbit fixed for the pot," a fat one shouted. "That's no man I see in the door but a coop full of chickens."

Urged on by the men, Father reached for both Desire and me, clutching at our arms.

"Leonard," Mother said, pulling us away from him. "You listen to me and listen well. Hannah's dying. Worked to death by that pig of a man that calls himself a husband. When the good Lord finally takes her, that man is coming for our Chastity. It's all your doing. You've sold your soul and now our daughter, all for this inn you built in hell with the Devil at your side. He's laughing right now, you hear him? You've done his work, and he's rightly pleased. But, Leonard, I'll not sell my soul, not any more than I have. We're going out that door to be with Hannah. Help her on her way out of this world where men like you and that swine sell their daughters and wives and laugh about it."

Mother blazed pure hatred at Father and the men who were laughing along the benches. She had lost the first war with Father, but she wouldn't lose this one. She recognized that Father was master of the family and his word was law—but not in everything. Not when a woman was dying and needed to be with womenfolk who understood her and her hard life in this world. She was going to be with Hannah, we were all going to be with Hannah, and no man was going to stop her. That was her law, a woman's law, and nothing in this world would keep her from obeying that law.

Father saw the anger in Mother's eyes and knew he couldn't keep her in his castle. But Desire and I were another story. If he couldn't stop Mother, he would stop us. As Mother pushed by him, he reached out for our arms and held firm. We were the last hope for him to maintain his dignity in front of the guests.

Mother had gone outside, but turned back when she realized we weren't following her. "Leonard," she said. "Let them go."

"I'll not," he said, drawing himself up to his full height.

Mother said nothing. She just returned and stood before him. She spoke quietly but I could just hear her. "If you ever want to touch me again, Leonard, you let those girls go."

Father looked around the room, hoping that no one had heard her. "Mary," he said just as quietly. "Don't force me."

"I mean it, Leonard. Let them go. We have a duty to Hannah. And to our God."

I don't know whether it was the mention of God or the threat of withholding herself, but Father released our arms. Maybe he suddenly realized that he had not really lost, not in this colony. Mother could not withhold herself from him even she tried. Other women had attempted to do so, and the magistrates had informed them that it was the husband's right to do what he wished with his wife. That no godly wife would ever withhold herself from her husband.

The three of us left Father in the doorway. "Don't turn around," Mother warned us. "Walk straight ahead. Don't give him the satisfaction."

I've often wondered what Father did after we left that morning. Did he fix breakfast for the guests? Did the guests leave immediately? Did they taunt him for his manly weakness in allowing his wife to leave her place?

We arrived at Hannah's, a large two-story frame house in Boston, but not far from us. A servant let us in and pointed us upstairs where Hannah was lying alone. Her husband was nowhere to be seen, and no other women had yet arrived.

"Hannah," Mother said, approaching her bed and taking hold of her hand. Desire and I stood behind her.

Hannah seemed to have already wasted away to little more than bones. I thought of her fat husband, waddling around the city, hoping for her to die. I wondered if Hannah knew that her husband had fixed his eye on me, and was waiting anxiously for her to die so he could marry me. Perhaps he was even poisoning her. I felt sick thinking about it.

Hannah smiled weakly at Mother. "God bless you for coming," she whispered. "I have a servant, but she's little help."

"I came as soon as I heard," Mother said. "Women need to comfort each other. You would do the same for me."

"I would, yes…" her voice trailed off.

"This is Desire, our help at the inn." She gently pushed Desire forward.

"Pleased to meet you, ma'am." Desire curtsied and stepped back.

Then Mother pulled me forward. I was afraid that Hannah knew everything and would curse me.

"Thank you, child," she whispered, taking my hand. "Such a comely girl you are," she smiled. "Are you married?"

"No ma'am," I said, trying to avoid her eyes.

"Well, you will be. We all must marry."

"Yes, ma'am."

She seemed more animated now that we were next to her. "My parents chose my husband," she said, sighing.

I could see Mother was growing anxious about the direction of the conversation and hoped to steer it in another direction. "Do you need medicine, Hannah? Or water? I can mix up some snail pottage."

Hannah wasn't thinking of medicine. She was thinking of her life and her approaching release from it. "My parents couldn't afford me anymore," she said quietly. "They thought I should marry into money and be secure." She closed her eyes. "Ah, secure. The good Lord never meant for women to be secure. Not in this world."

Mother was looking more and more anxious. She wanted to be with Hannah in her final days, but she didn't want to hear what Hannah might have on her mind.

It is not often in life we are granted permission to speak our minds. Only in childbirth and dying can women speak and be heard. But we are heard only by other women. The men, who should be listening, are too busy with their work.

Perhaps God hears us, but I didn't think so. If he did, he would have done something.

Desire and I tried to stand behind Mother, but Hannah from time to time would motion for us to step forward and stand next to her bed with Mother. She wanted all of us to hear what she had to say.

I glanced sidewise at Mother, who was debating what to do with us. Finally, she said, "Why don't you girls go back to the inn and help Father?"

Hannah opened her eyes. "No, please, Mary, I'd like them to be here."

Mother hesitated for a moment. "Well, they have work…" But then I suppose she realized she was being like Father, avoiding the painful. "All right, girls, you can stay. Father will get along just fine without us."

Hannah nodded weakly and closed her eyes again.

I watched her tired face relaxing. I realized she was still a young woman, made old before her time.

Just then a large blue fly, which had been buzzing around my head, landed on her face. And then another joined it. I leapt forward, faster even than Mother, to chase it off. Hannah had hardly even noticed the flies. She had more important things on her mind than flies. But we noticed them. They made me sick to my stomach. Hadn't the woman suffered enough in this world without the dirty flies punishing her more? I hoped that in Heaven there would be no more flies. Not for Hannah anyway. Not for women.

Pigghogg was another matter. Flies were too good for him.

Hannah opened her eyes again and smiled at us. She was gathering her strength to tell us something important. "I had two children with my first husband," she said. "Both were girls. They were stillborn." She turned her head toward us and motioned that she wanted to hold all of our hands. She took mine and Desire's in one hand and Mother's in the other.

Suddenly I had the feeling she knew I was the woman her husband had chosen for his next wife. I think it was the way she looked at me and not at Desire or my mother. I could hardly breathe. I wanted to be home again. But I also wanted to hear what she had to say.

"God forgive me," she said, staring at me. "May the good God forgive me."

"Of course he will," Mother said. "He forgives all sins and sinners."

I wasn't so sure about that.

"God forgive me," she said again. Then so quietly we could hardly hear her, she said, "I was happy later they didn't live. I didn't want them to live."

I wished she hadn't said that. I wished she hadn't said anything.

"You don't mean that, Hannah. It's your fever." Mother freed her hand and dipped a cloth into a basin next to the bed and wrung out the water. She pressed it on Hannah's forehead.

"As God is my witness, I do mean it."

"It's the fever," Mother said again, this time more to us than to Hannah.

"That's why I'm dying," she said. "God is punishing me for my sins."

"God loves you," Mother said. "He took your daughters to be at his side."

I don't think Mother really believed that. She just said it because it was what people said. What kind of God would take a woman's daughters away from her to be with him?

Hannah paid no attention. Nothing Mother said would change her mind. "I knew I wouldn't live long. I didn't want those children to be raised by Pigghogg alone. So I was happy he never had the chance to hurt them. As he hurt me."

Mother couldn't say anything to that. Desire and I both wanted to pull away, but Hannah was clinging to us as if she were slipping over a cliff and we were all she had to save her from falling onto the rocks below.

But we couldn't save her. And she couldn't save me.

"Dear girls," she said, squeezing our hands more tightly. "Dear girls…" She couldn't go on. She let go of our hands and we pulled away.

She was drifting off to another world, a better world I hoped.

But she opened her eyes one last time and looked at us. I couldn't be sure, though, but I think she was still looking at me. "Give me your ear, child," she whispered, and I bent over to hear her better.

"Flee, child," she whispered. Or was it free? "Be free, child." I couldn't tell.

Those were her final words. Her eyes glazed over, and Mother closed them gently. "God bless you, good woman," Mother said. "You deserved better from this sad world."

Mother sent us home and found some neighbor women to prepare the body for burial, which took place in the churchyard two days later. Mother and Desire and I left the inn again for the burial, and this time Father said nothing.

Only a few other neighbor women joined us at the burial. As the gravediggers shoveled dirt on her coffin, I hoped she was finally happy. It was kind of her to be thinking of me when she was dying, and I loved her for such kindness.

Pigghogg arrived late for the service and left early. He was a busy man and had much to attend to.

Before he left, he looked across the newly dug grave at me and smiled. I didn't smile back.

CHAPTER 5

Mother and I walked home from Hannah's burial with much on our minds. We both knew we had to obey Father or face severe punishments from the magistrates for unruliness. But Father likely would be punished as well for not controlling his wife and family, for not being master of his house.

Of course the master of his house had to be reasonable. He couldn't beat his wife and children for no reason—or because of drunkenness or a fit of anger.

It was reasonable to require your wife to submit to your request for a daughter's marriage. And it was reasonable to expect your daughter to marry the man you chose for her regardless of who the man was.

It was also reasonable to expect a man, especially a magistrate and a man of the church, to be married. I had heard of a law in another town that required a man to kill three blackbirds and six crows and pay a handsome fine if he remained single, thereby setting a bad example of selfishness and licentiousness.

Pigghogg's wife had died, so the entire colony probably expected him to be married again quickly so as not to set a bad example. I assumed that no one but Mother and Father knew he had settled on me to be his wife. But even if they did know, I would receive no sympathy. People would expect my family and me to be thankful that a girl of my station would have the opportunity to move up in the world, to be married to a man of such wealth and respect.

Silence descended on our family like some great bird had plucked out our tongues. Mother and I and Desire did our work with little talk among ourselves and no talk with Father, who began to feel the weight of our silence. He spoke more quietly himself, and soon stopped reading the bulletins that were posted daily by the door. Our guests had to read them for themselves, and if they couldn't read, they would request that Father read to them.

When I passed Mother and Father's room at night I could hear nothing. Not at first anyway. Then I heard angry words from Father, something about doing your duty. I wondered if Mother had told him that he could touch her no more, as she had threatened when he wouldn't let us visit Hannah on her deathbed.

Desire and I went to bed each night, saying nothing about Hannah or what was going to happen to me. Suddenly, one night I couldn't stand it any longer, and began crying. Crying for Hannah and crying for myself and what would happen to me shortly. Desire turned to me. "What is it, Chastity?" she whispered.

"Pigghogg," I said.

"I'm sorry," she said. Then she started giggling.

"What's so funny?" I said, angry that she would find my situation amusing.

"Pigghogg," she replied, unable to stifle her laughter.

"Let you marry him, then, if you think he's so funny."

Finally she quieted down, and I turned away from her, facing the window overlooking the street. If I was going to escape, it would be on that street, which led out of town and finally out of the colony.

"He's not a man, you know."

"What?" I turned to her again.

"He's not a man."

"Who's not?"

"Pigghogg."

"If he's not a man, what is he?"

"Half a man. Maybe less."

I shook her. "What are you talking about?"

"His cord was cut too short."

"Cut short?" I remembered what the women had said at Goody Johnson's house. "How would you know that?" I said. "Have you lain with him?" I was angry with her for laughing at my plight.

"No, but Sally Thorp has."

"Sally Thorp sleeps with her sisters. Four to a bed. Everyone knows that."

"Only one to a bed that night. Her sisters were gone. So was her father."

"So what happened if you know so much?"

"Pigghogg came over, pretending he was there on business. Sally's mother said that her husband was gone and wouldn't return until the next day. 'My business is with your daughter,' Pigghogg said. 'How's that?' her mother asked. 'I came to court her,' he said."

"So he was courting both of us?" I don't why that should have surprised me or made me angry.

"Successfully, it seems."

I couldn't believe what Desire was telling me. I laughed and told her she should write books.

"Do you want to know what happened or not?"

"Well, if you must. What happened? Pigghogg went home and drank his sack?"

"He'd already drunk his sack. He told Goody Thorp that since he was courting her daughter, he needed to try out the merchandise before making a purchase."

I didn't think even Pigghogg would do such a thing. "It's not true."

"But it is. 'What is your meaning, sir?' her mother asked."

"'My meaning is clear,' he said. 'I mean to lie with your daughter.' So he did."

"Did what?" I still couldn't believe he could be so brazen.

"He lay with her. Her mother couldn't say anything because he was a magistrate and could make trouble for them.

I took Desire's arm. "You mean he lay with her and her mother was in the next room?"

"In the next room, listening to everything."

"God…"

"That's when they both learned he wasn't a man."

"Wasn't a man? What does that mean?"

"Just what I said. It seems the midwife had cut his cord too short. Sally told me she tried to fight him off, but then she realized he wasn't a man and laughed in his face. That's when he bit her on the shoulder. It's what he does. He bites." She laughed again. "At least there'll be no children."

I was going to ask what Sally's father did when he found out, but then I thought of my father and knew that he had done nothing. What could he do? Pigghogg had the power to have him beaten and imprisoned if he protested too loudly.

We didn't say anything for a while, each of us thinking her own thoughts. I pulled the blankets up over my head, hoping that Pigghogg would disappear forever from my life, but he didn't. He remained the same loathsome creature I had known from the first day he came to the inn and pinched me in the rump when I left his table to get his drink.

I didn't know what to do. I was afraid to run away, having no experience in fending for myself. Other women had tried it, and most had been captured and brought back. Only one woman that I had heard of, a relative of Governor Winthrop, had managed to escape and that was probably because she *was* a relative.

But I was just as afraid of Pigghogg. So he wasn't a man. What did that matter? He was a biter, and I knew there were as many ways of biting as there were mosquitoes in our swamps. When a swarm covered us in the evening, as they often did, there was no defense. You couldn't run and you couldn't hide, though there were times when we and the guests would retire to bed early, hiding under blankets even on the hottest days.

I cried myself to sleep many nights, especially on those days when Pigghogg came by and made advances to me. I tried to get Desire to attend to him, but now that he had fixed his attention on me, I was the only one he would tolerate waiting on him. He would request his sack or beer or his corn pudding and soup, and then he'd put his arm around my legs and pull me to him. "Fine legs," he'd say. "They require tender care that only I can give them." "I'm not a horse, sir," I'd say and begin to pull away, but then I'd see Father shaking his head angrily at me, and I'd hesitate.

Finally, Mother called me to her room one night when Father was talking with one of the guests by the flickering candlelight. "You'll need to decide, Chastity," she said. "Pigghogg wants to post the banns."

"Will you guide me, Mother?"

She shook her head sadly. "I have no guidance to offer. I can't bear to think of you running off, alone, pursued by man and beast. But neither can I think of you married to that beast of a man. I don't know what to tell you."

That's when I told her what Desire had told me, that Pigghogg wasn't really a man. He was just a biter.

"That explains much," she sighed. "He's the worst kind. He'll do everything to demonstrate he is a man. There'll be more than biting. Lord, one might wish he were a man. There's some pleasure for us in that."

"Pleasure?" What was she talking about?

She smiled sadly. "When the time comes and there's no worry about children."

Mother had never said anything like that before to me. I remembered that she had told Father he was not to touch her anymore, so I realized then that she was denying herself for me. I loved her for it. But I couldn't imagine the pleasure she was talking about.

I decided that night I didn't want to leave Mother. She had lost a child already in childbirth and could have no more. I was her only child, and she loved me as I loved her. She had lost enough in her life. I resolved not to be another lost child, though I didn't know then there are many ways of losing.

I made my decision. I would marry Pigghogg and make the best of it. I told Mother my decision.

"Are you sure, Chastity? Your heart tells you this?"

"I'm sure," I said, trying hard to smile.

She held me to her and looked into my eyes. "All right, then. We must put our trust in God. If we show our faith, he will give us strength to find a way. And you'll be with us, as you are now. That will be a blessing. To me. And to father."

"Father? He's the cause of this."

"He is. And knows it. But he does love you. He knows no other way. Perhaps there is no other way. I can't see far enough to know." She looked out the window, as if trying to see the way. "Well…" She couldn't finish. She started crying, and I did too. For myself. For her. For all women who must make such choices.

CHAPTER 6

So it was decided: I would marry Pigghogg in the summer. The banns were published on each of three Sabbaths, and Mother and I were required to be at the Boston meeting house to hear them. Pigghogg sat ahead of me, along with several other distinguished men of the town, and seemed quite pleased with himself. He would occasionally turn slightly to smile at me, behind him, making sure that the rest of the congregation was aware of his magnanimity in agreeing to marry one so below him in station. I didn't return his smile and pretended to be listening to Reverend Wilson and his interminable sermons, wishing that the hourglass would crack and the sand would carry me to the seashore and away from my chosen fate.

One Sabbath, before the second reading of the banns, I was feeling so malicious that I asked Father if he would attend the service with us. "No," he said. "Someone must see to the guests' comforts." He wouldn't look at me when he said that.

I wouldn't let him off the hook that easily. "You should be there," I said. "The Reverend Wilson will think you oppose the marriage to one of his most respected deacons."

"It's none of my business," he said sharply, vigorously polishing the mugs for the spirits he would be serving later in the day, much against the colony's laws.

"None of your business? None of your business? Is it my business, then," I said, turning on him spitefully, "that Pigghogg has chosen me and I must marry, though the man makes me want to vomit every time I see him?"

Father had a gift of tongue. He could answer any question put to him and at great length. He could entertain our guests for hours with stories, real and imagined, and I could remember in detail many of the stories he had told me when I was a child. But he had no response to this question. He stood in the kitchen, cleaning what he had already cleaned, saying nothing.

Finally, he turned to me, and I could see the pain on his face. "Chastity…" he said, but could say no more. He held out his hand to take mine, but I pulled away. "You'll not touch me," I said as viciously as I could, remembering that Mother had said much the same thing when she confronted him about attending Hannah's dying.

I had struck at Father with a knife of vengeance, and there was no retracting that knife. It had penetrated to his heart, and he almost reeled before the blow. The warm relationship we had once had dissolved in the acid of my words that day.

Some people, like the Reverend Wilson and Pigghogg, deserve that knife, though they are no better for the receiving it. We are the ones who feel better, though later the feeling passes and we are left with a hole in our own hearts, while those we attacked are unchanged by the thrust, protected by the armor that kind always forges.

Father was not Reverend Wilson or Pigghogg. But I couldn't see that when I was young.

I turned away in disgust and spent the rest of the day in sullen anger. That evening I retired to my room, where Desire was already preparing for bed. It was a hot summer night, and she was debating how best to protect herself. "If I sleep naked," she said, "it will be cool but the mosquitoes will attack. On the other hand, if I wear my shift, I'll be hot, but the mosquitoes will have less of me to feast on. What shall I do, Chastity?"

"I don't know," I said, paying her little attention.

She laughed. "Well, you'll be sleeping naked soon enough when Pigghogg attacks you."

His name caught my attention.

"He won't touch me!" I said angrily. "Just let him try!"

"Ha. You won't keep him away any more than the mosquitoes. He'll bite every bit of tender flesh he can find." She looked me over carefully as I removed my underdress and stood in my shift. "And you have much to find, Chastity."

She gave me the strangest look, as if she wanted to bite me herself. I shuddered to think of Pigghogg biting me, but as I watched her remove her shift and stretch before me, naked, I tingled inside. It was something I had never felt before. I didn't know what to make of it.

In bed that evening we could hear the murmuring of voices in the great hall below. Now and then a voice would rise to a shout and then die down as the shouter was stilled with a hearty drink offered by another guest. Sometimes I supposed that the silence meant the men were making wagers. They would wager against most anything that came to mind. Who had more land? Whose house was more finely furnished? Whose wife was more comely? Or more satisfying in bed? Sometimes they would look at me when they made these wagers. A month ago a man had wagered that I would be more satisfying than another man's wife, and the other man said, "How do we know unless we sample the wares?" "Look and judge for yourself," the first man said. "If those aren't the juiciest melons you've ever set eyes on…" I escaped to the kitchen when I saw them looking hungrily at my bosom.

I turned to Desire who was lying on her back, naked, the sheet pulled up to her belly. I could see her breasts rising and falling as she breathed in the warm night air.

"Desire?"

"Hmm."

"What will he do?"

"What will who do?"

"Pigghogg."

"Oh. Him." She turned to me. "How should I know? I'm not married to him. Nor will I be. I'll be married to no man. I'd rather be a thornback than a wife to one of that kind."

"But you know about these things. You told me about the biting."

"I only told you what I heard."

"But you know…what happens. What will he do? When I can no longer flee him?"

"You'll find out soon enough."

"Desire, please." I knew that she was more experienced than I was. After all, she had older sisters who had been with men, even if she hadn't. I had no sisters to guide me, and I didn't want to ask Mother. She had enough problems with Father, especially now that she had told him he couldn't touch her anymore.

"Desire, what will he do?"

I really wanted to know what Pigghogg would do. But I think I also wanted to know what she would do.

At first Desire just looked at me, smiling. Then she opened her mouth, just a bit, and slipped her tongue out between her lips and drew it in again. Her eyes sparkled.

She pulled herself toward me. "What will he do? What do you think, silly girl?"

I didn't say anything. I didn't know what anyone would do, much less Pigghogg or Desire.

"He will do what all men do, except that he's not a man and will never be one no matter how hard he tries. The midwives made sure of that."

"Show me," I said, not realizing what I what saying.

Desire just gazed at me, and then the look in her eyes changed. They were burning now, as hot as our room was with no breeze coming through the open windows. "Yes. I'll show you. I'll show you, Chastity, just what he'll do."

She moved closer to me, tugging at my shift. "You must take off your shift. No man will be satisfied unless he sees you naked."

I sat up and pulled my shift over my head as she directed. Desire watched me, smiling with pleasure.

"There now. You're ready for the plucking."

She pushed me down and pinned my shoulders against the bed. It was strange because just then I could smell both her and the straw which filled our mattress. It was a pleasant smell, and I breathed in deeply.

Then she climbed atop me, as if I were a brother she was wrestling with. "First, he'll do this," she said, lowering herself on me. "Then he'll caress your breasts. Like this."

She took one breast in her hand and gently rubbing it, lowered her head and ran her tongue lightly over it. I didn't know what to say or do, but I enjoyed what she was doing. "'Like a ripe melon,' he'll say, and fill his mouth with your breast, tasting its sweetness. Like this."

I lay there quietly, allowing her to have her way. She said nothing, gently caressing my breasts and running her tongue over each one. I put my arms around her back and held her firmly to me.

Then, just as I felt an urgency and began to move under her, she sat up.

She looked angry.

"Desire, what's wrong?"

"Now he'll realize he's not a man. He'll be angry as a bull. Snorting and bucking his legs out in rage. He'll roughly seize you, like this, and turn you over."

She took my arm turned me on my stomach.

"He'll mount you again. Burning with rage and shame that he can't finish what he started."

She sat astride of my buttocks as if I were a horse and she would ride me to the next colony. I thought of her being the rider, the wind blowing in her hair as she urged me over the flatlands surrounding us. It was exciting, and I responded with pleasure.

Desire broke into my thoughts again. "Ashamed of himself and his manhood, he'll be dangerous like a mad bull. He'll bite you now, Chastity. But he'll look at you no more that night. Not again until he's filled with his passion. Or rage or whatever it is that moves men to do these things."

I could feel her lowering her face to my naked shoulders. I waited for her to bite me, wondering what it would feel like.

She took my flesh in her mouth, and I could feel her teeth. She closed them on my skin, but gently, just pricking my skin. Then I could feel her tongue gently washing over the bite.

Desire slipped her arms around me, holding my breasts, and we lay there quietly for the longest time. Sometimes she would whisper some silly thing in my ear, and I told her that she should ride me to Reverend Wilson's house and we might prance all night before his window.

"Reverend Wilson's heart will fail him at such a sight," she laughed.

"Good," I said, smiling at the thought.

Desire bit me gently again. "And what of his wife?" she asked.

"She would remember that her husband is no man himself, despite their children. She might join us in prancing," I said, even more pleased at the thought.

"Ah, that would be a sight. The minister's wife prancing on the Boston Common."

"We could summon others," I said. "Let all of the women, tired of their husbands, prance together. What pleasure that would be!"

Then, as I lay there, enjoying myself as I never had before, a dark cloud passed over me. I couldn't make it go away. I thought of Hannah, Pigghogg's wife, who never had the opportunity to prance gaily on the Common. In her short life she had only the anger of her husband's teeth to endure, for they could have brought her no pleasure as Desire's did to me. In her dying words she had told us she was glad her children died so that her husband could not hurt them as he had hurt her.

Then I thought of Mother and Father in ways that I had never thought of them before. They were always just…Mother and Father, two beings who were there like the trees or the swamps or the ocean. I wondered if Father bit Mother and whether she enjoyed it. I wondered if Mother no longer allowed him to touch her, if he felt himself less a man. And if that put him in such a rage that he might want to bite and hurt her, as Pigghogg did with his wife.

The tears of joy which I had felt with Desire turned into tears of sorrow. Why couldn't we have more joy in our lives? Why did Pigghogg and Reverend Wilson and even the Governor, John Winthrop, want to deprive us of joy when there was so little of it in the first place? Did it make them feel better about themselves? Did they find pleasure in it? Did it make them feel more like men, and if so, why was that? Why did feeling like a man mean that you deprived others of whatever joy they could find in their short lives? Poor Hannah. She never had the chance to find any happiness. Her husband and the other men had kept it from her, as parents might put a bottle of poison beyond the reaches of their children.

It wasn't right, and it made me angry.

Maybe Desire was thinking the same thing because she rolled off me and lay against my back, breathing softly into my neck. "Well, Chastity," she whispered, "we've had our little ride. You'll be leaving soon for another sort of animal. Will you remember me?"

"Of course I will. I'm not moving to Connecticut or New York."

"No. Something worse," she said, and I could tell she was crying softly. "You're moving to Pigghogg's house."

"That's not far."

"It might as well be the old country or eastern lands across the sea. We'll not be together again. Not as we were tonight."

I tried to deny what she was saying, but I knew she was right. We would be together no more, not, at any rate, like we were on this delicious summer night.

We fell asleep shortly after, dreaming our own dreams. I don't know what she was dreaming, but I do remember mine. And they were dark indeed, nightmares of dark woods and angry bulls and thundering, angry voices forcing me to bend to the ground. I wanted to free myself, to escape to the sun on the seashore, but the voices in the darkness kept me in the woods. I couldn't reach the sunny shore no matter which way I turned.

CHAPTER 7

A week before the wedding Pigghogg demanded I wait on him at his private table. When Desire tried to accompany me, Father took her arm and told her to mind her own business.

I stood before his table, saying nothing. He looked like a fattened pig, grinning in his slop food.

"It will be a smock wedding," he said.

"Sir?"

"You heard me. It will be a smock wedding."

I didn't know what he was talking about.

"Are you so ignorant, then?" he snarled.

"Is it drink you want? Or food?"

"In time, woman. In time. I'm speaking now of our marriage next week.

"Our marriage?" As if I had forgotten.

"You've not heard of the custom?"

"No sir." In truth, I had not heard of such a thing. Stories of strange customs were widely circulated, especially in the taverns and inns, but I couldn't remember such a story being told.

"I've arranged it with your father. We are to be married in the inn."

No one had told me where it was to be held. But then I wasn't important enough to be informed of these things.

"And, as I said, it will be a smock wedding. To avoid your debts."

"I have no debts, sir."

"Your father does. And his debts are yours."

"But his debts are to you."

"Some of them, yes. But there are others, incurred in building the inn and supplying its furnishings."

"They will be paid, I'm sure."

"They will not be paid," he said, his voice rising. "That's why we're having a smock wedding in the inn where you live."

"Sir?"

"You're dumber than a chicken," he said. "Friends told me this marriage to you was foolish. I sometimes think they're right."

I didn't think I was dumber than a chicken. I was curious about the marriage, and chickens are curious about nothing. They just cluck and eat and then are eaten themselves. But then I thought of Pigghogg and his biting, and I wasn't so sure I wasn't going to be the chicken.

"If I might ask, sir, what is a smock wedding?"

"Until the magistrate marries us, you will remain unclothed in your closet."

"Unclothed? In my closet?" My spirits rose. Pigghogg had gone mad, and I wouldn't be forced to marry him.

"It will be warm enough that you'll manage quite easily. Be happy it's not winter."

First I was a chicken. And now I was to be an undressed chicken hiding in my closet. But my mother was preparing a wedding dress for me. Was I not to wear it after all?

"In a closet, sir?"

"In a closet, sir?" he mimicked me. "Of course in a closet. Do you think I want my finest possession to parade naked in front of these lusting men? You are mine and only mine, Chastity. You will need to remember that."

He took my wrist and held it tightly. "You *will* remember that, won't you?"

"Yes, sir. But the closet. How can we be married in the closet?"

"*We* will not be in the closet. You will be in the closet, and the magistrate marrying us and I will be outside."

Now I knew he had gone mad. I looked for my father, but he had his back turned to me.

"Then we cannot be married," I said, thinking that I was to be saved after all.

"We will be married, as I said. Your father will have a hole cut in the door of your closet. You will take my hand through the hole, and we will say our vows."

"But I'll have no clothes on."

"You'll have no clothes on that night either," he leered. "So consider it a rehearsal for the evening's festivities."

"But my wedding dress…"

"Oh, don't worry about your confounded dress! You're like every woman. You think of nothing but show. Hannah was no different. But I'm a considerate man. You'll have your dress in the closet. When we've repeated our vows, you'll put it on and join me and the guests downstairs."

I was getting angry at all this nonsense. "Is this a game, sir?" I said. "Because I'll make no game of marriage. Even to you."

"Now listen to me, Chastity," he said, squeezing my wrist tighter. "This is what you will do whether you like it or not. Once you are married unclothed, you and your father will have removed your debts as you removed your clothes. It's the law." He paused and smiled. "And I, above all, respect the law."

I didn't know about the law, but I knew about chickens. No chicken was dumb enough to observe a law like that.

In the kitchen I told Desire about his plans. She laughed and told me I was lucky. Some women had to stand naked or in their shifts on the highway to have their debts forgiven. Their lovers would meet them, together with a magistrate, and the marriage would be performed on the highway. Travelers would often stop and join the activities.

I didn't believe any of it. I should have.

"What are you doing to my door?" I asked Father the next day as he brought his tools into my room and began work.

"You see what I'm doing," he said quietly, not bothering to look at me.

"I see you're cutting holes in my door," I said. "Are you letting the moths out?"

He kept at his work, saying nothing.

Desire and I both watched him. Desire seemed to think it humorous.

"It's a holy door you're making, sir," she said.

He mumbled something but kept on working.

I was losing control of myself again, what with his boring the hole and Desire snickering at his foolishness. "Only a stupid chicken would bore holes in a closet door," I said.

He stopped his work. I wondered what he'd do or say. But he soon resumed his work, saying nothing. To see him calmly boring that hole made me more furious than anything he had ever done.

I screamed at him. "It's stupid! Stupid! Stupid! Not even a chicken could be so stupid!"

Such talk to a parent, especially a father, could lead to severe punishment. Five, ten lashes at the post. But I didn't care. I had become a pot of bubbling grease and lye, boiling over but making no cleansing soap. I screamed into his ear and began to hit him with all my strength. I was defending myself from the man who meant to kill me.

Father dropped his tools and put his arms up to protect himself. Then Desire rushed over and held my arms. "Chastity! Stop it! Stop it! It's your father!"

Of course it was my father. Who else would sell his soul and his only daughter to a Pigghogg? And then cut a hole in her closet door so she could be married inside, naked as a baby, to free him from his debts? Who else but a stupid chicken of a father?

Father still wouldn't look at me. All he said was, "It's the custom." That's all he ever said about it. "It's the custom." God help us all if it's custom to marry your daughter to such a man through a door hole.

Later, I asked myself what he could have done at this point. Probably nothing. He had already put his foot into the swamp, and now the other was being drawn in as well.

It's a good thing to avoid putting the first foot in.

Good advice, I thought. But if it was such good advice, why didn't I follow it myself? I had decided not to run away to free myself of Pigghogg. So now I was to marry him, and marry him I did, just as Father and Pigghogg had decided—in a closet. And then in the darkness to put on my bridal dress which Mother had so lovingly made for me.

I stepped out of the closet a new person with a new name. I was now Chastity Pigghogg, no longer Chastity Hoar. If that was an improvement, it wasn't evident to anyone.

Desire and Mother helped me arrange the wedding dress, which was much askew from my dressing in the darkness. Father, Pigghogg, and the magistrate had withdrawn themselves downstairs to await my arrival.

I think it was going down the stairs, with Mother on one side and Desire on the other, that I began to sense the changes that were about to come in my life. I was a married woman now and would be leaving my home and family for the first time. I had repaid my father's cruelty in marrying me with hard and hateful words, breaking whatever bond we had. I was even angry with my mother for allowing it to happen, though of course there was little she could have done to prevent it. She, too, had put her first foot in and was now seeing the other being dragged in to join it. If you were born a woman in these times, you already had the first foot in. All you could do was resist as long as possible the other being dragged behind it.

Most of Boston and Roxbury had been invited to the wedding party, including the magistrates and church officials. That meant that Reverend Wilson, who, like the other ministers, was not allowed to officiate, watched me with vulture eyes as I came down the stairs. Other ministers from the area made their appearance, though it was apparent from their scowls that they disapproved of the boisterous activities of the revelers. I watched as they sampled the wedding cake, but refused the sack-posset they were offered. They stood aside, talking to themselves and several other silent, frowning men. But I couldn't hold that against them. There was much to frown about.

Watching them, I had the feeling they were recording everything that happened so that it could be used as evidence when one of us, even Pigghogg, should make a mistake and break one of their iron laws. They would then pounce on their prey, and there would be no stopping them. They would produce the evidence they found on this day of sorrow for me and joy for everyone else.

Well, it wasn't joy for everyone. Desire, who wanted me to stay with her longer, cried when I held her to say goodbye. "Come back to visit us, Chastity," she said. "We can still hold each other when the pig's not looking. Pigs have bad eyes, you know." I told her I thought this pig had very good eyes.

And Mother. We had had many good times together. And talks late into the night. It was no joy for her to see me off with Pigghogg. She disliked him almost as much as I did. "Courage, child," she said and turned away, unable to watch what she had no power to stop.

As for Father, I didn't think at the time it made any difference to him. I believe I was wrong about that. But I was too young to understand how we cannot always walk the most agreeable road before us, and choosing the fork lying at our feet will bring pain no matter what fork we choose. We choose our forks in the road, but the pain is chosen for us, as the mosquitoes on the way to Pigghogg's house chose us, swarming from the swamps toward the fine black horse Pigghogg had ridden to the wedding to demonstrate his wealth and prestige in the colony. I walked behind him, and saw Mother and Desire waving at me. Father was behind them, standing in the doorway, fiddling with a message posted on the wall to his side. He was only half looking at the poster.

Then they were all lost in the cloud of mosquitoes, whining and buzzing through the heavy air toward us. Pigghogg swore and brushed them off his arm toward me. On me they found a home. They bit me mercilessly all the way to Pigghogg's house, which fortunately was only a short distance away. We both could have walked there, as I was now, but walking was for common people and Pigghogg felt himself no common person. It was bad enough he'd married a common girl, who was now dutifully walking behind him.

I had been in Pigghogg's house once before, to help Mother care for Hannah in her dying, but I had not really seen it. Now that I was to be mistress of the house, I saw it more clearly.

The house stood like a fortress or castle on the corner of the dusty street. It was huge, larger than the inn, and it was dazzling in the afternoon sun, which had just broken through the clouds and was reflecting off the bits of broken glass mixed into the stucco when the house was built. As my eyes drifted over the exterior, from the latticed windows with the heavy shutters to the prison-like arched wooden door, I felt that the house was indeed a fortress that once entered would allow no escape. That heavy door would close on me and would remain closed forever.

In my mind as we approached the house I thought the horse would turn away, frightened by its fearsome appearance, and take himself and Pigghogg into the woods and beyond, far beyond into the next colony, but it stopped, docile and respectful, at the front door.

The door opened at our approach and a man and a woman appeared in the doorway, both of them dressed in their finest clothes. They bowed to Pigghogg as he strode toward them, pulling me along with him. "This is my wife, James," he said to the man who bowed slightly at his approach. "You will treat her with the respect she deserves. You will address her as Mistress Pigghogg. Is that clear?"

"Yes, sir," James replied, nodding his head.

I believe I saw the slightest of smiles cross the man's lips. When Pigghogg was admonishing the woman, I looked more closely at James, who didn't lower his head as his master expected him to. I thought I saw a brief flicker in his eyes that told me he loathed his master as I did and that he would be a friend to me if I needed friends, as I surely did.

The woman was another matter. She had ushered us in before and seemed unpleasant even then, so it was not surprising she was just as surly in greeting me now. Since Pigghogg didn't mention her name, I had to ask her name later in the day. She informed me coldly that her name was Dorothy, and she would be pleased if I called her by her rightful name. Surprised by her hostility, I replied in kind. I told her I would indeed call her by her rightful name and would be even more pleased if she did *not* call me by my name or anything that suggested I was Pigghogg's wife. "What should I call you, then?" she asked, her face in the perpetual frown I came to expect. "Just call me Mistress or Madam," I said, since I disliked the name Chastity as much as she liked the name Dorothy.

I wondered why she disliked me so much and supposed that being Pigghogg's servant had given her a bitter crop to harvest. But I couldn't be bothered with Pigghogg's bond servant. I had enough to contend with in Pigghogg himself.

Since we had eaten at the inn after I was married through the hole in the door, Pigghogg decided I required no more food for the day. "It's too hot to eat," he told Dorothy. "I plan to retire early," he added, smiling. I could see that pleased Dorothy, who would be spared the hot work of preparing dinner.

Pigghogg drew me to the stairway that evening to show me his family, all now shadows of their former selves. The heavy-framed portraits of the frowning men and women of the Pigghogg family surrounded me like dark ghosts guarding their kingdom from common intruders such as me. Pigghogg was pointing out one old man, dressed in a black suit with a white ruff around his neck, when he looked back at me. I was gazing out the window at a passing horse and cart, wishing I were on it.

Pigghogg became angry. "This is my family," he snapped. "Respect them."

"I do, sir."

"Do you know who this is?" he said, pointing to portrait above him.

I looked closely. "A dead man," I said.

He whirled and grabbed me, squeezing my arm so hard it hurt. "That man is my revered grandfather. A much respected judge in the old country."

"Yes, sir."

"Now, tell me, Chastity, who is the man?"

"A dead judge," I said. "From the old country."

Pigghogg squeezed my arm harder. "That is Judge Pigghogg, Chastity," he said. "You will remember that. You will study each of these," he said, sweeping his hand over the surrounding pictures, "and you will remember the name of each one. I will question you every morning."

"Yes, sir. I'll try. But I have a poor memory."

"It will improve with practice. Now who is this man?"

"Judge Pigghogg," I said.

"Very good."

"But he's still dead," I added.

"He is *not* dead!" Pigghogg sputtered. "None of these men are dead. Do you understand me, Chastity? None of these men are dead. They guide me every day of my life."

"If you say so."

"I do say so. And you will remember it. These men are more alive to me than…you are."

He pulled me to the portrait of the judge. "More alive than you are, Chastity. Remember that."

"You've given me much to remember," I said.

In truth he had. I would remember that we were married through a hole in the door. I would remember he thought these frowning ghosts more alive than I was. I would remember what he did later that evening. I had thought he was mad when I thrust my arm through the door hole to marry him. Now I knew he was mad. Mad as that woman in Boston who swept the streets each morning, calling out to anyone who'd listen that she was the bride of Jesus, and she was sweeping up our sins to save us all from the fires of hell. Or the man who beat his cow in front of the meeting house on lecture day, thinking it possessed because its milk dried up.

Suddenly, Pigghogg turned from his ghost family. "We're retiring," he said. "Prepare yourself."

I was real again. So much the worse for me.

I am shamed to think of that night. I could not even imagine what was to happen. Neither Desire or Mother, despite what they had told me about men, could have prepared me for what Pigghogg would do.

Or couldn't do.

Pigghogg led me into his upstairs bedroom, holding me as if I were a horse he was taking to pasture. At one end of the room was a beautiful bed, such as I had never seen before, draped with the whitest of silky curtains. The headboard and endboard were carved with figures which I couldn't quite see from the door. Later I found they were naked men and women, in many exotic and unseemly poses.

"Undress," he ordered me.

I looked around and saw the closet door. I walked to it.

"Where are you going?" he barked.

"To the closet. I thought to undress there."

"Why would you undress in a closet with your husband waiting for you?"

"I was married in a closet," I said.

His face darkened. "Take care with your words," he said. "Loose talk is severely punished in this colony. And I am a magistrate, you'll remember."

If I remembered everything Pigghogg told me to remember, my head would be like the stuffed scarecrow Mother put in the fields each summer, with as little use for the stuffing as the scarecrow—or the birds that paid it no heed, eating their fill every morning when we looked out on the fields.

I was not allowed to undress in the closet—or in another room. Pigghogg demanded I undress in front him, one piece at a time. Seeing no alternative, I did as he asked. He sat in his straight-back, caned chair, hands in lap, and watched me, smiling his greedy little smile.

I felt sick. I stopped undressing and looked for the chamber pot.

"What's wrong with you?"

"My stomach hurts."

"That's hardly my problem. Blame your parents. It was their food."

It was then I decided, pain or no, I would show him no more weakness. My pain was mine and not his to find pleasure in. He would see no more weakness in me. I would show him only strength.

I closed my eyes and my mind and continued undressing.

"On the bed," he ordered when I was naked.

I lay on the bed.

"On your stomach."

I rolled over.

"Good. Hmm. Ripe enough for cutting open."

Good god, what was he thinking? What would he do? I kept my eyes closed and my head buried in a soft pillow.

I heard him cross the room and return. He stood next to the bed.

The fire burned my buttocks. I tried to roll over but he held me down. The fire burned again. He was whipping me with his riding whip.

I was about to plead with him to stop when I remembered my resolution. I would show him no weakness.

Again and again the whip burned me. I held my head into the pillow. I dug my nails into my palm to keep from screaming.

Then it stopped. I waited for the next blow but it didn't fall.

He was doing something, I didn't know what.

I lay there for minutes, waiting for another blow, but none came. Instead, he took me by the arm and rolled me on my back.

"Close your eyes," he commanded. "And sit up."

"They're already closed," I said. "What is there I might want to see?"

He said nothing but tied a large handkerchief around my eyes. Then he pushed me down on the bed, this time on my back.

My back and legs burned. I was buried in a dark, flaming pit.

I tried to think of home and softer things, but I couldn't hold them in my mind. They kept wiggling away like fish from a net.

I kept wondering what he'd do next. Desire had told me something about Pigghogg and his desires, but none of this sounded familiar. Not knowing what he'd do next frightened me, and I began sucking in air, trying to breathe. Please, please, I thought, anything but more beating. I'll do anything you want but no more beating.

But then I thought of Pigghogg, his fat and greasy belly, burning and smothering me like an overturned leach barrel, its foul contents pouring over me. I felt sick again and longed to turn over and relieve myself of the sickness.

Then it happened. I could hear the door open softly and footsteps approach the bed. There was a pause, a muffled sound, a forced breath, like when you're hit in the stomach and can't breathe.

I tightened my muscles and waited for the blow.

At first nothing came. And then I could feel his knee on the bed, close to me. And now his body settled on me.

I clawed at the sheets, determined I would not cry out or show any weakness—or any pleasure. I would be no more than a piece of wood, cold and hard, on which Pigghogg had laid himself out. If I only could have brought an ax to his skull and laid him open as I would a pig ready for fall butchering.

His weight was not what I thought it would be. It seemed lighter. His body seemed firmer. All of it. That was surprising, given what Desire had told me about him.

I wanted to push him off and free myself. But I did nothing. I kept my arms to my side and made no movement. I hid my heart and soul in the darkness. I would show my soul to no one, least of all Pigghogg. Deep inside I was safe. He couldn't reach me, no matter how long his arms or great his prestige.

He groaned and then was finished. It didn't take long, not as long as the beating. And it was not nearly as painful as I had thought.

"Take off the blindfold," he commanded.

I took it off and could see in the flickering candlelight only the dark outlines of his body, bloated like a dead cow. His shadow hung over the bed, touching me on the leg. I moved away.

"Next time you will show more pleasure."

"I cannot show what I don't feel."

"Sinners at the whipping post feel no remorse until the lash descends. It teaches an admirable lesson on feeling."

He turned and walked to the door.

At the door he turned back to me. "You will remember that, Chastity, won't you?"

God help me. What more would I have to remember?

CHAPTER 8

My duties in the house were simply to satisfy Pigghogg's many appetites. I was required to make his meals at various times during the day, whenever he returned in need of nourishment. Actually, I was not allowed to make the meals or even go to the market to fetch the ingredients. I was allowed only to plan what we were to eat. Both Dorothy and Pigghogg made it clear I was to do no more. At first that seemed a kindness, but I finally grew bored with nothing to do. I asked Dorothy if I could help with the preparation, and she ordered me from the kitchen. When I asked why, she said, "You'd as like to poison Mister Pigghogg." The thought had never occurred to me, but now that it had, I pushed it to the back of my mind where it could simmer quietly.

It was in the evenings that my services were required, and I was expected to satisfy Pigghogg's bedroom appetite as I had that first night. It was always the same: lying on my stomach to feel the sting of his riding whip, then turned over like venison on a spit. Next, the handkerchief, the muffled sounds, the footsteps and finally Pigghogg satisfying himself.

That part of the ritual was always puzzling to me. Why the handkerchief? Was Pigghogg so ashamed of his body that he would allow no one, not even his wife, to see it? Did he have some hideous growth, a black, hairy mole, for example, that he wished me not to see? I began to carefully feel around his back, an inch at a time, to find it, taking care not to let him think I was enjoying myself.

Each night I expected the biting I'd been told about, but I never felt it. In fact, it seemed as if Pigghogg kept his face as far from mine as he could. If he could keep his entire body from me I would have been even happier, but such was not the case. Night after night it was always the same. I felt no pleasure, and I couldn't imagine that I gave him any.

Pigghogg also forbade me leaving the house during the day, unless, he said, it's ablaze. And even then he ordered me to remove his ancestors, still more alive than I, from the house before I removed myself. If any of them were lost in the fire, I would feel the consequences on my bare back in the front parlor—or at the whipping post in the marketplace, a spectacle for all to enjoy. And if several ancestors were lost, the rest of the colony would personally be invited to take part in the whipping, so all would have their pleasure as justice was fairly exacted on my back. He would deliver the first blows himself as long as he was able, to be assisted by the constables and other noteworthies as the situation required.

His ancestors were my only companions, such as they were. They were a strange lot with dreary names. Dudley Pigghogg. And his father Eziekiel. His sister Dorcas and their uncle Cornelius. Esborn and Joseph and Mercy—the names spun around in my head like a swarm of black flies, buzzing against the walls to escape but never quite succeeding. I would memorize one and then another, but by noon I would forget both and remember a third, though I couldn't remember who he was cousin to or his place in the great Pigghogg family tree. Despite their silly names, I began talking to them when no one could hear me. "Well, Dorcas, how is it with you today? Was your husband gentle with you last night? Did he satisfy you? No? Well, perhaps, he was too occupied with the wills and deeds to remember himself. Maybe tomorrow. And as for you, Dudley…"

So it went. I was talking with dead people. I began to think Pigghogg was right about them. They were more alive than I was.

There were generally only two live people in the house during the day, and Pigghogg had ordered me not to speak with them, except to give orders on food purchases. Dorothy took my orders, never saying more than was necessary, though it was clear she didn't approve of my orders—or even my presence in the house, for that matter.

When she was gone I was left with the servant James, who avoided me whenever he could. Apparently, he was also following orders not to speak with me unless it was necessary to complete his duties. But since I didn't know what his duties were, except to tend to Pigghogg's horse, I saw him very little. I had the feeling that the chief responsibility of both James and Dorothy was to guard me and report any unusual activity on my part.

I was a prisoner in my own house.

Three or so weeks passed, sometimes without the beatings at night but never without Pigghogg lying on me and having his way. I managed never to show any pleasure, which was easy enough since I didn't feel any. One evening, though, in carefully moving my hand to Pigghogg's left shoulder, I felt a mole. It was a small one, hardly enough to be embarrassed about, but it was a start. I would find a bigger one and then a bigger one and then…I didn't know what. Perhaps I would tell him that his moles were ugly and repulsed me and I would show no pleasure until he had them removed. Maybe he would lose interest in me as he had in Hannah.

I was so bored with my life that I began to think of jumping out the upstairs bedroom window just to see what would happen. What would Pigghogg do if I was hurt and unable to fulfill my duties? What would my mother do if she knew I had been injured falling out of a second-floor window? Maybe she'd think that Pigghogg had pushed me, and she would come to my rescue. That pleased me for a spell, but gradually I came to realize that no one, not even my mother, could rescue me. I was truly slipping into the swamp one foot at a time. At the realization I slumped to the floor and cried my heart out.

I longed to see Mother. And Desire. I was so unhappy that I even wanted to see Father, though he was the one responsible for my situation. Maybe it was just to show him what he had done to me, his only daughter, but I can't deny I wanted to see everyone.

Pigghogg had told me he stopped by the inn to see how his investment was doing, but he said little more. He knew I was desperate to know how my mother was, but I had determined to show him no weakness, and to ask about her would have been seen as weakness. So I bit my tongue and said nothing.

Then, when I was standing at the window one dark morning in late summer, thinking about how far the drop would be and how much it would hurt, I heard a voice.

"Chastity…Chastity."

It was Desire on her way to the market. She was looking up at my window. I was never so happy to see anyone in my life.

"Chastity, how are you?" she called. It was the sweetest voice I'd heard since my marriage in the closet.

"Desire," I called, not caring if the servants or even Pigghogg, busy at his work some blocks away, heard me.

"I've come about your mother," she called up to me.

"Mother. How is she?"

Desire shook her head. "Not well."

"Not well? What's wrong?"

"She worries about you. I told her you could take care of yourself, but it makes no difference." She smiled up at me. "You are taking care of yourself, aren't you?"

Oh my God, taking care of myself? I couldn't even care for the dead Pigghoggs surrounding me on the walls, how could I care for myself? Hearing this, I broke into tears again.

"Chastity? What's wrong?"

"I was about to jump from the window."

"Jump? Chastity, what's come over you? Have you heard about your mother? Come down here. I need to talk with you. And don't you dare jump," she added.

I did as she asked, sneaking out the back door when Dorothy wasn't looking. We fell into each other's arms, mindless of the people passing by on the street. Let them think what they wanted to think.

Desire held me at arm's length. "Now, Chastity, what is this about jumping from your window?"

"Never mind about that. How is Mother?"

Now it was Desire who began to cry.

"Desire, what is it? Tell me now." I held her hands tightly.

"She's not herself. She cries herself to sleep every night."

"You see her sleeping?"

"She sleeps with me now."

"With you?" I couldn't believe it. Mother would never sleep with anyone but Father.

"She moved out of your father's room shortly after you left. She sleeps on the floor in my room. I told her she could sleep in the bed with me or I could sleep on the floor, but she insisted. She talks strangely, sometimes to me, but often to no one.

"Does she speak of me?"

"At first. But then something happened. Something terrible."

"What? Desire, what?" She closed her eyes. She seemed as if in a trance. I shook her. "Desire! What happened?"

"I don't know."

"Of course you know. Tell me now. What happened to Mother?"

"She rolls on the floor. She brings a knife to bed with her."

"A knife? To bed?"

"And she speaks of Pigghogg. Or the ministers, Wilson and Cotton and the rest of them. It's a terrible thing to hear, Chastity. She screams and claws the floor or the bed as if she'd rip them apart. Sometimes I must close my eyes and ears."

I couldn't imagine what was happening. My mother leaving my father's bed, where she had slept all the years since her marriage. Sleeping on the floor in a servant's room. And now this talk.

"Oh, Chastity, she's in terrible danger."

"For screaming and rolling on the floor?"

"It's what she screams. The guests can hear her from downstairs. She screams that she'll cut Pigghogg in pieces and feed him to the pigs. 'Pigghogg to the pigs,' she screams. Sometimes it's Wilson and Cotton too. Then she stabs the floor with her knife."

"Oh, Lord."

"Pigghogg comes to the inn, you know. He'll hear what's she's screaming. Oh, Chastity, I think she's gone mad with grief."

She didn't have to say more. I knew what madwomen could do and what would be done to them if the magistrates learned of their behavior.

I could see in Desire's eyes that we were thinking the same thing, but were afraid to say it. The ministers had never approved of our family, especially of mother and me. And Pigghogg tolerated us only because of Father and the inn.

Witchcraft was what we were thinking but were afraid to say the word. Witchcraft. That could mean, depending on the person, more than the whipping post or the stocks. Mother was in danger if Pigghogg should hear her crying his name. Women had been hanged for less—and burned in the old country.

I couldn't help but think that being Mother's daughter, I was also in danger, especially if I displayed no more enthusiasm about my duties than I had each evening. Pigghogg was forever warning me about my obvious lack of pleasure in accommodating him. And then, the next morning, about my inability to remember the names and ranks of his dead, but now oddly come-to-life, ancestors.

I needed to help Mother. I would have no more time to think about jumping out my bedroom window.

But first I needed to set Pigghogg's mind at rest. If he was pleased with my performance each evening, he would be less ready to attack my mother should her crying out become known to him, as it surely would.

My help came in the most unexpected of ways.

One afternoon in wandering around the house, thinking it to be deserted, I came upon James at work on a worn saddle strap in a back shed. He didn't hear me, and on an impulse I crept up behind him. I gently touched his neck with my finger. Without looking up from his work, he swatted at the touch, thinking it a fly or mosquito. I pulled back so he missed me. I did it again, but this time he swatted my hand.

"Oh," he shouted, not knowing what he had done. He probably thought he had swatted his master and was in for a vigorous beating.

He whirled around. "I'm sorry," he stuttered and then saw who it was. He was relieved it wasn't Pigghogg, just his master's wife, but that was almost as bad. "Oh, ma'am, it's you. I didn't know."

I pretended to be angry with him. "Well, you shouldn't be swatting people without looking," I said, trying not to smile.

"I'm sorry, ma'am," he repeated, looking down.

"I shall tell your master," I said.

That frightened him terribly. "Please, ma'am. Please don't tell him."

"And why shouldn't I tell him you're swatting your mistress's hands? He's ordered me to inform him of what happens around the house when he's gone. This certainly happened when he was gone."

"Ma'am, please." He tried not to show his fear, but his eyes betrayed him. He was blinking uncontrollably.

"You'll need to give me a good reason not to tell him," I said, continuing my little game.

He didn't want to say anything, but the fear of his master overpowered his reserve. "Ma'am, if you tell him, it will be worse for both of us."

"Both of us? How is that, James? You were the one doing the swatting. I was the victim."

"He'll beat me terribly, ma'am. Worse than ever."

"I doubt that, James. Besides, how does that affect me?"

"He'll beat me terribly," he repeated, looking away.

"Your master is a good man. He wouldn't beat you. Only his wife," I said under my breath.

"He does, ma'am. He surely does."

"Ha," I said. "Prove it."

"Ma'am?"

"I'll not tell your master you swatted me if you can prove he beats you." I was enjoying my little game with him. I didn't for the moment consider how he must have felt.

"Every night, ma'am. After…after…"

"After what?"

"When I'm finished with my duties, ma'am."

"Well, I'm going to tell him if you can't prove he beats you."

"Don't tell him, ma'am. He'll not just beat me. He'll increase my debt. I have five more years in service to him. He'll make it ten—or fifteen. I couldn't endure it, ma'am." He looked so forlorn at the prospect I almost relented and ended my play, but I was too angry at my own situation to think of his.

"Well, then you know how I feel, don't you?"

"Ma'am?"

"I'm in his service for the rest of my life, think about that."

"Yes, ma'am."

"How do you think it makes me feel?"

"I'm sorry, ma'am."

"He beats me every night, you know. So don't think you're the only one to suffer at his hands."

James only looked down, afraid to face my anger.

"And that's not all he does, you know." I shouldn't have been saying this because it could get me in serious trouble, but I had no one else to talk with, and it felt good to speak aloud to someone other than the dead Pigghoggs on the wall.

"But you, being a man, wouldn't know about that, would you? You may be a servant but you're not a woman. And you're not a wife to Pigghogg and never will be. You'll have your own wife, when the time comes, and you'll do what you want with her."

He said nothing, his head still down.

"So I'm going to tell your master just what you did. Then maybe you'll know a little of how I feel."

"I do know, ma'am," he said, still not looking at me.

"You don't know anything!" I shouted at him. "How could you? You're a man. You can do what you want with your life. You don't have a father telling you who to marry. You don't have a husband who's little better than the pig of his name. A husband who whips you every night for the pleasure of it and then forces his beastly body on you to satisfy himself. I could drive a knife through his heart!" I cried, not thinking of what I was saying and who I was saying it to.

I stood there glaring at Pigghogg's servant. I didn't care if I was hurting him. I was hurting, too.

"So I will tell your master as soon as he arrives home."

"Yes, ma'am." He had given up his fight.

"Unless you prove to me he beats you."

He looked up again. "If I show you…? You'll promise not to tell him?"

"I said so, didn't I? Why should you doubt me?"

Of course, he had every reason to doubt me, especially after living with his master all these years. Why would he think I was any better than his master?

He looked at me briefly and then gave up. He was so afraid I would tell his master that he unbuttoned the loose shirt he was wearing and turned away from me. He pulled the shirt a bit down over his shoulders. His long hair flowed over his back. I reached to him and pulled the hair aside. There, as he had said, were the stripe marks from his shoulders on down. They were clearly recent.

"Ah, so you were being truthful."

He said nothing, but I could also see that he was shaking with the pain and humiliation of showing me his stripes.

He was about to pull up his shirt when it happened. I was standing very close to him so I could examine the stripes. Suddenly, I experienced a strange sensation. It was familiar, like when I was lost one time as a little girl, but in wandering through what I thought was an unknown and frightening field I suddenly felt at home, even though I didn't recognize anything about me. I sensed I should keep walking in the direction I was walking. It turned out I was much closer to home than I had realized, and I had walked in this field many times.

Just as James was pulling his shirt up, I glanced at his left shoulder.

I gasped and stepped back. I could hardly breathe. I felt faint and grabbed at a post to steady myself.

James turned to me. "Ma'am. Are you all right?"

I nodded, still unable to catch my breath.

"I shouldn't have shown you," he said. "Better that I had accepted my punishment."

I shook my head and held firmly to the post.

He pulled his shirt up and buttoned it. "I should have been a man," he mumbled. "I shamed myself."

I hardly heard or saw him anymore. I clung to the post, trying to get my bearings. The floor of my world had just dropped away, and I was hanging on to the post as if my life depended on it. Perhaps it did.

What I had seen on his shoulder was a small mole.

Then I knew, with little doubt, that James, not Pigghogg, was the man having his way with me each night. James the servant was serving his master in ways that he could never have imagined when he went into service.

"Are you all right, ma'am?" James asked, coming to my side.

I shook my head. I was not all right. It would take some time for me to digest what that little mole had taught me about men.

I staggered back in the house, refusing James's offer to help.

I needed time to think about what I had learned—without Pigghogg nearby, or even James.

Once again I forgot my mother as I considered my own life and the new road I was walking. This time it was indeed an unfamiliar field at the end of which I would find no welcoming home.

CHAPTER 9

I've never been so confused. My mind was swirling like the butter churn, but no sweet butter was forthcoming. I wanted to help my mother, who perhaps was going mad and in grave danger because of Pigghogg, but I had to help myself first. That was the problem: I didn't know how to help myself.

As I was walking to my room, I glanced up at the Pigghoggs scowling at me from their perches on the walls. I wondered if they knew what was happening in my room at night and if the male Pigghoggs had been doing the same things to their wives. Perhaps it ran in the family. So, Cornelius, I thought, was it you or your accomplice that exercised your rights on your wife, and if it wasn't you, then who was the father of your son, Percy, who hangs next to you, unknowing of his real father?

I stopped in the midst of these thoughts when I realized that the Pigghogg family was becoming more alive than I wished them to be. And also, Dorothy happened to be passing by.

"Learning your place?" she observed with the faintest of smiles.

I jumped when I heard the voice. It occurred to me as I looked at her sunken face that she herself might be a Pigghogg. I noted that her face was not unlike that of Pricilla Pigghogg's. Prunes, both of them, without any of the sweetness.

"And you should learn yours," I said with as much authority as I could summon. I fixed her in my glare.

She said nothing and was turning away when I accosted her. "Tell me, Dorothy, how is it you came to Mister Pigghogg's house?"

She stopped and slowly turned to face me. "Ma'am?"

"You heard me. How is it you come to be here?"

"Where, ma'am?"

Her blank face and stupid replies infuriated me. She obviously knew more than she was letting on. "In this house!" I shouted at her. "How is it that you're in this house?"

She stood there, clutching her dust cloth, and gave me the blackest look I've ever seen from a woman. Only Reverend John Wilson could match it for blackness. She drew herself up, standing as tall as she could, though I still could look down at her. "I came with my husband," she said slowly.

"Ah, you're married then?" I was surprised at the admission. I couldn't imagine anyone wanting to marry such a plain woman.

"I am." She said it proudly, as if it were an honor to have someone forced into marrying her, as I was forced into marrying Pigghogg.

"And who might that unfortunate man be?" I said as maliciously as I could.

"You know him well." There was the slightest of cracks in her black stare.

I continued the pursuit, sensing that she would break into tears shortly. "I can't imagine who that might be. The men I'm acquainted with would set their sights higher than a Pigghogg servant."

She flinched briefly, but my words seemed only to make her stronger and more resolved. "Higher than a Pigghogg wife, then?" she said, letting each word sink in.

It was my turn to flinch. The woman had more mettle than I had anticipated.

"I shall speak with Mister Pigghogg about your unruly tongue," I said. I could not imagine that years later the same thing would be said about my tongue, and it would lead me to greater grief.

She said nothing, and her haughty carriage suggested she felt herself superior to me. This angered me even more. I resolved to humble her so that she would remember who was mistress and who was servant.

"You're married to the governor?" I said, smiling. "Or perhaps it's the Reverend Wilson or Reverend Weld of Roxbury. Which man is so blessed with your presence in his marriage bed?"

Just then James passed by on his way, still holding the unrepaired saddle strap. He stopped and looked oddly at me and then at her. It was a look of surprise and not a little disturbed. He gave her the slightest of nods.

In the moment she gave him a restrained smile I understood. How could I have been so blind? Prune-faced Dorothy was married to James the servant and my nightly visitor. Once again I could hardly breathe and leaned back against the wall for support. My head touched and moved a Pigghogg portrait just behind me.

"You'll need to adjust that portrait," Dorothy said, turning and walking past James with an air of triumph.

James watched her leave and then turned to me. "I'm sorry to interrupt, ma'am," he said.

"What is it you want?" I was angry with him as well.

"You won't tell Mister Pigghogg, will you?" He was still frightened of me, as his wife didn't seem to be.

"I've told you already I wouldn't. If you ask me again I will."

I had had enough of both of them for the moment. I turned and raced up the stairs and down the hall to my room. I closed the door quickly behind me. More than anything I needed to be alone.

I walked to the window and gazed out. There was no Desire waiting for me. No Mother either, ready to take me in her arms to comfort me. Nothing but several carts filled with garden vegetables and drawn by plodding, unthinking horses to the marketplace. I felt sympathy for them as their masters swatted their backsides to keep them moving.

I sat in the chair and felt a warm breeze blowing over me. I was too angry and confused to think of jumping out to see what it would feel like.

I needed to sort out my feelings and put things straight in my mind.

First there was James, standing before me, his broad, bared shoulders reflecting the sun through the shed's small window. And the little mole possibly identifying him as the man quietly entering my room each night, Pigghogg at his side and leading him to the bed where I awaited, blindfolded, for the ordeal. Of course, I could be mistaken. Another man could have just such a mole. I would need to confirm my suspicions. But one thing I was sure of: my nightly lover was not Pigghogg, the man whose cord had been cut too short at birth, unmanning him for life.

But then an odd thing happened. I found it hard to catch my breath at the suddenness of the realization. It's true that I was being whipped each night. It's true that a man was nightly forcing himself on me, and that I was at first disgusted with the whole ordeal. But suddenly, it didn't seem an ordeal any longer. It seemed...exciting in some strange way. It was the same man as before, but somehow it wasn't the same man. It was not the fat Pigghogg but a muscular, broad-shouldered man, much like James the servant, who cowered at my command and my threat to speak to his master about him and who perhaps was married to the repulsive Dorothy. That was quite another matter.

I wondered what James thought that first night when he was ordered to my bed. Was this simply a duty he performed with no more feeling than he would having in grooming the horses? Or was he excited by the prospect but needing to mask his excitement lest his master beat him for it?

I thought about it. The handsome James and the ugly Dorothy. What did he see in her? Was he perhaps forced to marry by her parents because she was with child? And if so, where was the child? Or had Pigghogg arranged their marriage as he arranged my own? Was James imprisoned with her as I was imprisoned with Pigghogg? The thought caught my fancy. We were Pigghogg's fellow prisoners. In that prison he must have found me a pleasant diversion from the brutal Pigghogg. And a welcome escape from his ugly wife, whose bed he would need to seek when he was finished with me.

What I couldn't understand was why Pigghogg wanted both of us to be excited by the evening's events. I had to admit I could not fathom what either man was thinking or feeling. But in those days I couldn't understand any man. Ministers, magistrates, servants—it didn't matter; they were all great mysteries to me, like the stars making their circles through the heavens, visible but cold and unknown.

I could understand the woman, though. Dorothy, James's wife, if she was his wife, had good reason to hate me. Her husband was with me, enjoying himself for all she knew, before he joined her in their bed. It occurred to me then that James and Dorothy slept in separate rooms, which is why I had never thought they could be married. Perhaps he didn't join her after leaving me. Perhaps he was too ashamed or too tired. Perhaps she wouldn't have him, knowing that he had been with me just minutes before. Or perhaps they didn't want each other, sleeping together or alone in cold silence, nursing their separate grievances against Pigghogg and, I suppose, against me.

Why, I wondered, did they have separate rooms? Did Pigghogg require the arrangement for unknown reasons? To punish one or both of them for some transgression? Perhaps it gave him an unnatural pleasure to control these marital arrangements. With Pigghogg everything was possible.

But then perhaps I was wrong about all of them. Perhaps my imagination, in the long silences of the house, was running adrift. James might not be my nightly visitor, and he and Dorothy might not be married. I would need more evidence.

Night would soon be upon us, and I needed to set my feet straight on the path that would lead me out of this house to save myself and then my mother.

There was one small, nagging problem—nagging like the vapors and the mosquitoes from the nearby swamp. I was no longer in such a hurry to leave the house. Now that I knew it wasn't Pigghogg crushing me every night, that it was possibly the broad-shouldered James with the deep-blue eyes, my feelings changed. I wondered what it would be like knowing that it was James, or at least another man, and how I would respond. He wouldn't know that I knew. Should I secretly let him know I had discovered Pigghogg's secret? How would that make him feel?

And what about Dorothy, his wife? I smiled when I thought about her lying in her room or perhaps passing my room, knowing that Pigghogg and her husband were having their pleasure with me. She didn't know what Pigghogg was doing, and she didn't know what her husband was doing. That must have made it particularly painful for her, alone in the dark hall outside my door. It served her right, I thought, for being so mean-spirited with me. She surely knew that her husband, as a servant, had to do what he was told, no matter how he felt about it, just as all our women, being treated as servants, had to do what they were told.

That night after dinner I hoped to retire quickly to my room, but Pigghogg had other ideas. He ate half of Dorothy's apple pie and then pushed it away, growling something about it not being up to his mother's standards. His mother had not made a pie for over twenty years, as she was resting in her grave in the old country, but her standards nonetheless seemed to get stricter each year.

Pigghogg wiped his mouth with his sleeve and then sat back in his chair, scowling at me. "I was at my inn today," he said.

"Oh?" He had my attention.

"It was not a pleasant experience."

I could feel my blood quicken. I said nothing, waiting for him to speak his mind.

"It was, in fact, a most unpleasant experience."

I braced myself for the bad news.

"Several magistrates were there. We had important business to conduct; we are most concerned with the increasing laxity of behavior in public houses, such as the one I've allowed your father to run for me."

I said nothing.

He sat forward in his chair, his arms on the table. "Are you listening to me, Chastity? You seem distracted."

"I'm listening." Of course I was listening. How could I have been doing anything but listening to the man who held the keys to my family's lives? Of course I had been distracted, as he surmised, but not for any reason he might suspect.

"Good. Because this concerns you."

"I'm listening."

"Yes." He gave a large belch, moved his tankard aside so he could better fix his piggy eyes on me, and continued. "We were, as I've said, conducting the important business of the colony. Your father had just served us our usual drinks." He paused and stared at me.

"Yes? My father? Is he all right?"

"I wouldn't know his state of health. He seems, like you, distracted."

"And the drinks? They were not to your satisfaction?"

"The drinks were acceptable."

There was no use in putting it off any longer. I had already suspected the problem.

"And my mother?"

His eyes narrowed. "Yes, your mother. I hadn't seen her for some time. People had told me she was talking, acting wildly. But I had no evidence and passed it off as idle gossip."

Of course he had never passed off a word ever spoken as idle gossip. Idle gossip satisfied his and the magistrates' tastes as food does a hungry child.

I turned away from his steady gaze, unable to face what I knew would be coming next.

"Chastity," he commanded.

I continued to look away.

"Chastity. Look at me."

I was boiling inside. I wanted him to spit his bile at my back, not my face. But I also needed to know about my mother. I turned to face him, shuddering when I saw the evil in his eyes.

"Your mother, Chastity, has become like the howling wolves in the woods and marshes. She is a danger to us all."

"Danger?" Of course I knew what had happened. Desire had told me, and she would have no reason to lie. But still I needed to hear him confirm it.

"How is that, sir? A danger? Surely not my mother."

"Blasphemy. Heresy. Sedition. It cannot be tolerated."

"My mother is a good woman," I almost shouted at him. "I cannot imagine a better mother or member of the community." I was about to tell him who the real danger to the community was when he quickly reached across the table, grabbing my wrist and holding it hard.

"Take care, woman. Your mother has shouted for all to hear that God should strike the magistrates dead for their sins."

As well she might, I thought. As well she might.

I was not prepared for what came next.

"She will be examined."

"Examined?"

"For witchcraft."

Oh, god, it was worse than I thought. Witchcraft. Nothing could be worse. Women were hanged on just suspicions of witchcraft.

Pigghogg could see the fear in my eyes. He was enjoying himself. I hardened my face, remembering my vow to show him nothing that might give him pleasure.

"Pigghogg released his grip and smiled. "She will be examined tomorrow."

"Examined?" At the time I didn't know what it meant. I assumed he meant the court would convene and she would have a chance to defend herself, as Mistress Anne had. But then I remembered what had happened to that good woman and her friend—they were banished from the colony. There was some hope in that. She could leave my father for another life. Perhaps I could join her, and we would live together, finding solace in each other's freedom from the men in our lives.

"Yes, examined. As custom and law require."

He took my wrist again. "You will join me, Chastity, at the examination. For your instruction." Then he left, almost knocking over Dorothy who had quietly entered the room. I hadn't seen her enter and hoped that she hadn't heard our conversation.

I glared at her, sensing she knew of my desperation about my mother, but I gave her no satisfaction. "Clean off this table," I said sharply, and rose to leave. "Yes, ma'am," she said, a faint smile crossing her face. Damn the woman, I thought. She rejoices at my misery.

I went to my room early that evening and found myself eagerly awaiting Pigghogg and James—or whoever the mysterious stranger was. I would rejoice at Dorothy's misery when she helplessly watched as her husband left his room for my mine to perform his nightly duties.

It was not to be. For the first time since our marriage, Pigghogg failed to enter my room. Apparently, he had satisfied himself thinking about the next day's events, the examination of my mother.

I could do nothing but lie on the soft, curtained bed and think of my bad fortune in marrying Pigghogg, and of my dear mother, accused of witchcraft. Tomorrow she would be examined, and I would finally be allowed to see her. I fell asleep, feeling hopeful that I would be able to hold her again. We would give each other strength.

It was my custom to rise late in the morning, after Pigghogg had left for his work as magistrate and landlord of several properties. But this morning I was up early, and putting on my best black and white skirt, I descended to the dining room. Pigghogg was a furnace of energy, ordering Dorothy and James to various duties to be performed during our absence, and striding around the house as he never did. I glanced at James to see if I could determine the reason for his absence last night, but I could see nothing. He listened only to Pigghogg and paid me no attention.

Scowling, Dorothy served me breakfast, the usual corn cakes and eggs. Pigghogg had already eaten and paced back and forth, waiting for me.

"Come along, woman," he rasped. "The women await us."

I didn't know what that meant, but it provided a good excuse not to eat Dorothy's food. "All right," I said, glancing at Dorothy, "the meal looks particularly unsuitable anyway." That was the truth. Dorothy tried to disguise her feelings, but I could see that my words had disturbed her.

James had retrieved the horse, its saddle now repaired, and we set off the few miles south to the inn. It was a hot morning, and the only breeze was the one stirred up by the horses on the road.

At the inn I could see several women in the windows, watching our arrival. I had no idea what they were doing there, especially since it was so early in the morning. Even later in the day, there would always be more men than women in the inn, and the women who were there were not known as respectable women.

I followed Pigghogg in, and suddenly I knew something was wrong. It wasn't just the women, most of them neighbors that I recognized from the times I went to market or sometimes saw at the inn if they came to find their husbands. No, it wasn't the women; it was the absence of the men. There were no men, not even my father.

"Where is she?" Pigghogg commanded.

"Upstairs, sir," one of them said. It was Alice Bracken from down the street.

"Take me to her."

"Yes, sir." She turned and motioned to the others and together we walked up the stairs. We stopped at Desire's room, which we once shared.

I didn't want to go in. I wanted to close my eyes and be somewhere else—at the ocean, in the woods. Anywhere but here, at the door of the room where I would see my mother for the first time in months. I didn't know what to expect.

The women parted as Pigghogg swaggered to a chair by the bed. Desire was standing next to my mother, caressing her shoulder and speaking quietly into her ear. "It's all right now," I could hear her say. "It's Chastity."

Mother turned her head slowly in my direction, and I stepped back, shocked at her appearance. I wasn't even sure at first it was my mother. Her beautiful black hair, which she had always combed and fixed so carefully, hung about her face, and her wild eyes searched the room as if she had never before seen it.

"Mother." I started to her, but Pigghogg stepped in front of me, blocking my way. I tried to move past him, but he flung out his arm against my chest, momentarily knocking the air out of me.

It didn't matter. Mother didn't seem to even recognize me.

Pigghogg pushed me back against the wall. "You are to remain apart until the examination. I'll not have you contaminated."

"Examination?" I said. "I see no court."

"For the moment, I am the court," he said and turned to the women. "Strip her," he commanded the women.

No one moved.

"Strip her," he commanded again.

Alice Bracken stepped forward. "If you please, sir."

"What is it?" he scowled.

"If you please, sir. This is a women's duty. It is custom."

Pigghogg stopped, considering the request. But only for a moment. "You reproach me with custom?" he thundered. "Remember who I am."

"We do, sir. But custom requires you to step out of the room while the women proceed with the examination."

"You will proceed with the examination," he ordered. "The court demands there be a reliable witness. And who is more reliable than an important magistrate?"

"Begging your pardon, sir. But it is custom—"

"It is custom that women not conduct themselves improperly in front of their superiors." He stared at each of the women until she looked away. "Is that not correct? Is that not what you learn each Sabbath from our ministers? Is that not the word of God?"

Alice lowered her head. Please, Alice, I thought. Lift your head. Look him in the eye. This is no man you're facing. The person you face was unmanned at birth and must use a surrogate to find his pleasure. He is not fit to sweep your floors.

"Yes, sir" was all she said. "Yes, sir." She turned to the other women and they moved to my mother, surrounding her so that Pigghogg and I couldn't see what they were doing.

"Be quick about it. I have work to do."

They were about to begin their duty when my mother leapt from their midst and ran to her dresser. She picked up a letter opener and faced all of them, snarling like a caged beast.

Pigghogg was furious. He moved toward her, intent on taking her weapon away. Stab him, Mother. Stab him and end our misery.

Mother was a wild woman, waving her weapon about her, eyes blazing, warning everyone to keep their distance. Pigghogg paused in front of her, and she reached for him, plunging the opener at his chest. He stepped aside and caught her arm in a grip so powerful that she screamed in pain and dropped her weapon.

Disarmed, in terrible pain, she crumpled against the wall and slowly slid to the floor. The women watched in horror, and even Desire seemed rooted to the spot.

I ran to her before Pigghogg could stop me. "Mother, it's me. Your daughter. Chastity."

I thought for a moment she recognized me, but then Pigghogg pounced on us, tearing her away from me.

"Strip her," he said to the women with ice in his voice. "Or I'll do it myself."

He pushed me back and was about to begin stripping her when Desire stepped forward. "I'll do it," she said quietly. "You step away."

Pigghogg considered her request. He was about to dismiss her but then thought better of it. He stepped aside, and Desire took my mother gently in her arms and led her away. She submitted weakly, her spirit destroyed.

The women surrounded her again and began removing her clothes. Mother seemed to offer no resistance. I could hear her crying softly, but when I tried to go to her, Pigghogg stepped in front of me again. I stopped, unwilling to risk another blow from his arm.

Mother, Mother, what are they doing to you? What have you done to deserve this shameful treatment? What does this horrid man want with you that he remains in the room? I looked over at the closet door through which I had offered my arm for marriage to Pigghogg. There was no hole. Nothing but a solid door. For a moment I wondered if the hole had ever been there, if I had imagined the whole scene because of my disgust with Pigghogg. Perhaps I wasn't really married to him. Perhaps it was all a dream.

The women had completed their task of stripping Mother. I couldn't see her, nor could Pigghogg. Then I heard a gasp, and one of the women was pointing at Mother.

"What is it?" Pigghogg growled. "What do you see?"

Alice turned to him. "Nothing, sir. She is free of signs."

"She is not!" he snarled, and moved to the group. "I'll see for myself."

As he moved to her, I followed behind. The women tried to protect her, but he easily pushed them aside. Mother stood naked before him, the women holding her firmly.

He looked her over like one of his horses and then his eyes fixed on her privates. "Ahh!" he cried in triumph. "There it is. The evidence that will send her to the gallows."

I couldn't help myself, and I pushed forward to see what he was talking about. I couldn't bring myself to look at anything but Mother's face. Her eyes were closed, and it seemed as if she was no longer alive, that her spirit had left her body, which remained upright only because the women were supporting her.

"The Devil's teat," he hissed. "Where he sends his familiar to suckle."

I followed his gaze and just as I looked, Mother let out a shriek which could have been heard in Heaven if Heaven were listening. "It comes," she cried, looking to the ceiling.

I looked up but saw nothing but the rafters Father and his men had so carefully lifted into place.

"The Evil One comes for her," Pigghogg said, "but he will not prevail."

I looked at Mother again, but she had collapsed and the women were bending over her. Pigghogg looked once more at her and turned away. He grabbed my arm and began dragging me away. I pulled back, reaching toward my mother. I wanted to hold her in my arms, thinking that I could heal her, that I could draw into me whatever evil spirits had found their way into her body and soul.

Pigghogg was too strong, and I found myself being dragged to the door.

"You will attend the trial," Pigghogg flung back to the women, "and testify to the horror we have witnessed today."

The women said nothing and turned again to my mother.

Pigghogg closed the door on them, and guided me forcibly from the inn. I thought I would never see it again.

CHAPTER 10

Pigghogg became a man possessed. The upcoming trial consumed all of his energies for the next week, and he seemed to forget I existed or that three people lived in his house with him. I might have considered that a good thing if it hadn't been for the fact that it was now my mother who had drawn his attention—my mother who would be on trial for witchcraft.

My evenings, which just a few days ago I had almost been looking forward to, were now spent alone in my room. No one spoke to me, even at dinner, and I found myself talking to the Pigghogg family and then answering myself in their voices. It helped pass the time.

Then one night at dinner Pigghogg finally addressed me. The trial, he said, was scheduled for Thursday following the morning lecture. It was to be at the meeting house because of the significance of the charges. He would be one of leading magistrates, offering whatever testimony was required.

I had vowed never to enter the meeting house again, for that was where Mistress Anne had been found guilty of heresy and sedition. She and her dear friend Mary Dyer had been banished from the colony. If Mary had known of Mother's trial, brave woman that she was, she would come to comfort Mother, as she had comforted Anne.

But that was no help to me now. Mother had no one except Desire, who was only a servant and carried no authority. Of course, there was Father, but who had he ever aided? He was the cause of all this trouble, marrying me to Pigghogg, which had led to Mother's madness and this trial for her life.

Pigghogg rode his horse—and I walked behind—to the meeting house though it was but a few blocks away. The drummers announced the meeting, and could be heard throughout the city. We came a bit late, I suppose so Pigghogg could make his entrance for all to see. He pulled me along with him into the building.

He motioned for me to sit with the women in the back benches along the side of the meeting house where the women were required to observe the proceedings. He signaled for a constable, an agreeable-looking man, to stand near the door, ensuring I would make no escape.

The men were on the opposite side with better seats to view the proceedings. The inside looked like a dark blanket had been drawn over the room, with the men and women, even on this warm day, all dressed in their dull, dark clothes. Pigghogg had allowed me to wear a brighter dress, to show me off, and I felt I no longer belonged among these people. I didn't know where I did belong, but it was not in that meeting house with these people.

The constable motioned to several women to make room for me. They were reluctant to do so until he approached them, indicating he was the law and they would be required to respect it. They looked about them for a more suitable seat, but finding none, they were forced to sit again. They scowled when I sat beside them.

Mother sat alone in the front with the magistrates ringed around her. Pigghogg, with great ceremony, took his place at the head table. I whispered to the hussy sitting next to me, asking who he was. She gave me a dark look and told me it was the governor, John Winthrop. I hadn't recognized him, so much older and sterner he looked. I had met his wife one morning when I was a foolish girl looking for Mistress Anne. Even then I had I wondered how she could have married such a man as her husband, but I quickly remembered how I had married Pigghogg. I gave it no more thought. We married the men we were ordered to marry.

I knew the man sitting next to the governor, smiling at the magistrates taking their seats. It was that foul minister, John Wilson, preening himself like a wild turkey, and enjoying his important place in the proceedings.

I looked more closely at Mother. She looked straight out in front of her. I stood a little, to let her know I was there. I wanted to run to her and hold her in my arms and tell her I loved her and all of this was not her fault or mine. It was Father's fault and that black Pigghogg's, but surely not hers. I had the feeling, though, that Mother saw nothing—nothing but blackness in which no form took shape.

I had been told as a young girl about the angels, how one or two would be assigned to watch over us and keep us from the perils of the world. I saw no white angels hovering over Mother. Her angels had more pressing matters on that stifling afternoon. Perhaps they were cooling themselves over the ocean waves not far from where we sat on that hot and steaming day. Perhaps they had found the meeting house, but thought the sea of black robes not to their liking. Whatever the case, they were not floating over my mother, keeping her from the danger surrounding her—the black vultures hungry for the carrion the colony gave them each day since our arrival on these bleak shores.

The governor opened the trial, his voice like thunder. "Mary Hoar," he said, his voice cracking only slightly at the mention of her name, "you have been charged with undermining the authority of the magistrates, with calling for their deaths. Pursuant to this, you have been accused of entering into a covenant with Satan and doing his work among us. These are serious charges. What say you to them?"

Mother said nothing. She seemed not to even hear him.

"You stand mute, then?"

Still she said nothing.

He stared at Mother, not knowing what to make of her stony silence. It was not what he had heard about her from Pigghogg. "Let the trial begin," he finally said, and nodded to the Reverend John Wilson to begin the questioning.

I glanced across the room and saw Father sitting behind two men whose heads seemed like orange pumpkins atop black posts and burning in the afternoon sun. He quickly ducked behind the pumpkins so I couldn't see him.

"If the woman will admit no guilt," Wilson said, "we will reveal it for her. Would Goodwife Bracken step forward."

The woman I had seen before at Mother's inspection rose and took her place in front of the magistrates.

"You examined this woman, did you not?" Wilson asked.

"I did as I was ordered."

"Tell the court what you saw."

Alice hesitated and then said quietly. "I saw nothing, sir."

"You saw nothing? Take care, woman. The court will not tolerate lying." He stepped forward. "Now tell us what you saw."

Alice looked around her, but saw no help. "I saw a little mark, a mole, a wart perhaps."

"It was more than a wart, wasn't it?"

"I have no knowledge of that, sir."

"And where was this monstrous growth?"

Alice hesitated, then quietly said, "In her private place, sir."

"Her private place. Yes. And who has the power to commit such a horror?"

"I have no knowledge of that, sir," she repeated.

"You have little knowledge, it seems," he said, the scorn dripping from his voice. "You will be better instructed the next time you appear before us."

Wilson drew himself up and addressed the meeting house. "It is well known that the Evil One sends his familiars out to willing women. A black dog. A bear. A wolf. These familiars need daily sustenance before they return to their master for instructions. It is Satan, and only Satan, who provides that sustenance. He finds a willing woman, such as the one being tried today, and leaves his mark." He paced the floor, arms behind him. Then he stopped and turned to us. "His mark is well known by those of us instructed in his wiles. The Devil's teat. Where his familiar comes each day to suckle as a child would suckle from the breasts of an innocent woman." He turned to Goody Bracken again. "You will take care the next time you appear before us. Or we may be persuaded that you have compacted yourself with Satan to do his evil work among our women." He stared at her. "Have we made ourselves clear?"

"Yes, sir," she said quietly.

"You are dismissed."

Goody Bracken took her seat on the bench in front of us. She said nothing to anyone and bent her head, ashamed of helping that devil of a man condemn Mother.

Satisfied with the results of his interrogation, he summoned several women this time. "Goody Shepard, Goody Preston, Goody Clap, would you step forward."

The three women quickly moved to the front of the room. Goody Clap was Desire's mother, and the other two women I had seen at the birthing with Mistress Anne several years before. From them I had learned, to my later sorrow, what happens when a man's cord is cut too short.

Wilson faced each of them and then fixed on Goody Shepard, the fat woman I had seen at Goody Johnson's. "Tell the court of the signs you've witnessed, Goody Shepard."

"I have seen wonders, your honor."

"Recount them for us."

"When she moved into the town," she said, pointing eagerly at my mother, "my churn made no butter. And the beer, your honor, it was not fit to drink." She screwed up her face. "Ugh. Tasted as if the Devil's familiar had shat in it."

At that, another magistrate, seated not far from Mother, said quietly, "And your husband, Goody Shepard, is he known for the quality of his beer?"

There was tittering in the assembly, and even some of the magistrates seemed amused. It was well known that Goody Shepard's husband brewed beer that was little better than cow urine, which accounted for his sour disposition. Besides, he had no license to be making beer.

I wanted to know the name of the magistrate that asked so sensible a question, but I dared not ask the women next to me.

"My husband makes…" She realized that she was condemning him by admitting to his beer making, so she said, "My husband makes no beer. He is a lawful man, your honor."

There was more tittering, and the questioning magistrate sat down. Wilson was not pleased at being thwarted and turned to the next woman. "What signs have you seen, Goody Preston?"

"My pig, your honor."

"Yes, what about your pig?"

Goody Preston, her voice rising so that all could hear, told of the strange events in her yard. "My pig, your honor, has mated with Goody Spencer's calf."

Even Wilson seemed surprised by this accusation. "And when did this unnatural mating occur, Goody Preston?"

"Not long after this woman moved into the neighborhood." She pointed to Mother, who continued to stare into the darkness in front of her, giving no sign she heard the accusation.

"These are fearful signs, Goody Preston. We will consider them."

The quiet magistrate broke in again, addressing Goody Preston. "And what was the issue of that mating?" he asked.

"Issue, sir?"

"You have testified that your pig mated with a calf. What was the issue of that mating? That is, what did the mating produce?"

There was more tittering, this time from many of the women. "A Pigghogg," I heard one of them whisper.

Goody Preston was confused. "I…I don't know, sir. I was not present."

"Were you present at the mating, then?"

"No, sir."

"Then how do you know of it?"

"My neighbor told me."

"How did she come to this knowledge?"

"She was told by her mother, who was visiting from Connecticut."

"Then let us summon her mother. The court needs to learn the truth of these accusations. So that we might keep our pigs from such dangers."

Goody Preston saw an escape. "Her mother died suddenly, sir."

"How convenient. And when was that?"

"Just last week. One day my chickens laid no eggs. The next day, they were black with maggots."

"The chickens or the eggs, Goody Preston?"

"Why the eggs, sir. The chickens were white. White as my baby's arse, I'd say."

The spectators laughed again. Wilson was growing anxious, unable to control the standing magistrate who continued with his questioning, and fearful that he was losing his case. He wished to continue his questioning, but the quiet magistrate held the floor. "Your chickens, then, were indisposed—such as I am with this trial. Is it possible, Goody Preston, that your pigs had entered the chicken coop?"

"Why would they do that, your honor?"

"Perhaps they had thought of mating with the chickens—after their success with Goody Spencer's calf."

Louder tittering this time. Goody Preston was flustered, not knowing what to make of the magistrate's question.

"Are you finished, Mister Thorton?" Wilson broke in. "Because if you're not—"

"I'm quite finished for now," Mister Thorton said and sat down.

I was growing more hopeful, with at least one magistrate asking sensible questions of these magpies who cared not a whit for my mother. Perhaps there would be others.

But Wilson impatiently dismissed Goody Preston and turned to Desire's mother. He didn't wish to speak her name, fearing more laughter from the spectators, so he merely said, "Woman, what terrible sights have you been witness to?"

I knew Goody Clap to be a better woman than the other two, and I now felt that the trial had turned against Wilson. Mother would be cleared of the charges.

Goody Clap said nothing at first. She looked at my mother for the longest time, and I could see her shudder. Finally, she spoke, in a whisper. "She came to my husband."

"Speak louder, woman. What is it you say?"

"She came to my husband. In the dead of night."

There was a gasp from both sides of the room, and even the magistrates took notice. Several of them spoke quietly among themselves.

Wilson sprang on her. "Ah, she came to your husband. At night when witches are about. Did you see her fly?"

"I did, your honor. On her broomstick. She circled the house, and thinking me gone to my mother's, which I had intended, she came through my husband's window."

"Sent by the Devil. What evil did she do?"

"I'd rather not say, your honor. It is a terrible thing."

"Come now, woman. The court needs your testimony. If the Devil is among us, we must know his work. What did you see?"

"I looked in his room. The door was open a crack." She paused and pleaded with Wilson. "My husband is a good man, your honor."

"Yes, yes. We know his reputation. But you must speak of what happened, though it burn your flesh." He was growing more excited and waved his hands as if he were swatting flies. Perhaps it was the Devil afflicting him as he was said to have afflicted my mother.

"My husband, he's a good man, your honor."

"Woman!"

Goody Clap cowered before the wildly waving arms of Reverend Wilson. She knew what could happen to her if she lied to the court. But finally she spoke, her hands wrung together in front of her: "Well, as I said, this woman, Goody Hoar, came through the window. She rested her broomstick by the bed. And then…and then…she lay on him. And pinched him, about his body. Like this and this." She pinched herself on the thighs and stomach. "And he was crying out and writhing and telling her to stop, but she wouldn't let up. She had her way with him." She looked angrily at my mother. "Whore that she is!"

I rose to my feet and started toward the woman, hoping to gouge her lying eyes from her head, but the constable restrained me. He held me tightly to him and said quietly, "Not now, Mistress Chastity. Your day will come." I relaxed in his arms and then returned quietly to my seat. The women stared at me maliciously.

I couldn't believe the woman had made such an accusation. My mother had always been kind to her when she came to the inn, looking for her errant husband and dragging her brood with her. She was not a comely woman, as my mother was, and her tiresome brood, except for Desire, made her seem much older than Mother, though she was probably about the same age. Her husband often came to the inn, no doubt to avoid her tiresome complaints.

Then it struck me. It all came back. I had often seen her husband, when he did come to the inn, looking at my mother. He'd turn away when he saw me watching him, but I could tell that he looked at her longingly, as well he might. She was not the hag of a woman his wife was, and he must have thought he had made as poor a match with his wife as Father had made a good match with his.

The quiet magistrate, Mister Thorton, began to rise, but the other magistrates motioned for him to sit. They were convinced by the woman's story that Mother had attacked the man in his sleep. Perhaps they were worried about their own wives watching them writhing on their beds at night as they dreamed of forbidden women.

"And she stole his money," Goody Clap said, as if she had just conjured it up.

Wilson was pleased with the unexpected accusation. "Stole his money, did she? The Evil One asks more than souls of his followers. He requires they bring him earthly wealth."

At that, the quiet magistrate rose again. "How is it you know the money was stolen, Goody Clap?" he wondered.

"My husband always keeps his wages in his pocket. He puts his pants over the chair when he retires. The money was gone when I checked."

"I've heard it said," the magistrate continued, "that your husband and his money are easily parted. On his travels. At the inns. Is that not true?"

"It is a lie, sir. My husband is a God-fearing man. He is careful with his money."

No one who had ever seen her husband would have believed that story, but it didn't matter. They believed my mother had stolen it.

The magistrate kept at her. "You're quite sure, are you, that in a moment of need, shall we say, to feed your many children, you didn't find it necessary to borrow the money from his pocket?"

It was too late for these questions. She had no need to answer that of course she had borrowed the money, as she had done since they were married, trying to keep the children fed and in respectable clothes. Everyone who knew her knew that her husband was as tight with his money as a wine cask is sealed.

The tide had turned against my mother. The other magistrates ordered Mister Thorton to take his seat. He reluctantly did, aware that he was losing the case.

"I have no fear of her," Goody Clap said, pointing to Mother.

"You should have great fear, woman, at what those who compact with the Devil can do to the righteous."

"I know that, sir. But I have taken precautions."

"What are these precautions?" He seemed doubtful that a simple woman could protect herself without his help.

"Why, I've done what we've always done. Goody Preston helped me. We've hung horseshoes over our door. And we've baked a cake, as we were told, with her urine."

"Urine?" Wilson was not pleased with this testimony, but Goody Clap was not to be denied. "Yes, sir, as our mothers taught us. All of our family—Experience and Wait and Supply, the older ones too."

"Yes, yes." Wilson wanted no more of urine cakes.

Mister Thorton did want more, though. "Ah, Goody Clap," he said without standing, "so you made urine cakes?"

"Yes, sir. To protect ourselves."

"And, if I might ask, how did the urine come into your possession?"

"My possession?"

Mister Thorton was even more exasperated than Wilson was. "You testified you made cakes with the accused woman's urine, isn't that so?"

"Yes, sir."

"Then tell the court how you obtained it. The urine."

Goody Clap was greatly agitated, and looked around the room for help. No one before had ever asked her such a sensible question. "I cannot say, sir. The Devil will come to me."

"I'll come to you with a switch, woman, if you don't tell us the truth."

"I speak the truth, sir, so help me God. The cake has protected me. Search me, if you wish. I have no marks on me as this woman has. I love only God, sir, not the Devil."

Wilson stepped in. "We believe you, Goody Clap. We do believe you." He had had quite enough of urine cakes, and abruptly dismissed her. "Thank you for your testimony, good woman, the court will consider it." But as she attempted to return to her seat, Wilson called her back. "One moment, woman. I have further need of you."

Wilson then called the liar's daughter, Desire Clap, my dearest friend. If there was any hope remaining, it lay with her. She would, I knew, stand with Mother and me against all accusations.

Desire looked briefly at me before she took her place in front of the magistrates. She seemed desperate, like a frightened fox caught in a trap. She wouldn't look at her mother.

Wilson could not restrain his delight. Nor could Pigghogg, seated at his side. They both looked hungrily at Desire as she stood humbly before them, her head down.

"You are this woman's daughter, are you not?" Wilson said.

"I am, sir." She still didn't look at her mother.

"Too bad for you." He motioned for Goody Clap to take her seat, and she quickly returned to it, not looking back. "But the court will offer you the opportunity to clear your name of any suspicions. You wish that, don't you?"

I didn't know what suspicions he had since it was my mother who was on trial.

"Yes, sir. I would have no suspicions on me. Or my mother."

"Hmm." Wilson paused to consider her demeanor. Then he began: "You are employed at the inn operated by the accused woman's husband, are you not?"

"I am, sir."

"Tell the court what horrors you have witnessed at the inn."

"None, sir. I've seen no horrors."

"You've seen no horrors? None whatsoever?"

"No, sir."

"Nothing at all out of the ordinary?"

"No, sir." She shook her head. "Unless you mean the wedding of Chastity to Mister Pigghogg."

I almost danced to hear those words. Horror, indeed.

Wilson glanced briefly at Pigghogg. Of course he had been at the wedding, as had the other magistrates, and thus knew of Pigghogg's marrying me through the hole in the closet door, though he didn't witness the act himself. Better to keep those horrors safely hidden behind closet doors, he must have thought, because he quickly changed the subject.

"Woman, I find it strange indeed that you worked at the inn, and even slept there, and find nothing unusual to report. There can only be one explanation for that. One explanation only." He glared at Desire. "Do you know what that is?"

Desire shook her head.

"Then let me inform you. If you claim to have seen nothing, it can only be"—here he paused to ensure that everyone was attentive to his words—"that you have succumbed to Satan's wiles yourself."

"Oh, no, sir." She now saw the danger she was in. Whatever suspicions hung over her head were there because she was close to Mother.

"Oh, no, sir. Never. I have no business with the Devil."

"Then you must have seen something. Tell us what you've seen, or it will go hard on you."

Poor Desire. She didn't know what to say because whatever she said would be twisted to condemn both her and my mother. She wrung her hands together, trying to think of a story that would hurt neither of them. No such stories existed.

I looked at Mother again, but she was still staring straight ahead. Then I thought I saw a slight movement of her head, a flicker in her eyes, but I wasn't sure. I turned back to Wilson. He was growing more impatient.

"Since you're unable to clear your name with voluntary testimony, then I shall need to compel you in other ways. The court will expect you to be as truthful in your response as you can be. Or else…" He didn't need to say more.

Desire awaited his questions, knowing there would be no escape.

"The court is concerned with the condemned woman's conduct in her house."

Condemned woman? Who had condemned her? Only silly and envious women who bore grudges against Mother.

"You will tell the court about her conduct," he commanded.

"Yes, sir."

"It is said that the condemned woman often orders her husband in his duties. Is that true?"

Desire looked puzzled. "Yes, sir, she does ask for help in the kitchen or clearing the tables when he's…he's talking with his friends."

"Does she do this often?"

"As often as she must." Desire smiled, thinking she was helping Mother. "That is quite often, you may be sure, for master is often talking."

Wilson put his hands behind his back, satisfied with her answer. Desire had condemned Mother without knowing it.

But he wasn't through with her yet. "I have heard it said," he continued, "that your mistress had taken another room. Is that true?"

Desire hesitated, not sure of the path he was leading her on. "Yes, sir. She has of late slept in my room."

"She slept with you?" He acted horrified at the news.

"Yes, sir. Of late. She slept on the floor."

"Did you ever see her leave the floor?"

"Yes, sir. She would often pace around the room. She was much distracted."

"I'm sure she was," Wilson said, relishing the moment. "Distracted by her lust, which she satisfied with a neighbor's husband, afflicting him as your mother has just testified."

Desire now saw that Wilson would take her where he pleased. "She never left the room," she said weakly.

"Your mother has testified otherwise. Do you call your mother a liar?"

"No sir," she said, almost in a whisper. She knew now she was lost and would not find her way again.

"And where was her husband when his wife was sleeping on the floor in your room?" He paused again for effect. "Or flying to your neighbor's house?"

"He was in their room."

"Ah, their room. And was he alone?"

"Yes, sir."

"You're quite sure he was alone? He had no visitors, coming to comfort him? Visitors from just down the hall?"

"No, sir. He was alone."

Wilson stopped his pacing and confronted her directly. "How would you know that if you didn't visit him?"

Now she was really trapped. She didn't know how to respond. Fortunately, Mister Thorton had had enough. He rose again, despite the surly look Wilson and the other magistrates directed at him.

"This questioning is outrageous," he said. "How can the young woman defend herself when every response is turned against her? If she claims Goodwoman Hoar remained in the room, you accuse her of lying. If she says she was alone and assumes that Goodman Hoar was also alone, you accuse her again of lying. There is no evidence, except from these silly women, that Goodwoman Hoar has done anything but assist her husband in his employment, which, I'm told, is a very good employment indeed, frequented as it is by members of this court."

I'm glad the magistrate defended Mother, but I wish he hadn't said what he did about the other magistrates because it made them angry. They must have thought some taint of witchcraft had rubbed off on them, being so close to the accused witch. "Sit down," one of them growled. "You're out of order."

Mister Thorton began to protest, but other magistrates repeated the order. "Sit down," another said. "This is a matter for those versed in the ways of the Evil One, which are sometimes beyond our powers to detect. Let Reverend Wilson continue."

Mister Thorton glanced up at the governor, who grimly shook his head. Finding no support, he sat down. He seemed lost.

Wilson waited until Mister Thorton was seated and a threat no more. Then, with great ceremony, he turned to his audience: "There is a threat to our community, let no one forget it. Dissension is foul in the eyes of our Creator, who has ordered us to guard our people that the Evil One can make no advances. One chink in the wall is all he requires to make his entrance among us. He has found that chink, and he walks among us now." Satisfied that he had the attention of all but Mister Thorton—and my mother—he proceeded with his attack. "You know, of course," he continued, "that a woman is not head of the house. When she usurps that role, she is vain and proud, no better than Satan the archangel, who refused to serve God and was cast out of Heaven. A woman's husband was meant by God to be master of his house, as God is master of the angels, expecting them to do his will. Who among us has forgotten that the first woman, Eve, was created as wife, as helpmate to Adam, and it was she, for pride, who was seduced by the Devil's wiles to disobey our God, seeking more wisdom than he had granted his creatures? For that they were expelled from Paradise." Wilson was triumphant now. "In our city upon the hill, we are threatened again, as we were with Mistress Hutchinson and her followers, who sought to overthrow God's ordained authority for their own proud desires. We have dealt with them as we will deal with this woman." He looked at my mother, who remained impassive. "The evidence is overwhelming that this woman who sits before us, in a trance induced by Satan himself, has signed his book. But," he said magnanimously, "to leave no doubt about the justice of these proceedings, I will ask our esteemed colleague, Magistrate Pigghogg, to address these charges."

He turned back to the governor, who said, "You may proceed, Reverend Wilson."

"You have valuable testimony, I believe," Wilson said to Pigghogg.

"I do." Pigghogg stood up and approached my mother. Wilson was on the other side. Mother paid no attention to either one. I desperately wanted to stand next to her, to protect her from those demons hovering over her, but one look at the constable told me I needed to remain in my seat, another spectator in this unholy business.

"She has performed her evil at your house, I believe," Wilson said. "In Satan's command."

"There is no doubt of it," Pigghogg replied, swatting away a fly or mosquito that was annoying him. "It was a great evil to me, of course, but to the community as well. She has torn the fabric of our lives."

"How is that, magistrate?"

Yes, I thought, how is that? What evil had Mother done to Pigghogg, except to speak vainly against his marriage to me?

"She came to my house when my dear wife was ill. I was not informed of her presence until much later, and then it was too late."

"Satan had found entrance, then?"

"He had, together with this woman, found his prey. My wife, dear woman that she was, could do nothing to defend herself. This woman sitting before us cast spells on her, and it was not long before Hannah left this world for a better one. May God bless and keep her." Pigghogg lowered his head, and Wilson shook his own approvingly.

I wanted to vomit Pigghogg's words over every inch of his ugly flesh. How dare him charge my mother with Hannah's death when it was Pigghogg himself who killed her? Why didn't God strike him dead for his lies?

Wilson touched Pigghogg on the shoulder. "Thank you for the testimony, magistrate Pigghogg. The court is in your debt."

Pigghogg looked at Mother and pointed his finger at her. "You," he growled, and then returned to his seat, his fellow magistrates nodding their appreciation.

Damn the man for his lies! If God is good, if he is the shepherd as we are often told, he will damn the wolf Pigghogg to everlasting hell.

I thought Mister Thorton would say something in Mother's defense but he sat impassively, looking at no one.

Then it occurred to me that I was with Mother when we visited Hannah in her dying, and if Wilson and the others thought Mother was a witch, they might also think I was one. Pigghogg, my husband, was the only one standing between me and the charge of witchcraft. I looked about me, thinking that others had already accused me. But then I thought, what does it matter? Let them hang me, with Mother at my side. Better to be out of this world than in it with the likes of Pigghogg and his friends.

Wilson interrupted my thoughts. He had not finished with his questioning, though there could not have been more than one or two in the room who thought my mother innocent.

"God demands that we be just in our judgment," he intoned, looking at the governor. "Let us call this woman's husband before us. That we be sure of the truthful testimony already presented to the court." Looking about and seeing no opposition, he summoned my father.

Was there no end to the man's villainy?

Father stood up and looked about him, blinking, hoping there was a mistake.

"Yes, you," Wilson called out. "Step before us."

Father moved slowly down the aisle, never looking at his many friends, all of them visitors to the inn. He seemed to have shriveled since I last saw him.

"Stand by your wife," Wilson ordered.

Father did as he was told, standing as far away from her as he could.

"Closer," Wilson commanded. "It is your wife, is it not?"

Father nodded and moved closer, never looking directly at Mother. She continued to look forward, into the darkness.

"You seem to fear contagion."

Father shook his head.

"There will be no contagion if you speak the truth. The truth and this court will stand between you and the Evil One."

Wilson looked at both of them and shook his head sadly. "It is a terrible thing to behold," he said, "what Satan can do when he comes among us. Terrible indeed."

With that he began the questioning. "We have heard this day of many horrors associated with your wife. You must have seen these horrors yourself, being as she is your lawful wife."

He looked at Father, expecting a response, but Father said nothing.

"You will tell of the horrors you've witnessed."

Still, Father said nothing.

"Man, you will speak to the court when you are commanded! Now tell us what you've seen!"

"Nothing, sir," Father said in a whisper.

"Man, your immortal soul is at stake here. You will tell us what you've seen or we can only assume you are in a pact with your wife and Satan to overthrow this court and this colony. The punishment for such offense is swift and certain. Now what say you?"

"My wife is a good woman, sir."

"That is for the court to decide. Tell us what you've seen."

Father was genuinely at a loss and cast about for words—words which had always helped him before in his many difficulties. But in this moment, they didn't come. Not until Wilson drew them out.

"We have heard today that your wife rules you, bringing discord to your house and defying God's commands for his people. Is this true?"

"No, sir. I rule my wife."

"How is it then she left the inn against your wishes to attend to Mistress Pigghogg, who, we have also been told, was afflicted by your wife and soon died wracked with pain?"

"It was not my knowledge, sir, that she left. I am sorry for it."

"You are sorry for it? Are you sorry she murdered the magistrate's wife, who was too weak to defend herself?"

"Yes, sir. I am heartily sorry. I meant no offense."

"So you admit your wife killed Mistress Pigghogg with your permission. Or without your knowledge."

"I gave her no permission to murder anyone."

"Take care, mister. You have admitted your wife left without your knowledge to murder the magistrate's wife."

"No sir. I said only I gave no permission."

"Then you do not rule your wife, as we have charged. You have disobeyed our God who has commanded that the husband rule his wife."

Father just shook his head, not knowing what to say.

Satisfied that he had befuddled Father, Wilson took another path. "We have also heard today that your wife has left your bed. That she sleeps with another woman in her room. Is that not also true?"

Father looked at mother and back at Wilson. He couldn't defend her for what must have greatly angered him. "She did, sir."

"She left your room for another?"

"Yes, sir."

"And freed from your rule, she has flown to Goody Clap's husband's bed and had her way with him, beating and pinching him about his body as witches are known to do."

"I have no knowledge of that, sir."

"Man, it is your responsibility to know what your wife does! Freed of your rule, she has brought death to Mistress Pigghogg and assaulted an innocent husband, depriving him of his wife's godly marital duties."

Father could say nothing to these charges. He wouldn't look at Mother or Wilson. He stared ahead, seeing only the blackness that Mother was staring into.

Wilson looked contemptuously at Father. "You are not fit to stand before this assembly," he spit out. He made a show of turning his back on Father. Then he whirled around, accusing him once more.

"The court has knowledge that your wife frequently speaks of the magistrates and the court. What does she say?"

"Nothing, sir."

"You lie, man! Let you know that lying in court is a sin against God, who has forbidden it. Your wife is an accused witch and you are lying to protect her. Men have been hanged for less. Now tell us what she says."

Something broke in Father then. I don't know how else to say it. He turned on Mother and accused her. And himself in so doing. "She cursed him every night," he shouted. "Pounding on the floor so that the guests heard her. They stopped coming and my business dried up. Mister Pigghogg. She wished his death. Just because my daughter married him. I loved her, I loved them both. I wanted what's best for them. For that she cursed him. And me. She wished us all dead. You. And him. My daughter. All of us. She wished us dead."

The spectators gasped in horror, but Wilson said nothing. He glanced up at the governor who sat forward now, listening intently. They both let the accusations sink in.

Everyone in the courtroom was staring at Father and Wilson, who stood before him, arms folded. He had all the testimony he needed to send Mother to the gallows.

Suddenly I noticed a movement to the side. No one else saw a thing. It was Mother. Something broke in her as well, and she was standing and advancing toward Father. Then we all saw it. She had drawn out from her sleeve a kitchen knife and raised it above her head. Before the constable or Wilson or anyone could do anything she plunged it down, striking Father, who fell to the floor, crying out in pain. Then she turned toward Pigghogg seated with the other magistrates behind the table. She drove the knife into the table, just inches from Pigghogg's hands, which he quickly drew back, nearly falling off his chair. The women screamed.

"Murderers!" she cried. "Murderers! I condemn you all!"

The constable finally reached her and took her arm with the knife and bent it back. The knife dropped harmlessly to the ground.

Mother resisted no more. She fell limp into his arms, and he led her back to her chair and sat her down. She didn't move, and only stared into space as she had before. All life seemed to have left her, and she had become only a ghost of herself.

Father was still writing on the floor. She had missed his body and hit only his arm, which was bleeding badly. No one moved.

The governor arose. "Attend to him," he called to the women's side. "What are you waiting for?"

They were waiting for permission, as women were expected to do. After all, hadn't we just been told that men were rulers of their women?

It was all a jumble after that. Father was taken from the building, the trial was dismissed, and the magistrates decided they would meet later to discuss the case. Pigghogg signaled for the constable to lead me from the room, which he did, holding my arm gently. "It will be all right," Mistress Chastity," he said as he led me out into the square. A puff of wind blew up a whirling dirt cloud, momentarily obscuring the scaffold and the whipping post. Then the dirt settled, and we were reminded again of the punishment for disobeying the authorities. And for witchcraft.

People hurried to their homes, looking the other way.

Pigghogg roughly took my arm and led me to his horse, which awaited us a short distance away. As we were about to leave, I looked back for Mother but saw nothing, only the scaffold awaiting its next victim.

CHAPTER 11

That evening I was in bed, planning a secret trip to see my mother, when the door opened and Pigghogg entered. He was accompanied by the smiling Dorothy.

"Over you go," he snarled.

"Sir?"

"Over you go. And remove your shift."

I couldn't believe it. He had always been alone when he asked me to strip, protecting his property from a stranger's eyes, and now he was asking me to strip in front of that hated woman. I was furious.

"You will need to kill me first," I said.

"That may come later." Pigghogg was amused at my defiance, and circled his hand in front of him, suggesting a rope around my neck.

He approached the bed, with Dorothy close behind. I looked for something to defend myself, but I had nothing but my hairbrush that I had left on the pillow beside me. If I had had a knife, as my mother did, I would have plunged it into his black heart.

Before I could do anything, Pigghogg was on me, trying to pin my arms to the bed. I kicked hard, hitting him in the stomach, and he squealed in pain. "You would do better to obey me," he hissed, "your mother's life may depend on it."

With that I stopped my resistance. I didn't dare do anything to harm Mother.

Pigghogg relaxed his grip. "Now off with the shift."

I did as he commanded, taking care not to look at Dorothy.

"Good. Now on your stomach."

I turned over and saw Dorothy step forward.

Pigghogg and Dorothy stood beside the bed. "Dorothy tells me you've been disrespectful to her," he said. "And if you're disrespectful to her, you've been disrespectful to me, since she's my servant and owes me allegiance until her bond is paid off."

Yes, I thought, and I'd plunge a kitchen knife into both of you if I could.

"More seriously, she tells me you've said incantations to my dear family."

"Incantations?" I didn't know what he was talking about. I thought he'd gone mad.

"She tells me she's seen you standing in front of the pictures and putting spells on them, hoping to get at me through my family."

"That's a lie!" I shouted and tried to sit up.

He pushed me down again as hard as he could. "That is what you told me, Dorothy, is it not?"

"Yes, sir. Plain as day. She was putting spells on the pictures."

"The woman lies, I tell you. I was merely talking with them."

He had me now. "Talking, was it? And what were you saying?"

I couldn't very well tell him what I'd been saying. Or that the talking was keeping me sane in that insane house. "Nothing," I said. "Nothing."

He found my response unsatisfactory and began to lecture me. I tried to shut out his hateful words, but it was about my mother again so I forced myself to listen. "Chastity, I need to remind you that your mother has been accused of witchcraft and undermining the authority of the magistrates. It is common knowledge that if Satan finds entry into one member of a family, he will seek out others in the family. You have been accused by Dorothy of speaking incantations. As your mother did. That is the Devil's work. If it comes out and is widely known, you will be in grave danger." He bent over me, pinching my ears as he did. "You will remember that I am the only one who stands between you and your mother's fate. If I say the word, you will join her and be accused." He stood up again, pleased that he had silenced me.

I said nothing and turned my head. I would not let him or Dorothy see the tears his words had provoked.

"Dorothy will administer the punishment tonight."

She did so with undisguised pleasure, bringing the riding whip down on my back again and again. Though she did not strike as hard as Pigghogg, the pain and humiliation were worse. Both of them delighted in each blow that burned my very soul.

When the beating stopped, Pigghogg took my ear again. "Turn your head this way."

"No."

He pulled sharply on the ear. "I said—"

"No."

The pain was so great I couldn't resist. "All right, all right." I turned my head.

"Now you will thank Dorothy for saving you from the peril awaiting you."

He pushed my head into the pillow, pulling harder on my ear.

"Stop it," I screamed.

"Well?"

I've never said more hated words, but I couldn't stand the pain and the thought of what he could do to my mother.

"Thank you," I snarled. "Thank you for the punishment."

"That's a good girl," he said and let go. "Is that satisfactory?" he asked Dorothy.

"Yes sir. Quite satisfactory."

The two of them left the room in high spirits.

I had never until that night felt such hatred or spoke such painful words. I swore then that I would never forget what the two of them had done to me. I would never forget, I would never forgive either one of those fiends who delighted in every blow. When I escaped, as I surely would, I would find a suitable revenge for such undeserved cruelty.

But first I had to find Mother. The next morning I waited until Pigghogg left and Dorothy was at work in the kitchen, preparing my breakfast. When I was sure he was gone and Dorothy was busy, I crept down the stairs, passing close to the Pigghogg family who scowled at my escape, and went to a side door. I could hear Dorothy in the kitchen.

I opened the door and stepped out into the warm air. The sun was already heating the air, and even the mosquitoes would be fleeing before its power. Seeing no one around, I started on my way to find my mother.

Suddenly, a voice called to me. "Mistress Chastity!'

I turned and saw James stepping out from behind the shed. I was relieved.

He approached me quickly. "Mistress, I have orders."

"Orders? What orders?"

"You're not to leave the house."

"And why not? I go to see my mother."

"Mister Pigghogg said you were not to leave. I'm sorry, ma'am, but you'll have to return to the house."

I approached and stared him in the eyes. "I am mistress of this house. I will go where I please."

"I'm sorry. But Mister Pigghogg was clear. You are not to leave."

I decided on another approach. "James, please, my mother is in grave danger. She needs me as I need her. You would not leave your mother, would you, when she needed you?"

He looked down. "My mother is in the old country. I am paying off her debts to Mister Pigghogg."

"Well…" I didn't know what to say. Debts had enslaved us both.

"Please, ma'am." He pointed to the house. "I only do my duty. If you were to leave, it would go hard on me."

"So this is how you treat—" I was going to say the woman whose bed you come to in the evenings, but I didn't want to give my secret away just yet. Besides, I wasn't absolutely certain he was the man.

I turned and quickly began running down the street toward the inn. There was only an old peddler with his vegetable cart in front of me. I glanced around to see James standing forlornly where I left him.

I crashed into a body, stone solid like a wall. It was another constable, whose name, I later learned, was Zeb Stubbs.

"Damn you," I shouted. "Out of my way." I clawed at his arms, which held me firmly.

The constable was an ugly giant of a man, pock-marked and red in the face. He was missing several teeth. I tried to peel off his arms, but he simply took my hand and bent it back until I was limp with pain.

He didn't say a word as he dragged me back to James and the Pigghogg house. Several neighbor women observed and turned away, embarrassed at my humiliation.

I was led to the door, which opened quickly. Dorothy had been watching the whole scene from the window. Pigghogg had known I would attempt an escape and had successfully thwarted it. For now, anyway. There would be another day.

I was growing more desperate to see my mother, to comfort her after the trial. Or, at least, find out if Desire knew how she was faring in the gaol, where there would be no sympathy for her now that she had become a possessed woman accused of witchcraft and thus a danger to the entire colony. But each day I tried to leave at a different time or from a different door, I would get no farther than the edge of the property and someone would step out to confront me. Sometimes it was James, but mostly it was the ugly giant who had held me the first time. No matter how I struggled with him or threw myself on his mercy, he was relentless, dragging me back to the house, where Dorothy awaited me at the door, smiling maliciously.

Finally, almost a week later, I was looking out my bedroom window when I saw Desire with her basket. I opened the window, knowing I wouldn't be allowed outside to talk with her. Desire walked on by, never looking up, and then I saw why. Constable Stubbs was following her, no doubt carrying out his instructions to see that I had no communication with anyone. I watched her closely, and saw her ever so slightly lower her head and shake it. Then she was gone. I knew then that Mother had not improved or escaped.

Pigghogg also said nothing about her, eating his meals in sullen silence. Finally, I could tolerate it no longer. I had to find out how she was. At one evening meal, Pigghogg having come home late as he had become accustomed to doing, I blurted out, "How is Mother?" He was lustily chewing his boiled pork and made no comment.

Thinking he hadn't heard me, I asked again, "How is Mother?" I added, "sir."

He belched loudly. "I wouldn't know," he said, raising his ale tankard again. I picked at my food, wondering how to pursue the matter. Did he really not know, or had he found a new method of torture? I didn't care. I needed to know. "Then perhaps I might be permitted to visit her?"

Pigghogg became furious, exploding in anger. "You will not be permitted to visit her! You will not be permitted to leave the house! There is strong sentiment about that you and your mother have contracted together to do us harm. The magistrates are concerned. There is sickness in the colony. Neighbor cries out on neighbor. Cows cease giving milk. Horses rebel and throw their masters. Babies are born and then die. Comets appear, flashing across the heavens, warning us of greater dangers. The ministers have told us that God is displeased. His kingdom is being polluted, spoiled. There is a cause, we're told." He pointed angrily at me. "Let me hear no more about your mother's health. It is my health we must consider." He emptied his tankard, wiped his lips, and pointed a knife at me. "Let me remind you again, Chastity, that you are my wife. If your mother is found guilty of witchcraft, as she was accused, then you are also under suspicion. If you are under suspicion, and you are my property, then I risk contamination along with the both of you."

I responded quickly, thinking I could make my escape through divorce. "Then perhaps I should no longer be your property."

His eyes narrowed. "Your mother is accused of being the Devil's property. Take care, Chastity, if those charges are leveled at you, you will receive your wish. You will no longer be my property. Or anyone's but the Devil's. You and your mother will hang together. Let Satan claim you for his."

With that, he left the table and retired to his study. I saw him no more that night. Or the following nights.

I was alone all night, a small comfort, and now alone all day as well. Dorothy and James continued to avoid me. I resumed talking with the Pigghogg family as I dusted them each morning. But I spoke quietly, whispering. I would give Dorothy no second opportunity to beat me.

As I spoke with them, I would ask what they thought about my plans for escape. Perhaps, I mused, I could throw a note to Desire or some woman passing by, promising them money if they could bring me news of Mother. The Pigghoggs laughed at my presumption. No woman, not even Desire, would risk contacting a condemned witch or receiving a note from her daughter.

I remembered another woman, one who had been kind to me the time when I first met Anne and Mary. She had directed me to them and made a comment that being a woman, a wife, meant little in those days. I still remembered that, finding it to be more true each day I lived. But the woman, I told the portraits, was Mistress Winthrop, the governor's wife. The Pigghoggs laughed loudly. The governor's wife? The governor's wife? Are you mad? The governor's wife will be deaf to the daughter of an accused witch. But she smiled at me, I thought. I saw much in that smile, but I didn't tell the Pigghoggs. I would keep that smile for another day.

Perhaps a man, I said to them. A man might have the authority no woman would have. The Pigghoggs nodded agreement. I remembered the quiet magistrate, Mister Thorton, the one who asked such sensible questions. But I could think of no way to contact him. He never passed by the house and probably never would. Besides, he was a magistrate, a powerful man, probably respected throughout the colony. He would not think to listen to such as me, the daughter of a condemned witch. The Pigghoggs smiled at my recognition.

But there was another man at the trial, the one who was assigned to guard me so I wouldn't escape. I didn't know his name at the time, but he was the constable who whispered that my day would come, and squeezed my arm gently. What about a constable? I whispered to the Pigghoggs. They laughed at my presumption. A constable indeed! Why would a man of the law have anything to do with a lawless creature such as yourself?

That was true. Still, there was some softness in his words and his arms as he guided me to and from my seat. I would remember that softness should the time come when I might meet him under more favorable circumstances. For now, though, I could think of no way to meet him or gain his attention. The Pigghoggs smiled at my plight: I would remain in the Pigghogg house, a slave to the family portraits and to Pigghogg himself.

I grew more desperate, and from that desperation grew more bold. What are you thinking? the Pigghoggs said in unison the next day, their dark brows furrowed. Be careful, young woman, or you court infamy and death. I didn't tell them what I was thinking. It was too risky, and Pigghogg himself might glean from his ancestors some hint of my intentions.

There were two men I did have contact with, and it didn't require leaving the house: Pigghogg and the man who came to my bed at night. I would need to work through them to find out about Mother and perhaps make my escape.

The Pigghoggs continued to watch me carefully as I planned, but I didn't let on what I was up to. I cleaned the portraits silently, or if they seemed overly suspicious, I allayed their suspicions with idle chatter about my clothes or the food I would order for the next meal. In the meantime I planned, telling no one.

It was dangerous, but I had no fear of danger anymore. The gallows on the Common, not far from Mother, quieted that fear. I had to find out how she was and what the magistrates had decided.

So I began the plot. That evening when Pigghogg returned I met him at the door. "Welcome home," I said, taking his arm and leading him into the house. I held his arm against my breasts, caressing it gently.

He was immediately suspicious. "What is it you want?" he growled.

"Nothing but your pleasure," I said. "I had Dorothy fix your favorite meal. Roast pork. Sweet potatoes. Apple tart. With the best of cream."

"Hmm." The thought of dinner momentarily quieted his suspicions.

I seated him in his favorite chair in the parlor and removed his shoes. "Was it a hard day?"

He looked at me suspiciously, but I had found his weakness. Like a baby, he loved to be coddled. "Why do you ask?" he said.

"You've been so tired of late. I worry about your health." I knelt at his feet, rubbing them and pressing them to my chest.

"You've never worried before. What is it you want?"

"Nothing," I said. "I don't wish to trouble you."

"What is it you want?" he repeated, looking more closely at me.

I kept rubbing his feet. "Well…no, I dare not ask."

"If it's about your mother…"

I looked shocked. "On, no, she's in your hands. You and the magistrates. You know best what must be done. For the good of the colony. No, it's not for me to question you about my mother."

He was not convinced. I would have to tempt him further. "I had another thing in mind. But I am—I fear to say it."

"Say it," he said and smiled. I had tickled his feet.

"I'm embarrassed to speak of such things."

"Speak it, woman."

"You'll not be angry?"

"I promise nothing. Say what you have to say."

I looked down, pressing his feet more tightly to me. "It's about you, sir."

"Yes, what about me?" He was becoming impatient, just as I hoped.

I closed my eyes, fearing it wouldn't work, and told him. "Well, I'm much alone these days."

"Yes. As you deserve."

"At nights as well."

"Yes."

I gritted my teeth and said, as sincerely as I could, "I miss your company. At night."

There, I said it. I kept my eyes closed, not knowing how he would respond.

He said nothing at first as he pondered my words. Then he stuck his big toe into my breast and wiggled it about. "So you miss my company?"

"Yes, sir. I am not accustomed to being alone." This was true, of course, but I didn't mean him. I meant Desire and Mother.

He looked hungrily at me. "I thought as much. Absence opens the heart, I've found in my experience. The legs as well," he added.

I almost laughed. Surely he couldn't believe I would feel deprived by his absence. I looked his face over carefully, expecting to see the mockery that lay behind his words. I saw nothing but lust. I had snared him, as I hoped.

"I don't mean to trouble you," I said, continuing to massage his toes.

"I am already much troubled," he said. "The magistrates have become contentious. The debate is wearying. What was once clear has become muddied. We play into Satan's hands."

I held my breath, thinking he would tell me more, but he had other things on his mind. That would have to be enough for now. I concluded my mother was still alive and the debate was over her punishment.

He indicated he wished to have his shoes put on. Then he motioned he wished to stand, and I offered him my hand. I stood close by as he steadied himself. "Well, enough of the unpleasantness. Let us repair to dinner and afterwards, if you're good, I might be encouraged to pay you a visit."

"I'm always good," I said as charmingly as possible. "Today I cleaned each of your ancestors and addressed them by name. They were pleased with the attention."

A frown passed over his face as he considered what I said. "You spoke no incantations?"

"Never, sir. I merely keep them company in my loneliness."

"I shall ask Dorothy about that. But in the meantime, in the meantime..." He saw the dinner Dorothy had prepared, under my direction, of course. He had no more to say about his ancestors or the magistrates as he stuffed himself with Dorothy's cooking, all the while mumbling about the energy he would be needing shortly.

Dorothy cast an evil eye in my direction. She knew something was wrong, but she didn't know what. And she didn't know how to find out without condemning herself in the process. So she quietly brought in the food, saying nothing, but watching the both of us for clues. I remained courteous to her and solicitous of Pigghogg as he greedily wolfed down his food.

Finally, at the end of the meal, when Dorothy was in the kitchen and out of hearing, he sat back in his chair and considered me. His eyes narrowed again as he spoke: "You're a good girl, you tell me. How do you propose demonstrating that you deserve my attentions again?"

I was not expecting this, and had not planned what to say. Or even exactly what to do, especially if he entered the room himself. I thought quickly, but having no experience in these matters, I was at a loss, not knowing what to say. "Anything you'd like," I finally said. "Whatever would please you."

"Hmm. Anything?"

"Yes. Anything." Of course, I didn't know what that meant. To a man like Pigghogg, it could mean anything. And it did.

His eyes narrowed more, and he was breathing heavily. "In the barn, then."

"Sir?" I had no idea what he was talking about.

"In the barn. With the animals. If you're a really good girl."

I said nothing, not understanding at first what he was suggesting. Then it hit me. I had heard wild tales when I was younger about men and women and animals, but I had paid little attention to them. I thought they were only stories that young ones told for want of better things to do. Now it was Pigghogg, asking me to join him in the barn. With the other pigs.

I had to control my anger or my plans would fail. "Oh, sir, I couldn't do that. You would not want it known that your wife, your wife was…well, you know. It would not be good for your reputation."

It was also clearly unlawful, and people were hanged for the crime, but I didn't know that at the time.

Pigghogg considered my words carefully. He despised being thwarted in his plans—he was used to having his way in all matters civil and personal—but he also was concerned about his reputation. He had a position to uphold, and any accounts such as what he was suggesting would severely tarnish that reputation. He was torn between his lust and his need to be admired.

I closed my eyes and prayed. Please, God, I know you're busy watching over your children, protecting them when they are in dire need, but I am your child as well. Please, please, tell my husband what he must do.

Pigghogg rocked back and forth in his chair, considering the dilemma I had created for him. He was unhappy about the problem, but for the moment, his reputation overcame his lust. "All right, we'll reserve the barn for another day."

I was saved until another day. I determined now that I would need to escape before that other day arrived.

"But, if you want me to visit you," he commanded, "you'll need to be in the bedroom."

"I will, sir," I said, a little too quickly since I didn't know what that might involve. "What is it you wish?"

He considered this for a moment. "We'll see when the time comes. But as a start, you might show more enthusiasm. This is not just a duty, you know. It's a pleasure."

"Yes, sir. It will be a pleasure."

"Good. Prepare yourself."

With that he left the table. Dorothy came in and observed me closely. She knew something important had been said, probably concerning her or James. I would never tell her.

I repaired to my room, anxious about what would be required of me. And who would require it. It was possible that, consumed with lust, Pigghogg would come alone to the room and attempt to perform on me what his shortened cord had heretofore made impossible. I could think of nothing more disgusting than showing pleasure to that beast of a man, unless it was being in the barn with the other beasts.

I prepared myself carefully, wearing my nicest shift and sprinkling a bit of the perfume Pigghogg had ordered from the old country especially for me. Then I waited, not knowing what to expect.

Night was deepening, and the crickets and frogs were singing in the swamp nearby. A slight breeze blew in off the ocean, a sign that the weather would soon be cooling as autumn arrived. I lay on the sheets, thinking of Mother and what was happening to her. Was she being fed properly? Were the jailers kind? I had heard stories of what happened to the beggar women who came under their care. Poor Mother, already mad, would not be able to defend herself.

I was becoming more and more anxious. Perhaps Pigghogg's ardor had cooled and his reputation required him to keep some distance from his wife who carried her mother's contagion. Perhaps he didn't think I'd be good enough to satisfy him, as I had previously shown no inclination to do so.

Just when I had given up, the door opened. Pigghogg entered, wearing only a robe. He came to the bed and regarded me.

"You will show pleasure this evening?" he said, threateningly.

"I will. As I promised."

"Good." He produced the usual blindfold, which I let him tie around my head. I heard him blow out the candle. And then nothing, except for his breathing. Would he whip me? It didn't seem likely, as he hadn't forced me to turn over.

I waited and waited, hardly able to breathe. Nothing happened. The darkness that engulfed me was unbearable. I tried not to think, to close my mind to where I was.

Pigghogg stood nearby, breathing deeply, but doing nothing.

Good God, I thought, maybe he has a knife. Maybe he'll do to me what Mother tried to do to him. Of course that would excite him, monster that he was. And who would care? A witch's daughter gone, a contagion no longer spreading, a threat to the colony removed.

I could hear him move. Now he was closer to the bed, his breathing labored. Oh God in Heaven, no one will help me. He will either stab me or fall on me. I would rather he stabbed me and got it over with.

He didn't stab me. I could feel his body pressing down on me. I tried to shut out the pain and shame, but I was overwhelmed. I wanted to scream and scratch and tear him off my body.

But then, in my anger, I realized Pigghogg wasn't moving. He couldn't move because of his deformity. That was a small satisfaction. If I could hang on, he would soon be off. But that would mean my plan would have ended, and I would learn nothing about Mother or be no closer to escape.

He didn't get off, and he didn't move. He just lay on me, breathing, but breathing more shallowly. And it seemed different. It was then I realized it might not be Pigghogg. I raised my arms up to the shoulders of the man who lay quietly on me. I felt a small mole, just where it had been before. It was James—or whoever had been Pigghogg's replacement before. I couldn't contain my excitement. My plan might work after all.

I pulled him to me, pushing Pigghogg out of my mind. I thought only of James and the pleasure I needed to show. And then, surprisingly, as I began to move under him, I began to feel a tingling inside of me. I pulled him more strongly to me, caressing his back and pinching it lightly. He began to respond as he never had before. He sensed my pleasure, and I, his. I could dimly hear Pigghogg enjoying himself, probably leaning over us, but I quickly forgot him. I concentrated on James and myself. Together. He was breathing harder now, and I groaned and cried out in pleasure. I had, at last, released myself, my anger and sorrow subsiding in the soft, warm pleasure of the moment. I let it wash over me, cleansing and refreshing as it did. I was at peace.

As James and I relaxed, I suddenly remembered the plan. I had nearly forgotten it in my carefree passion, thinking only of myself. I didn't know how close Pigghogg was; I sensed he had pulled back in his chair, enjoying himself in whatever unnatural manner he had devised. This could be my last chance. I might never again have James so close.

I pulled my head quickly and stealthily up to his ear, not knowing for sure who it was or what the consequences might be. "Please help," I whispered. "How is Mother?"

His hands were around my shoulders, and I could feel them tighten again. He had heard me. Then he pressed my back two times in quick succession, which I took to mean he would do what he could.

I had done what I could on that strange, disturbing night. I had awakened for the first time, and I knew that I would never be the same woman again.

As James and Pigghogg left, neither saying anything, I wondered if Mother would ever be the same again.

CHAPTER 12

The next morning was cool and cloudy, a sharp wind blowing in off the ocean. Pigghogg often ate his breakfast alone, seeming to prefer the company of Dorothy to mine. Perhaps he was ashamed of his inability to perform and didn't wish to see me. I was a constant reminder of his deficiency in those matters.

My own feelings were similar. I also preferred eating alone, though I had to endure the presence of Dorothy, who said little to me, but whose silence was filled with contempt. I, too, was ashamed of what I had allowed Pigghogg to do so often and so painfully.

But last night was different. I had finally done something to help Mother, or at least find out how she was. I was going to make contact, and from that contact I would be able to help her. My old dreams appeared again: I would help Mother escape, and I would escape with her.

Last night had awakened me in other ways I hadn't expected. I couldn't fully understand my feelings yet, but I felt stronger, more sure of myself than I had ever felt. I had satisfied a man and myself at the same time. It was a good feeling.

Thus emboldened, I walked confidently past the Pigghogg family, their pinched faces suspecting that something was amiss, to join their descendent at the breakfast table.

I quietly approached the dining room and heard low voices. At the doorway I paused and looked in. I couldn't believe what I saw. Dorothy was standing next to Pigghogg, serving him. Pigghogg was seated, facing the other direction, his arm pulled tightly around her hips, which he was stroking.

I was furious. Were all of us no more than Pigghogg's playthings? What right did he have to assault his female servant, force his male servant into unnatural acts, and treat his wife as if she were no more than a servant herself?

I strode into the room. "I see no breakfast," I spit at Dorothy, who quickly moved away from Pigghogg. I sat at the other end of the table, glaring at the two of them. Neither turned away from my angry stare, and I realized then how little I knew of what Pigghogg and his servants were capable of. For a moment, I felt that all three of them, even James, were allied against me.

Pigghogg nodded to Dorothy who quickly turned to fetching my breakfast. He continued eating, paying me no attention. This made me angrier. I was determined to attract his attention.

"Why was my breakfast not prepared?" I asked him.

He said nothing and kept eating.

"Your ancestors were not pleased," I said.

Pigghogg looked up. "What was that?" he growled.

"I said your ancestors were not pleased. They scowled as I passed them."

His face darkened. "You mock me, then?"

"Your ancestors mock you. You have disgraced them."

He grew darker. He stopped eating and leaned toward me and spoke quietly and deliberately, his words as cold as the wind blowing in from the ocean. "You mock me, Chastity. I have warned you before what I can do. And I will do it, you may be sure. I am a man of my word."

He finished his meal and left the table. He went to Dorothy and stood at her side, speaking quietly to her, but I couldn't hear him. The two of them were planning something, but I didn't know what. All I knew was I had carelessly endangered myself. And then I remembered. Pigghogg, as he often reminded me, stood between my mother and me, and between her and her fate. At one word from him, she would go to her death on the gallows.

I wanted to go to Mother to warn her, but I knew the ugly constable was waiting nearby. I would be forced to remain in the house. For the day. For the rest of my life, for all I knew.

I went to my bedroom and threw myself on the bed, where I remained all morning, fitfully sleeping and dreaming of Pigghogg eating, consuming everything in front of him. I screamed when I saw Mother appear before him, pleading to spare her life. Her pleas awoke me and sent me to the window facing the back of the house. I saw James on his way to the barn. I knew then what I had to do.

I went to the mirror and looked at myself. I looked a wild woman, much like my mother at the trial, but I couldn't waste time improving my appearance. I went downstairs and heard nothing. Dorothy would be shopping. I slipped out the back door and walked to the barn, where Pigghogg kept his two allotted cows, two horses, and a number of pigs and goats and chickens, as did others in town. I knew he had more livestock and property at other locations some distance from the city, but he had never told me where. He preferred it a secret.

I stopped at the door, remembering. This was where Pigghogg wanted me to go with him for whatever unnatural acts he had planned. I didn't want to enter. He might be waiting inside, with James, to force me to his will. I became convinced that was exactly what he'd done. It was all part of his plan to work his unnatural acts on me and then accuse me of witchcraft and send me to the gallows with Mother.

I shouldn't have gone in. But I did. I needed to talk with James, and that need was greater than my fear of Pigghogg.

It was dim inside, a little light coming through the loft. The cows had been taken to pasture on the Common as usual, but Pigghogg's horses were there. He had not ridden his horse to work as he often did, though work was but a few blocks away. I knew then he was waiting for me, somewhere in the barn.

But still I didn't leave. I walked quietly through the barn, looking in each stall and behind every post. The goats were pleased to see me and clustered around, nuzzling me. I reached down to pet one when I heard a noise behind me.

I stood up and turned to face my fate.

"Mistress Pigghogg?"

It was James. Pigghogg was still hidden.

"You frightened me."

"I'm sorry. I didn't hear you enter."

I looked past him but saw nothing. "You're alone?"

He looked at me oddly. "Yes, of course," he said. "Except for these." He motioned to the goats, which now circled both of us.

I didn't believe him. He seemed uneasy. Alert. Expecting something to happen. Pigghogg ready to assault me.

I needed to act quickly. I stepped forward, but he moved back, afraid. I held my hand up for him to stop. "Wait," I whispered. "I need to talk."

He shook his head.

"Please. What have you learned?"

He shook his head again, backing farther away.

I moved quickly to him, looking him directly in the eyes. I looked for recognition that he had been my lover, the man I had held fiercely to me and responded as I had never before responded to a man.

I saw only fear. Fear of me or fear of Pigghogg waiting behind him. I didn't know. I didn't even know if he was my lover the night before.

I heard a sound in one of the vacant cow stalls. Looking into James's eyes and seeing no recognition, I moved quickly to the door, passing the stall where I had heard the noise. It was dark, but crouching in the corner, I saw a figure, dimly outlined against the wood. I didn't look closer, but ran quickly to the door and passed into the yard. I didn't look behind me, even when I was safely in the house. I didn't want to see what I had just escaped.

But I was curious, and the more I thought about it, the more curious I became. Was it Pigghogg crouching in the corner, and if it was, how did he know I would be coming to the barn? It was another question for which I had no answer. And none immediately forthcoming.

All of my dreams of escape with my mother ended in the barn. James was a servant, a cowardly one at that, and would find out nothing about Mother. I was destined to remain in the house with the dead Pigghoggs, their grim faces a reminder of the life my father had chosen for me to save his inn. I didn't care if it burned to the ground. If given the opportunity, I would set fire to it myself.

The days went by, one after the other, in a dull and heavy darkness. I saw little of Pigghogg or James, and my evenings, like my days, were spent alone. I could hardly drag myself from bed each morning, and I had no appetite. Food that before so delighted me seemed putrid, and I ate only enough to keep myself alive. It passed through my mind that with little effort I could stop eating altogether, saving Pigghogg the expense of keeping me alive. What did it matter to him? He could find another man like my father who would sell his soul and his daughter to keep his business. Better a live business, even if it meant a dead daughter.

But just when I was most despairing a remarkable thing happened. My friends Anne and Mary would have said it was Providence, but I had no faith in Providence, which had turned blind when my mother went mad and was sent to prison to await her terrible fate.

I was lying in bed one morning, thinking how pleasant it would be to lie there at peace, eating no more and sleeping forever, when Pigghogg charged in.

"Get dressed," he growled.

"I'll not go to the barn if that's what you're thinking," I said, pulling the sheets more tightly around me.

"You'll go to the barn if I demand it," he said. "But I have other plans for you."

"I'll not go anywhere," I said, and meant it. I would stay in bed forever just to thwart him.

He ripped the sheet and blanket off. "I said get up. Now. You are to display yourself."

"Display myself? I've done with that. I'd rather die."

"You will die soon enough if you don't dress immediately." He took my arm and pulled me to my feet and held my wrists so I couldn't scratch him.

I saw in his eyes what his plans were. He would drag me naked, screaming, to the barn, where I would display myself in whatever disgusting manner he had now devised. I tried to fall to the ground, but he held me firmly.

"You're going to town," he snarled.

"No. Never."

"You will wear your finest clothes. And be seen by everyone."

So great was my anger I didn't hear him at first. "I'll not go to town. With you."

"You're not going with me. You will be attended by the constable. And you will wear your finest clothes. Now dress!"

He turned and left the room.

Then I realized what he had said. I was to be dressed in my finest clothes. I would be going to town, attended by the constable. I could hardly believe my good fortune, if it was good fortune. No doubt Pigghogg had another plan to humiliate me and send me to the gallows. Or have me murdered along the way.

But at least I would be out of the house.

I paid no attention to the Pigghogg family when I descended the stairs, dressed in my finest clothes, but I could hear them talking among themselves. They suspected I was escaping their clutches.

Dorothy was no better. I had now begun suspecting her relationship with Pigghogg, though I didn't know what it might involve. I knew only she couldn't be trusted. As she placed the corn cakes and sausages in front of me, she sniffed, "Master says you are to be ready at nine." She left, saying no more, but I knew she disapproved of my leaving, escaping her surveillance.

At nine came a knock on the door. Dorothy answered it, informing the visitor I would be ready shortly. She wanted to speak more to him, but coming into the hallway, I interrupted. "I'm quite ready," I said, and indeed I was.

I didn't know who it would be. There were three constables in town: the ugly giant who guarded the house, another I didn't know but had only heard about, and the one who had spoken nicely to me at the trial.

"Mistress Pigghogg," the constable said when I reached the door. It was the gentle one, Thomas Brattle. He smiled and offered his arm, which I took, sweeping my skirt past Dorothy and out the door.

I breathed in the cool morning air, which had seemed so oppressive a few days before. I welcomed the fresh salty breeze, as I welcomed Thomas. They both refreshed me.

Thomas was a young man, a little older than I was, and possessed a friendly countenance, which put me at ease.

"What is the meaning of this?" I asked him.

"Of what, Mistress Pigghogg?"

"Of this walk. I've been in prison for several months, watched by blood-thirsty men."

"Ahh. Well, that's a story."

"Yes. Tell me. It will pass the time."

I could see him struggling with himself and I pressed closer to him. "I shouldn't tell you this," he finally said, "but say nothing to anyone, especially Mister Pigghogg, and I will. Promise me?"

"Yes, of course. I would not speak to my husband if my life depended on it."

He looked over at me, wondering at my words. "Well," he said, "it seems that the court and others think it's rather improper for an important magistrate and man of the town to be keeping his wife hidden in the house."

We nodded to several men and women passing. I recognized one of the women who was at the trial, sitting next to me. She stopped talking to the man accompanying her, and held his arm more tightly as we passed. I stared at her, saying nothing.

A cart rumbled by on its way to the marketplace.

So, Pigghogg was afraid of public opinion. That was the best news I had heard in some time, except that I didn't know what public opinion was and expected little of it. It had, after all, given evidence that my mother had contracted with Satan to cause Goody Preston's pig to mate with her neighbor's calf.

"Thank you," I told Thomas. "I'll say nothing."

We were approaching the marketplace, filled with men and women and bustling with activity. Once there we would not be far from the prison, and I hoped that we might walk down Prison Lane. We were also not far from the

Reverend Wilson's house and the hateful instruments he loved so well, the whipping post and the pillory.

A group of men and women were gathering at the old wooden scaffold, on which were the stocks and the pillory, and Thomas pulled me in that direction. I wanted no part of those machines, not knowing at the time what part they would play in my future.

"No," I said. "Not there."

"I'm sorry, Mistress Pigghogg. I have instructions."

I tried to pull away, but he firmly held my hand. "No," he said quietly but firmly. "We must attend to the proceedings."

We pulled closer to the scaffold, Thomas pushing gently through the crowd so that we could see more clearly.

Oh, God in Heaven. It was a woman. The ugly constable who often guarded me had just forced her head into the unyielding wooden notch and had pulled the heavy top over it, locking her head and hands in place. I recognized the woman as she stared angrily at the crowd. She had often come to the inn, she and her shiftless husband, and there was little peace when she was there. Her shrewish and sharp tongue would provoke Father, who often asked her to leave for fear that a minister or magistrate would hear her profane talk and close the inn.

Then I saw him, climbing the stairs from the other end. It was the Reverend John Wilson. I had not seen him since the trial, and had no desire to see him now. But when I tried to pull away, Thomas held me firmly. "Be careful, Mistress Pigghogg," he said quietly. "We must witness this."

I closed my eyes. I had no interest in more punishment of our women. I wanted to find Mother and flee with her from the colony.

"Abigail Murdock, you know why you're here?"

"For your pleasure," she replied in a mocking voice.

I opened my eyes, surprised at her tone.

Wilson was angry. He was not used to be spoken to in this manner. "Woman, do you know who I am?"

"Indeed. You are the man who beats women."

"I beat no women. It is God, working his way."

"Oh, God is it?" she said, still mocking him. "His arm is stout then. I would have it caressing me at night."

Wilson was furious. "This is blasphemy, woman."

"What is this blasphemy you slaver over? In truth, you are like my dog with a bone."

Wilson could not restrain himself. He pushed her head down against the hard wood, causing her to cry out.

"Woman, you are here for lewdness. And drunkenness. Now it is blasphemy. You are a sinner, a blight on the colony." He stood back, shaking his finger at her. "You know what we do with sinners such as you?"

She said nothing at first. Then she smiled, "You save them, I believe."

"Save them? Hardly. Not such as you"

"I have no soul, then?"

"All of God's creatures have souls."

"All of them?" She smiled again, her eyes dancing with pleasure though her head was bent in pain.

"Does my pig, then, have a soul? And you will save it?"

"God saves only those men and women justified before him."

"Ah, poor pig. She's harmed no one, and will provide a fine meal for a slavering man such as yourself. Your God is wicked if he will not save my Sarah."

"He will save your Sarah. But not your pig."

"But Sarah is my pig."

Wilson was exasperated beyond endurance. He had wanted to make an example of the woman, but he had produced only sympathy. Several of her friends were laughing loudly at her responses, and others were speaking among themselves, amused.

Wilson turned to face the crowd, then turned back to the woman. Before he could say anything, she spoke again. "Will your God save no women, then?"

"Our God saves women," Wilson said angrily. "That is his word."

"Then he will save Sarah. She's a fine woman. If you saw her litter, you would save her yourself. And her litter. Feed a hungry man properly for the winter."

Wilson composed himself. When he spoke to her again, he spoke with authority. "Abigail Murdock, there is a woman in prison now charged with witchcraft. She is known to have signed the Evil One's book, and done his foul deeds among us." He stepped back and addressed his audience standing quietly now around the scaffold. "These are perilous times. God is angry with us. Each day brings more evidence of his displeasure. We cannot allow this contagion to spread." He turned back to Abigail. "Woman, you will remain here until nightfall. You will be given water to drink, but no food to eat. When you are released, you will be called before the court."

"For what, your honor? I have done nothing but speak the truth."

"For witchcraft!" he hurled at her. "For witchcraft."

Now she matched his anger. "I would rather go to hell than see the court," she spit at him. "Not that there's a difference."

Wilson said no more. He turned and left the platform, going past me as he did. I tried to look the other way, but in stopping to greet my guard, he saw me.

"Ah, Mistress Pigghogg, I'm pleased to see your interest in the law. Have you been well instructed?"

"I have. I have indeed." Little did he know how well instructed I'd been.

"Good. It would have been a mercy if your mother had been so instructed."

"My mother is well versed in the law, Reverend Wilson. It is a millstone around her neck."

He smiled maliciously. "Indeed. The Devil listens to no other law."

I was about to ask how it was he had become so familiar with the Devil, but Thomas sensed my impudence and squeezed by arm. "We should be off," he said, nodding to Wilson.

I wanted to walk down Prison Lane, but Thomas guided me in another direction. We walked through the marketplace and came upon the spring where I had met Anne and Mary. Two young girls were fetching water for their families.

I don't know why but I stopped and knelt on the rocks that lined the gushing water. The two girls stopped their work and observed me. The smaller one said softly, "Why is it you kneel, Madam?"

I looked at her, so young and innocent. I wished I could be her age again, in the old country with no fears, no Pigghogg or Reverend Wilson tormenting me. "I kneel for you, my dear," I said. "And pray that your fate be more agreeable than mine."

She was puzzled, so I took a handful of the pure water and touched her forehead with it. "Let it keep you safe from our men," I said and thought of Anne and Mary, both now gone. The girl looked at her friend and quickly moved away, frightened. Perhaps she had heard of Mother and thought I had also contracted with the Devil. I was very sorry I said anything to frighten so young a child. She would have enough to frighten her when she became a woman.

Thomas nodded that we should be on our way again. I smiled and said, "You'll not sit with me here and rest?"

"No, ma'am. It would displease Mister Pigghogg."

"Ah, well, another day then. I have many."

"Yes, ma'am."

I got to my feet and he offered his arm. "Have I displayed myself enough for the day?" I said, lightly pressing his arm.

He looked about him, as if I had broken one of the Commandments: Thou shalt not squeeze the constable's arm.

No one paid us any attention. "You have displayed yourself fittingly, mistress," he said. "We should return." We moved away from the spring, but not to Prison Lane. He shook his head when I looked in that direction.

I glanced at the pillory, where Abigail Murdock stood alone, the crowd having departed to more pleasant activities. She saw me looking at her. "Come this way," she called.

Thomas didn't seem to mind, so the two of us walked to the edge of the scaffold. "Up here," she said. "I would speak with you privately."

Thomas resisted, but I implored him. "Please, there is no danger for me."

"Be quick," he said, looking around. "Mister Pigghogg didn't speak to this."

I climbed the stairs and walked to her. She was younger than I first imagined, and there was a fire in her eyes, though the infernal instrument held her head and arms in its unyielding embrace.

"Scratch my cheek," she said. "I cannot bear the itch."

I hesitated for a moment and then did as she bade. "This one?"

"Aye."

I rubbed it softly.

"Is that better?"

"Aye."

"The other one?"

"If you would."

I rubbed that as well, softly touching her cheek and pushing her rich black hair out of her eyes. I ran my hand over her forehead."

"You have a fever," I said.

"Aye."

"I'll tell my husband. He'll have you released."

"No one will release me."

"He has great power in the colony.

"The dark angel will release me. I can hear his wings above us now."

I looked up and saw a dark, jagged cloud pass over the sun. I shuddered, thinking that it was an omen.

She saw my concern. "You see him, too, then? I thought as much. We are sisters."

"Oh, no…no. You'll be fine. I'll help you."

She looked me in the eyes. "I've seen you before," she said.

"Perhaps."

"Hmm. You dress as a fine lady, but you are not a fine lady. Am I right?"

"Why would you think that?"

"You would not stand here with such as me if you were."

I glanced down at my guardian, who nodded that I should leave the scaffold. Perhaps I should have. But the woman held me in her spell.

"It was not in prison, was it? I've been there often."

"No, not there."

"Take my hands," she ordered.

I glanced at Thomas again. He was getting more agitated. Several others in marketplace had noted me, and had stopped their activities.

I did as she ordered. She gripped my hands hard, so that I almost gave a little cry. Then she closed her eyes, as if in a trance. I waited, not knowing what to expect.

Finally, she opened her eyes and smiled. "You were at the inn, weren't you?"

"Yes."

"A MAN'S CASTLE, I recall. Beastly name."

"Yes. I never liked it myself."

She relaxed her grip a little. "Ah, now I know you. You were his daughter, a maid, that's why I didn't recognize you."

I nodded. "Yes. I was that girl. But I am no longer, God help me."

"God will not help you any more than he helps me. Or those like me. He has no time for us." She gripped my hands more tightly and looked me in the eye. "Chastity Hoar," she said quietly. "Now Chastity Pigghogg. Married to that pig of a man." She relaxed her grip, as if she knew what I suffered. She knew my name and she knew me.

I nodded and lowered my eyes. I couldn't bear to look at her. "I must leave now," I said. "The constable is impatient."

"Wait. I have powers."

She was frightening me. "I must leave. Quickly. Pigghogg is waiting."

"Look at me."

I raised my head again and saw her burning eyes, searching me out, reaching for my soul. I wished to leave, but she held me fast.

"Chastity Pigghogg, I see your life. It is narrow and long. You will one day live as I live. One day stand where I stand. There will be others."

I couldn't breathe. "Who? Who stands beside me?"

She was quiet for a moment, seeking out the future. "I cannot tell. They are shadows. I see no faces." She paused and then said, "But they are women."

"Women? My mother?"

"Ask no more."

"You see no one?"

"You must leave now. Or it will go hard on you."

"Yes. My husband is a beast of a man."

She released my hands. "But wait."

"Yes?"

"That man. The constable."

"What about him?"

"He will be with you."

"Here?"

"Somewhere. Perhaps here."

"Do you see more?"

"No. The curtain is drawn."

"Then I must go. To Pigghogg. I would that he stood here. In your place."

She smiled grimly. "He will come to a fitting end. But not here."

"Could you…?"

She shook her head and looked to the stairs where Thomas had come to fetch me. "No more." She didn't want me to leave. "Touch my face again, if you would."

I did as she asked and I saw tears.

"You are kind," she said. "I thank you."

I wiped away a tear, almost crying myself.

"But listen. Kindness will kill you quickly in this world. You must be hard and strong. Do you understand?" She was desperate for me to believe.

"Yes. I understand."

She closed her eyes and said no more.

Thomas took my arm and led me off the scaffold. I noted then that several people were standing close, watching us and murmuring among themselves.

Thomas was angry with me. "You should not have stayed so long," he said. "I should not have allowed you."

"It was worth my time," I said. "She saw my life."

He stopped, stunned, and turned to me. "Tell no one," he said. "No one. Only those who have contracted with Satan himself can read the future. If Mister Pigghogg or Reverend Wilson discover this, it will be the end for her." He paused and then said, "Be careful, madam, very careful. You've been seen with her."

"Thank you for the advice, Thomas," I said, making light of his warning. "I shall do as you ask."

He said no more, and we walked silently back to the house. I had started the day feeling stronger, more assured than I had ever felt. My mother and I would soon be escaping from this doleful colony.

I ended the day much differently. My fortune had been told, and it was dark and terrible. I would not escape, nor would the shadow women Abigail had seen.

I had much to think about.

CHAPTER 13

Abigail had told me to be hard and strong, but I found that easier to say than do. At dinner with Pigghogg my mind was all in a jumble, thoughts swirling this way and that, twigs in a rushing river after a sudden storm. I saw Dorothy hovering near Pigghogg, watching every bite I took. I figured she was trying to poison me, but what could I do? I had to eat food, and I couldn't watch every meal she made. I would need to take my chances and eat if I wanted to be strong as Abigail had demanded of me.

Pigghogg seemed more spirited than usual. He stuffed himself, using his hands when his utensils wouldn't suffice, and spoke frequently to Dorothy, asking every manner of question. She responded amiably, smiling at each question and answering with great spirit. They seemed to be speaking in code, and I didn't know the code.

After a while I paid them no attention and thought about my own situation and the road I was now treading. I hadn't yet seen my mother or found out her condition. I assumed she was still alive, though in great danger, as turmoil seemed to be increasing in the town. She had been accused of witchcraft but not yet found guilty, which was a small solace. Accusations, I was learning, were little different from guilt in this town ruled by Wilson and Pigghogg and other men of their nature. Even the governor, John Winthrop, listened to their howling voices and was loath to intervene if it meant showing kindness or mercy to those less fortunate than were his family and friends. Still, I hoped that his wife, the woman who had smiled at me, might have influence on him, interceding for Mother and for me, if that should become necessary.

My thoughts drifted to the scaffold where Abigail was perhaps standing, her hands clamped in the wooden vise, her neck bowed but not yet broken. I thought I could hear her voice, still crying out at the men who taunted her and held her in their instrument of torture. I had thought her a shrewish woman in the inn and had little respect for her, but perhaps I had judged her unjustly. She had called me her sister and condemned her accusers in public as I had condemned them in private. She did not tremble before them, even with knowing what fate her words would bring down on her. She was strong like my mother but unlike my mother had no daughter whose marriage would drive her mad.

I had touched her face and saw the tears as I comforted her. Had anyone else in her broken life ever touched her face, softly as I did, and listened to her words? Was I not her sister, married to a pig of a man no different from the knave of a man she had married and who was nowhere to be found now that his wife was in danger.

I shuddered as I thought more deeply about my encounter with Abigail. If I were her sister, as she said, would I walk the road she walked? She had looked into the future and seen a dark and narrow path for me, one that led to the scaffold where she now stood in the gathering darkness, alone, forsaken by everyone. Had she seen correctly or was it a mirage, such as the one I saw looking out onto the bay, shimmering in the sun, when it seemed that silky sea creatures were dancing on the waves?

I was dancing on the waves and didn't hear him speak. "Chastity!"

I drew myself back to the table.

"Chastity, I'm speaking to you."

"Hmm. Yes?"

"You are distracted again. As you are much of late."

"Yes. What do you wish?"

"I wish your attention. As your husband and ruler, I demand no less."

"Of course." My husband perhaps, but no more my ruler, if I had sufficient mettle.

"I asked if you were soberly instructed today."

"Soberly? I've had no drink if that's your meaning."

"You've had no drink because I've ordered that you have none. I'll not have you talked about in town for drunkenness."

"There is no danger in that I would think."

"But you are talked about. In town." He stopped his eating and watched my reaction. I showed him none.

"The town talks about everyone it seems," I said as calmly as I could. There could be danger lurking behind his words.

"You were seen talking to that demon of a woman in the pillory."

There was little use in denying it since he might have seen me himself. "I was, that's sure." I looked at him and smiled. "It was sobering, indeed."

"You are not to talk with accused women such as her! Have you no regard for my reputation?"

"I do, sir. That is why I mentioned you when I spoke with her."

"You uttered my name in her presence?" he thundered. "How dare you be so foolish? Do you ever think about the consequences of your acts? Do you ever…?" He was overcome with anger.

"I said only that you were a powerful and respected man in the town. Was that so wrong?"

"You said nothing else?"

"Nothing but idle talk of the weather. And her health."

"Hmm. I'll speak with Thomas about that. He should never have allowed it. I'll need to have constable Stubbs take you next time."

"Constable Stubbs?" I could never allow that to happen. Never. I spoke almost without thinking: "That would be much appreciated," I said, with as much sincerity as I could summon. "Thomas is too harsh with me. He turns me like a pig on a spit."

That pleased Pigghogg no end. "Like a pig on a spit, is it? I'll need to reward him for his service."

"Please, not him, my husband. I implore you. I could not endure it. I'll do whatever you like."

"Whatever?" His eyes narrowed. "The barn then."

To his side I could see Dorothy smirking. What did she know about Pigghogg and the barn?

I couldn't be worried about Dorothy. I had to think of myself. "Your reputation, sir. It should not be compromised."

He searched my face for the meaning behind my words. "I think you worry more about yourself," he said.

"No, sir. I worry about you. It's not good for there to be whispering."

He was silent for a moment. Then he shook his head. He was not at all pleased. "All right. All right. I'm persuaded. This time. But you'll not put if off any longer."

"No, sir. I seek only your reputation be spared."

"In bed, then. Tonight. As before."

"Yes, sir. I will be enthusiastic. Did I not please you the other night when you favored me with your presence?"

"Modestly. No more than that."

"I will do better this time. Trust me. I enjoy the pleasure of your company. At night."

I almost gagged, but it was becoming easier with each speaking of the lie. Besides, there was the reward to be anticipated.

True to his word, Pigghogg visited me later than night. I thought to test him when he produced the blindfold. "I would see my husband if he thought it proper."

That surprised him, but in his lust he was blinded to what I was truly seeking: the identity of the man who had become my lover.

"It is not proper," he said after a pause. "My reputation must not be tarnished by foolish women who talk like magpies when no men are present to guide them."

"Very well," I said. "But I would see my husband if I am to show pleasure."

"Perhaps when you submit to my pleasure in the barn, I will make allowances. Until then, it will be the blindfold."

"As you wish," I said as he tied the handkerchief even more tightly than he had before. I would need to be guided by touch.

I lay there quietly, listening for each sound. First the footsteps, heavy like his, though he was walking as quietly as ever. Then lighter footsteps, so light I wasn't sure I even heard them. Then a slight scraping of the chair, close to the bed. Closer than before. I could hear his heavy breathing.

I waited, excited now by what I would soon feel.

His body was soon on me. This time he didn't lie on me, unmoving, hoping to be finished with his unwelcome duty. This time I could feel the excitement throughout his body. I held him fiercely to me and he responded to my urgency with his own. I forgot about Pigghogg again as I opened myself to his powerful thrusting into me. Over and over and over, until I was but a weak vessel, accepting what was freely given in the darkness of the room. And, in truth, the darkness of our lives.

My pleasure came quickly to an end. I felt James's body, his shoulders, the mole, his hands, but something was wrong. I stiffened. There was another hand running over my breasts and down my body, eagerly exploring, unsated by our passion. It could only be Pigghogg.

I screamed.

The body was quickly off me. And the mysterious hand was withdrawn.

One pair of footsteps scurried to the door and was gone. The other didn't move.

What would he do now, his pleasure interrupted? I tightened my body, waiting for the lash of the whip.

I waited. And waited. Nothing happened.

I could hear a faint sound, at some distance now from the bed. A groan. And breathing. And then nothing.

The door closed behind him, and I heard no more.

The next morning he was gone when I ate breakfast, and James was nowhere to be seen. Dorothy was more dour than ever, no doubt furious that her husband was now enjoying himself in my bed. There was some pleasure in that thought for me, but the silence that filled the house was ominous. Frightening. Even the Pigghoggs on the wall seemed to sense that a fire was smoldering somewhere, in the house, in the town, and it would soon burst into flame.

As it did. The next day.

Pigghogg was at my door early, throwing it open and shouting for me to rise. I thought the house on fire.

"You must be ready by nine," he said. "In your best clothes."

He was gone before I could ask him why.

I dressed quickly and went to breakfast. He was still wolfing down his food, unaware I was sitting across from him.

He finally looked up and saw me.

"He'll pick you up at nine."

"Who will that be?" I said, sure that he had seen through my ruse and had secured constable Stubbs to drag me to town.

"The man who turns you like a pig on a spit," he laughed, coughing out a half-eaten sausage on the table in front of him.

"I begged you for constable Stubbs," I said. "Did you not enjoy yourself the other night?"

"You were quite unsatisfactory," he said. "Thomas Brattle will be your punishment."

I groaned. "I cannot endure it. You are unjust."

"You will endure it. And more. Much more."

"More than him? How could that be?"

"Be in the marketplace at nine and you'll find out. Today you will be instructed as you were not the last time."

"Sir?"

He said no more but finished his meal, gave Dorothy a friendly caress on her thigh and left. I could hear his horse clopping as it passed the house and galloped the few blocks to the town center.

I met Thomas at the door, eager to accompany him to the marketplace. What awaited me there could be no worse than what I endured at home. It would probably be much better.

I said as much to Thomas who didn't answer. He said nothing as we walked side by side to the town center.

It was a beautiful day, brisk, a cool wind blowing in off the ocean, but the sun was bright with hope. What could have excited Pigghogg and silenced Thomas? Was it the glorious beauty of this day?

I found out quickly enough and was sorry for it.

As we approached the scaffold, a crowd of people were milling about, some talking excitedly. Others said nothing and seemed to wish themselves elsewhere.

Thomas and I approached the crowd, stopping only when I stood next to an old woman.

"What brings everyone here, Goodwife?" I asked the woman.

She turned and saw who was speaking. She pulled away, moving to the other end of the crowd.

"Thomas, what is it?" I was becoming alarmed.

He said nothing but nodded toward Prison Lane. I looked and saw the ugly giant and another constable approaching, leading a woman whose hands were tied before her. She appeared at a distance to be no more than an animal being led to pasture by the town's cowherd.

Oh, God, let it not be Mother. Not Mother. Not yet. I'm not ready.

As they drew closer, I could just make out the woman's features. It was Abigail. Abigail Murdock. The woman whose face I had touched in the pillory, whose tears I had wiped with my sleeve. Though the men would yank the rope, forcing her to stumble, she walked upright, gazing at each person along the lane. She smiled and nodded at the women, as if she knew what they were thinking. As if she knew what her fate was and would face it as they should face their own.

When she reached the scaffold, I looked up and saw that Reverend Wilson was already standing there, awaiting his prisoner.

Abigail was led up the stairs. She fell to her knees going up and was pulled to her feet and dragged onto the scaffold.

"Wait, you bastard sons!" she shouted. "I would walk aright to this man."

She pulled herself to her feet, pushing the constables back with her tied hands. She stood before Wilson, fiercely staring at him so that he turned away.

The smoldering fire was now alight.

Wilson regained his composure, but I noticed he wouldn't look at her as he spoke.

"Abigail Murdock," he said. "The court has met and found you guilty of gross crimes against the colony.

"Pssh. I spit on your court."

Wilson continued, still not looking directly at her. "You are found guilty of lewdness. And drunkenness at many times in many places, even after being so warned of the danger. And, finally, you are found guilty of disrespect for the magistrates who rule you. For undermining their God-given authority."

"I curse your authority," she hissed. "And you, John Wilson. Your authority is from hell where you are bound."

"Silence, woman! For this talk you are to be punished!"

Abigail lunged for him, but the constables pulled her back before she could reach him. "Look me in the eye, John Wilson. If you dare. Tell me what you see."

Reverend Wilson couldn't refuse the challenge or he would seem a lesser man. He turned to face her directly.

"What do you see?" she asked, her eyes blazing hatred.

"I see the Devil," he said. "The archangel himself, filled with hatred for all that is good."

"I think not," she said. "What you see is what all men see when they look in my eyes. They see themselves and their fate."

"I see nothing but darkness," he said, but not as strongly. He was weakening in the fire of her gaze.

"It is darkness, surely. Of your own making. You will fall into it, and no one will pull you free. You will cry out, and no one will hear. You will—"

"I said silence, woman!" He reached for the rope binding her hands, but as he did, she raised her hands, striking him in the face. He backed off and turned away, stung by her words and now by her hands.

They stood together on the scaffold, burning with hatred, each for the other. Neither spoke, such was their anger. No blacksmith's forge had ever seen so hot a fire.

The crowd waited, hardly breathing. I leaned against Thomas, fearing for Abigail. Fearing for myself. She had looked into my eyes as well and seen my future, no different from hers, she said.

Wilson broke the spell. "Take her to her fate," he shouted. "Let her know how we punish those who bring evil to God's chosen people." He pointed at her. "Abigail Murdock, in the name of the court and of this colony, I cast you out into darkness." He motioned to the constables. "Take her."

We all backed away as Abigail was led off the scaffold and dragged through the crowd. I turned away, afraid she would see me and the fear in my eyes.

We all followed behind as she was led to a small wooden cart with a horse and rider in front. I could see a few corn stalks stuck in the corners.

"Strip her to her waist," Wilson ordered.

The two constables looked around, as if to be certain they were to follow the orders. They were unsure themselves what would happen. I could feel Thomas stiffen next to me. He thought Wilson was speaking to him.

It was then I saw Pigghogg, standing on the other side of Abigail and the constables. He was watching her closely, smiling. He looked away and saw me. Even from that distance, I could see the lust in his eyes. He would satisfy himself on this poor woman.

The constables were still looking around the crowd, as if seeking approval from the citizens. Wilson was furious. "Have you not heard me?" he cried. "Strip her to her waist. The court has so ordered."

Now sure of his orders and the approval of the crowd, the giant moved to Abigail to carry them out. He bear-held her in his vise-like arms, bringing his head down hard on hers. She raised it quickly, cracking it against his head, and he howled in pain. "Bitch," he snarled, lifting her off the ground as if she were a goose whose neck he would wring. She fought him furiously, bringing her elbows into his stomach, but it was no use. He was too strong for her and squeezed her so tightly she couldn't breathe. Finally, she collapsed in his arms and he relaxed his grip. He motioned for the other shorter man to strip off her blouse while he held her. The man hesitated, unwilling to strip a woman in public.

The crowd was tense, expectant. No one moved.

Wilson could bear no more. "Tear her garments from her," he cried, "as she has torn the fabric of our laws."

At the command, the giant ripped her blouse and underclothes from the neck down, exposing her body to the gasping crowd. I turned away, as did many, unable to face her shame.

When I turned back, Pigghogg had moved closer to her, enjoying the spectacle as he enjoyed his nights with me. I could have ripped his garments from him if I had the strength, but I had none. I was weak, almost fainting, and leaned against Thomas for support.

"Tie her to the cart," Wilson ordered, whereupon the smaller constable tied the rope to the tail of the cart. Abigail didn't resist, her spirit broken.

Wilson approached, satisfied now that he controlled her. "The Lord smiles on us this day," he said, addressing the crowd. "We are doing as he commanded, punishing the wicked who seek to endanger the lives of our people."

He motioned for another man to come forward, which he did, bringing with him a freshly cut, thin branch of a tree. Wilson took it and held it up for all to see.

"God's instrument," he said, turning slowly so that we all could see it raised like a sword above his head. Then he turned to Abigail, holding the whip directly in front of her face, which she had lowered in her shame. He lightly placed it under her chin and forced it up. "Abigail Murdock," he intoned, "this stick will be your just punishment. May it drive the wickedness from your body and bring you to repent of your evil ways." He moved closer to her. "You are to be driven from town to town until the colony is rid of you forever. But—" and now he turned triumphantly to the crowd—"the Lord has spoken to his people, asking that we be mindful of his eternal love for his children. Our God has asked to stay our hand that this woman be given time to repent. If she repents now, of her words and deeds, she will be driven untouched from the colony. If she persists in her wanton ways, she will be whipped with this stick from town to town and her blood will stain the ground for all to see and learn by." He turned back to Abigail and pushed her chin up again with the stick, waiting for her reply. "What do you say, woman? Will you repent now of your evil ways, kneeling before us, and escape the scourge? Or will you persist in these foul ways and thus redden the dust with your blood?"

Abigail said nothing, and I thought she had gone mad, like my mother in her grief. Her face was blank, but as I watched, her face came slowly alive, as if a banked fire were brought to life by stirring the slumbering coals. Wilson waited for her answer, as did all of us. We could not have expected what that answer would be.

She was breathing heavily now, as if gathering strength from some hidden depths. She lowered her tied hands, which she had raised to partly cover her naked chest, and brought forth from deep within her the foulest phlegm she could summon. It hit Wilson full in the face, and he backed quickly away.

"I spit on your court and the evil God you worship," she cried out. "I spit on you and all your kind. May you rot in hell."

The crowd gasped in horror, and I was about to turn away when Wilson lashed her breasts before she could bring her arms up to defend herself. A red line appeared, and Abigail shook in pain. Then she gathered her strength again. "I curse you, Reverend John Wilson. And you magistrate Pigghogg," she snarled, turning to my husband as he pressed even closer.

Wilson held the whip out for Pigghogg. "Whip her!"

Pigghogg took the stick gladly and brought in down on her back. She stiffened but didn't cry out. He brought it down again. And again. But still she made no sound. Once more with all his strength. Her knees buckled, but she didn't fall.

"Enough," Wilson said, taking the whip from Pigghogg. "Let others share in God's punishment."

Many of the crowd had turned away, unable to endure such pain inflicted on one of their own. I wanted to leave and nudged Thomas to return me to my home. Wilson looked at us, and divining my intention, called out to Thomas.

"Constable Brattle," he said. "Let you carry out the court's orders as magistrate Pigghogg has done."

Thomas froze next to me.

"Constable Brattle," he called again, moving in our direction. "Did you not hear me?"

"Yes, sir. I heard you."

"Well, then, step forward and show us your diligence. As a servant of the court."

"Yes, sir."

I stepped in front of him. "His responsibility is to accompany me back home," I said. "As I have requested him."

"Nonsense. Your husband is here. That is his duty if he should desire it." He glanced at Pigghogg. "I see that it isn't," he said.

I looked desperately at Pigghogg, but I could see there would be no escape. For me. Or for Thomas. I backed away.

"Besides," Wilson said, looking directly at me, "this is for your edification as well."

"Thomas." Wilson held out the whip. "Do your duty."

Thomas stepped forward, slowly, torn by the unexpected and unwanted demands made on him. He took the whip from Wilson and looked around, pleading with his eyes. He looked to heaven, but saw only a blank blue sky, the morning sun falling now on the spectacle. Finally, he turned to Abigail, who was watching as well as she could.

"Thomas," she whispered so quietly only a few of us could hear. "Be brave. Do what you must." She turned again to the tail of the cart, her back to Thomas and the rest of us.

"Begin," Wilson said, "or we'll think you have qualms."

Thomas brought down the whip on her back, grimacing as she staggered in pain.

He was about to give the whip back to Wilson, who shook his head. "Again, Thomas. You've hardly begun."

Thomas hesitated and was about to quit, but Wilson would have none of it. "Again, Thomas, unless you wish your position with the court to be forfeit."

Thomas swallowed hard and turned back to Abigail. He brought down the whip again, this time with greater force. He seemed angry at something.

"Very good, Thomas. Once more and we'll give others an opportunity. Show us your strength."

Thomas brought the whip down again with even greater force and turned quickly away from Abigail, who had nearly fallen beneath the blow. He staggered over to my side, saying nothing.

I stood away from him, ashamed that he had beaten an innocent woman.

The crowd was growing restive, especially the women, who knew that an unguarded word, an act done in haste, might bring them the same punishment.

Sensing that he might lose control, Wilson changed plans. "Proceed," he called to the horseman pulling the wagon. "We will follow along side until we reach the Neck."

"What then, sir?" the poor rider asked. He wanted no more part of this than any of us.

"You will then proceed to Roxbury where you will be met by the local magistrates They will continue the journey until such time she no longer walks our land."

The rider had no choice. Or thought he had none. "Yes, sir. If those are the orders of the court."

"They are the orders, and you will follow them to the letter."

"Yes, sir." He turned away.

"Constables," Wilson said. "Beat her every foot of the way. Show no mercy. Evil will learn in no other school."

Pleased with himself, he cast one last look at Abigail and strode off. He seemed to have forgotten he was to follow along. Perhaps he was worried that Abigail would find some other way to humiliate him.

Abigail didn't see him leave or in her anger she would have spit again. She prepared herself for her long journey out of the colony.

The horseman urged his horse forward, and the sad procession began through the colony, ending I knew not where.

Thomas didn't want to move and looked away, not daring to face Abigail and her fate, which he had contributed to himself. I moved to Abigail's side, wishing to have no more of Thomas and his cowardice.

Pigghogg reached out, hoping to remove me from her side, but I pulled away. Pigghogg couldn't decide what to do, but fearing he would be compromised if I didn't obey him, he returned to his office near the marketplace. Good riddance, I thought.

Several other women joined us as we passed along the dusty streets leading to our home and beyond that to the Neck. The giant and the other constable continued with the whipping, taking turns by passing the whip between them.

Finally, I could bear it no longer, and I stepped behind Abigail just as the whip descended. It fell on my shoulders with a burning that shook me to my soul. I faltered but didn't move away. I had endured beatings before, from Pigghogg and Dorothy, and I would bear this one as well.

Abigail turned and saw what I was doing. She shook her head. "Save yourself, friend," she said.

"No," I said.

But it was no use. Constable Stubbs threw me aside. "Off with you," he snarled. "This is not your business."

I tried to step back again, but this time Abigail resisted. "No," she implored. "No."

"What can I do?" I asked. "Is there nothing?"

"Reach in my pocket. Quick, before they drive you off."

I did as she asked and found a small locket.

"Take it." She gave me a wan smile. "Chastity." She looked deeply in my eyes. "And remember me."

"Yes," I said. "I will remember you. Always."

I stepped back and the small procession moved on, the whip descending with terrible regularity. I stood watching until it passed out of sight, raising a small cloud of dust which hung in the air and then settled to the earth. A few stragglers who had followed her returned and went their separate ways, not speaking, ashamed that they could do no more than I to stop this unspeakable cruelty.

Thomas was quickly at my side. "I'll take you home," he said.

"I'll take myself home," I said and walked away.

"Mistress Pigghogg," he called. "It will go hard on me." He hurried to catch me.

"That's nothing to me," I said and continued walking.

I wanted no company but my own.

And the memory of Abigail Murdock.

CHAPTER 14

You are an evil one, Cornelius Pigghogg said when I passed the scowling faces on the stairs. The others agreed: I had disgraced the family and my husband. I deserved whatever happened to me in the future, one of them said. Look at what happened to Abigail Murdock, another said, and I would see what would happen to me. So, let it be known, they all said, that I could no longer count on their wise counsel, which I had so foolishly ignored.

I care nothing for your counsel I told them as I brushed past and ascended the stairs. I could hear their angry voices following me to my room, where I firmly shut the door on their eternal lecturing. I had experienced enough of the Pigghoggs to last me to my grave. I wanted no more.

In my room I sat at my little dresser and looked at myself in the mirror my husband was so proud of. It had been his mother's, and he had brought it with him when he came to the new country. I thought of his mother sitting at this very dresser and gazing at herself in the mirror. What had her life been like? Had her husband abused her as mine abused me? Did she go to her grave, grieving for a life with so little happiness? What had she thought of her son, my husband Pigghogg? Was he cruel as a child, shooting animals for sport and taunting the boys who would be his friends?

And Hannah, too. She had also looked in this mirror. Hannah Pigghogg, that frail, bird-like woman whose only happiness was that her two children died before they would have Pigghogg, her new husband, as their father. What more had she sacrificed, never to see again, when she became a Pigghogg? Poor Hannah, with no children to mother and care for. Only a husband to serve in this sad new world at the end of the long voyage across the ocean. We had hoped for so much and found so little.

I felt I was falling into a black swamp, like the one near the seashore a short distance from us, that had opened its mouth to swallow me like the whale swallowed Jonah. I was falling and falling, and there was no end. Soon I would disappear from sight.

Was that such a bad thing, to disappear from sight? It seemed not to be. Not at all.

I reached in my pocket and pulled out the locket which Abigail had asked me to draw from her own pocket. Inside was a small wisp of hair—two actually. I noted that one of the wisps was much darker than the other. It was the color of my mother's hair.

I was struck again. How could I be so thoughtless, so concerned with myself? Mother was still in gaol, her fate undecided. What had happened to Abigail had poisoned the water we all swam in. If Abigail were driven from the colony for no more than her harsh words, what would happen to Mother, an accused witch, whose madness and threats to the colony would seem even worse? Abigail had been accused of drunkenness and waywardness, but Mother had been accused of causing butter to spoil and beer to turn bitter and Goody Preston's pig to mate with her neighbor's calf. She was thought to have flown in Goody Clap's windows, attacking her husband in the dead of night. And worse, she had been stripped and found bearing the Devil's teat on her body. Abigail had not been accused of these things. How much worse, then, would Mother's punishment be?

I vowed to think of myself no more. It was important to find Mother and comfort her.

I closed the locket and slipped it around my neck, hiding it under my blouse. Then I went to dinner with a firm resolve, passing the grim-mouthed Pigghoggs on the way. I didn't look at them. I would give them no more of my time.

Pigghogg was waiting for me. He hadn't begun eating yet and said nothing to Dorothy when she served him. His anger had seized him as the giant had seized Abigail, nearly crushing the life out of her as she struggled in his grasp. I could tell he'd been drinking.

"You have disgraced me," he shouted. "I could throttle you."

I decided not to oppose him. "I'm truly sorry," I said, thinking more of Abigail than of him.

"Disgraced me before everyone. Wilson is furious, as he should be. The magistrates have all heard by now, many of them witnesses with their own eyes."

"I meant only to honor you," I said as plaintively as I could. "That is my only wish."

"What do I care for your wishes? They are poison to me. You brook me at every turn. I ask you to display yourself respectably in town, and you consort with that woman who threatens us all."

"I only spoke of your high position in the colony."

He didn't hear me. He could hear only himself. "I expected you to be instructed by her punishment, and you seek to thwart it by lying to our esteemed minister."

"I never lie. That is the truth."

"The court has decreed she must be punished—severely punished. She is to be cast out of the colony, beaten from town to town that her stripes might appease our God, who in his righteous anger demands no less. To save his people, he has told us, we must punish those who transgress our laws."

I kept calm, though it was difficult. Pigghogg's blustering made him seem a madman wandering the streets seeking alms.

"And what do you do in front of our good saints? You place yourself between the woman and her punishment. You lie to Reverend Wilson, our respected preacher, and you tell him you are required to return home, accompanied by the constable, when you were required only to witness the woman's punishment—for your edification. For your edification, Chastity."

"Yes, sir. I was edified. Very much so."

He rose from his seat and approached me. "I'm told you did more."

"More?"

"I'm told you walked with her. I'm told you placed your body between the woman and her whipping and received the lash yourself. Is this correct?"

He came around the table and stood behind me. I was terribly afraid of him, so I looked ahead, at the empty chair and the untouched meal. Then he put his hands on my shoulders close to my neck and dug his fingers into my flesh. "Is this correct? Speak the truth."

His wrath was a terrible thing. I didn't know what he was capable of, perhaps murder. He might, as he said, throttle me at the table and who would care? I thought quickly. "No. It is not correct."

"You didn't protect her?"

I closed my eyes and lied. "I think her a witch."

"Witch? How is that?"

"She pulled me to her. It was like a spell I couldn't resist. I tried to stand away, but she was too strong. She wanted to punish me for being your wife, for giving you pleasure. She wanted me to feel the whip that was meant for her. To punish me. It was terrible. I've never been so frightened."

I raised my hands to his and caressed them. "It was Thomas, though he hurts me fearfully, who pulled me away and brought me home. I thanked him for his service, for saving me from her grasping hands. Thomas serves you well. You should thank him."

I kept my eyes closed, afraid he would see in them the gravest lie I'd ever told. If lying is a sin, as we were told at Sabbath services, then I had damned my immortal soul. I waited, tense, expecting him to see my soul and know me for the sinner I was.

Finally, he relaxed his grip. His anger was spent. "If you're lying, Chastity…"

"She is a witch, I tell you. The colony is well rid of her."

"Hmm." He thought for a bit. But his fear of witches and their power was so great he decided I was being truthful. "Let those in Rhode Island suffer her presence," he finally said, removing his hands from my neck and shoulders. "They deserve no less for their malicious talk of freedom."

I stiffened. What was this? Freedom? So that is what Rhode Island was. And where Abigail was bound, if she lived so long. It was something to think about.

I retired that night, hoping to lose myself in James. I longed for him to pull me to him and make me his, to carry me from this hated land. But he didn't come, not that night or the next.

I couldn't get Rhode Island out of my mind. If I could find it, if I could free Mother, we could go there together. I had no idea how far it was, only that it was south through Roxbury. It might have been in another land for all I knew. But if it was through Roxbury, that meant Abigail would have passed the inn, where she had spent so many hours. Would my father have watched her, naked to the waist, bleeding into the dust before his door? Would he have raised a hand to stop the beating? Would he have offered water to quench her thirst? Or, more likely, would he have offered to assist the constables, seeking to break Abigail's spirit as he had broken mine?

For the moment I had no desire to go south, to the inn, to seek out Rhode Island, wherever it was. I needed first to go north, several blocks to town, to the marketplace and Prison Lane. Before I could be free, I would be a servant, in the marketplace, at the meeting house and scaffold, where no one was free.

Though Pigghogg, and even Dorothy and James, was free to go north to the center of town, I could not, for the giant still guarded me. I could see him from my bedroom window, day after day, leaning against a house, talking with passers-by, but always with one eye to the prison where I lived. Had the town no better employment for its constables than guarding my house so that I might not walk freely as other women did? Was Pigghogg so afraid I would leave him? Or, perhaps, he thought I would find a broomstick, as my mother was accused of, and fly into the bedroom windows of the ministers and magistrates, men who were men as he was not. Men who would enjoy my company in bed in the darkness as he did not. Men who would not think to force me to the barn to satisfy their unnatural desires.

Thinking this amused me. What would the Reverend John Wilson do if I should enter his room and press him when he slept? Desire and I had thought about him when I was a child at the inn. Was he a man as Pigghogg was not? Would he pull me to him as James did when I urged him with my body? I thought not. So cruel a man would desire no woman, in a natural way, as none would desire him. Even his wife, I was told, had been dragged from the old country to serve him in the new.

Then I thought of Thomas. He was pleasant to look at, to be sure, and I had once thought him kind, but he was no man I could desire. His heart was faint, soft as the marshy ground near us, and he had sorely abused a woman who had done him no harm. How was he different from John Winthrop or John Wilson or the other men who had condemned her to the pillory and then to be lashed, naked to the waist, from town to town until she was out of the colony?

I didn't wish to see him again. He was no better than the other men. But I could think of no other way to go to town. He would need to accompany me, or I would be trapped in the Pigghogg prison for the rest of my life.

My path was clear. I would need to approach Pigghogg.

The next morning I did. "What are the people speaking?" I asked at breakfast.

He looked up from his eating. "Speaking? What they endlessly speak. Pigs running free, fences broken, cows dried up. It never ends."

I needed to be careful. "Is there no talk of my absence from the town?"

He looked closely at me, suspecting something. "There is some, yes."

"Perhaps I should be on display again. That the people know your generosity."

"The people know my generosity."

"And that you have a dutiful wife."

"There is no question you are my wife. Whether dutiful is another matter."

"Then you will not permit my leaving?"

"Not at this time."

"If that is your wish, I will be dutiful. Ever your dutiful wife," I smiled.

He shook his head. "Not in all things, Chastity. There is another matter I've spoken of."

I knew he was thinking of the barn, so I quickly changed the conversation. "And the court? Does your work there go well?"

"Why do you ask?"

It was, I knew, a dangerous thing to ask. He never talked about the court and his work there. I didn't expect a reply, but I received one. "We are moving to resolution," he said, smiling. "It is only a matter of time."

I was afraid to ask, but I did. "Resolution of what, my husband?"

"Your mother," he said simply, and began eating as if nothing had happened in the last few weeks. As if Mother were still at the inn, providing food and drink for him and his friends. I picked at my food, which Dorothy had rudely set before me. Finally, I could wait no more. "What of Mother?" I asked.

"You will know when it's fit for you to know. And not before."

"Well…" I stopped, knowing I would provoke him if I asked more questions. I still had hope that the magistrate defending her at the court trial might have prevailed at the meetings to decide her fate. Or that Pigghogg, fearing for his reputation if his wife's mother were found guilty of witchcraft, would seek to lighten her sentence. Maybe even the other magistrates, their lust for punishment sated by the cruel punishment of Abigail, would relent and reduce her sentence.

In those days I could always find hope, like a child looking for bright stones along the seashore.

Nothing was said for several days. Whatever I said or asked fell into a great pit of silence. I began to worry. I ate less and less, not caring if Dorothy was poisoning me or not. I wanted only one thing: to know how Mother was.

Finally, a week or so later, Pigghogg awakened me early in the morning. "Today you will be at the scaffold. Your questions will be answered." He said no more at breakfast, except that Thomas Brattle would escort me.

"Thomas? I beg you, husband. Not Thomas." This time I meant it.

"It will be Thomas. You will dress well. And you will comport yourself in the manner appropriate for the wife of an important magistrate."

I couldn't tell from his voice whether I would be finding bright stones or bitter drink. But at least I would find something.

I met Thomas at the door. Neither of us spoke, and I noted he didn't hold out his arm as he once did. He just began walking toward the town center, expecting me to walk with him, which I did.

It was a chilly day, the clouds obscuring the sun one minute and then floating off, blown by a sharp wind from the north. Autumn had arrived late this year, having given us a reprieve of many warm and sunny days. But I knew that winter would soon be upon us, whipping through our lives, bringing us to our knees as it had done since we arrived in this dismal new world.

A number of people, dressed in their Sabbath meeting clothes and pulling their capes about them, were moving in our direction. A few glanced at me, but no one spoke. They seemed to move as far from us as the road would allow.

Thomas stopped. "Ma'am. I must speak with you."

"I have no wish to speak with you, Thomas," I said and tried to move on.

"Ma'am. Please. It's important."

I stopped, angry at the delay. "Yes, what is it?"

I thought he would apologize for the whipping, but he didn't. It was just as well because I was in no mood to forgive him.

"Ma'am. It's about your mother."

"Yes. Of course. She will be sentenced this morning."

"Something else," he said.

"You know her sentence? Is that it, Thomas?"

"No ma'am. It's not that."

"Then what? Be quick about it or we'll be late."

I looked him in the face and saw that he was deeply troubled. "Thomas, what is it?"

He swallowed and began his story. "Your mother, ma'am. She's not well."

"I know that, Thomas."

"She's…worse."

"What did you expect, living in that darkness with no one to comfort her?"

"I did my best, ma'am."

"As you assisted Abigail Murdock?" I said sharply. "Now let us go."

"Ma'am, it's worse."

"Worse? Stop speaking riddles, Thomas. Tell me what happened."

"Yes, ma'am. It is difficult. Very difficult. I have no gift for words."

"Thomas!"

"Yes. Well, you see, last night, ma'am, after I had done my duties and was going home, I thought to stop by, just to see how she was. I do that nightly, you know."

"How would I know, Thomas? You've told me nothing. Nothing at all. You've made me suffer all this time, knowing how she was. What have I done to deserve such treatment?"

"Forgive me, ma'am. There were reasons. But hear me out."

I was growing impatient, and had little wish to hear more from this cowardly servant of the court. "Well? Speak your mind."

"I arrived at the gaol. Quietly. I don't like to frighten her. She shakes like a leaf, you know." He didn't want to go on.

"Yes...yes. What is it?"

"Well, I was just outside...oh, ma'am. If I had come sooner."

"Thomas! What are telling me?" Now I was truly frightened.

"I heard a scuffling, a scream, and then muffled sounds. She often talks to herself, you know, but this time it sounded different. So I went inside. To the door of her cell. And...and, good Lord in Heaven. Forgive me, ma'am."

"Thomas, what happened?" I shook his arm fiercely. "What happened?"

"It was Zeb Stubbs, ma'am. The constable. He was attacking her."

"Oh my God. Thomas. Oh, my God." I shook his arm, violently, as if I were attacking the giant myself. I held on to Thomas while I trembled, unable to control myself.

Then I began to hit him. On the arms, on his body. When I hit his face, he stepped back. I tried to it him again, but he seized my arms.

"I pulled him away, ma'am. I told him I'd report him to the magistrates. 'Just try it,' he sneered. 'And I'll have a few words with them myself. You and Pigghogg's wife. A cozy arrangement, if you ask me.' Then he left, kicking the fire pail through the door. I could hear him cursing a long while after he left."

I couldn't speak. The thought of that filthy man attacking my good mother was too much. My knees felt weak and I began to fall. Thomas caught me just in time. "Ma'am. I'm truly sorry to tell you this. But I thought you would want to know."

"So I'd feel sorry for you?" I spit at him. "So I'd be grateful you saved her from the door of hell, and forget that you lashed a naked woman unable to defend herself? I curse Stubbs. I curse you. I curse all men."

I tore my hands from his grip and turned to town. I noticed several people were standing nearby, watching the two of us. "I curse all of you," I shouted. "Go home and pray that your God forgive you. Because you may be sure, I won't. Not in this world."

I proceeded on to town, picking up my skirt and walking as fast as I could. Thomas struggled to keep up, but I pushed him back. I couldn't bear to see him next to me. I didn't want him to touch me. I blamed him for what happened to Mother.

A block away I could hear the drum roll, announcing that today the court would reveal its sentence. I hurried faster, Thomas panting behind.

The marketplace was filled with people, all of them excited for any diversion from their dreary lives. No victory in battle had ever brought such excitement. They were pushing up against the scaffold, talking loudly among themselves, the women as well as the men.

Then I saw him. Constable Stubbs. The monster who attacked my mother. I pushed my way through crowd. I would rip his eyes from his head. I would tear his flesh, with my teeth if need be. There was no pain I would spare him.

Thomas restrained me, catching my arm and holding it tightly. "Mistress, not now. Please."

I tried to pull away, but he held fast. "Please. It will only go harder on your mother."

Despite my anger, I knew he was right. I paused, and he relaxed his grip. Constable Stubbs was staring down at us, smiling wickedly.

I had no time for him or for John Wilson or Pigghogg standing next to him. The drum roll beat louder, and we all turned our attention to Prison Lane, where a small procession was approaching slowly, making its way down the narrow, shadowed street toward the sunlight of the marketplace.

I strained to see who it was. I couldn't tell from this distance, but apparently it was unexpected, for Wilson and Pigghogg had bent over and were conferring with other magistrates. They seemed concerned, angry at this change in plans.

Finally, the procession was close enough for me to make out my mother, led by the other constable and the town beadle. But there were others, walking apace. I could see several women and two men, on each side of Mother, steadying her, their arms around her as she stumbled along, hardly able to hold up her head. First the constable and then the beadle would turn around, trying to fend off the intruders, but the women took whatever blows they received and kept on, step by step. The men tried to protect the women, but were forced to the side each time they advanced on the guards.

The drum roll rattled and rattled, louder now as they approached the scaffold. The women's faces were mostly covered by the hoods of their capes, and I couldn't see who they were. "Who is it?" I could hear murmuring from several women in the crowd. "Who are those people?"

A woman standing in front of me with the rough voice of a man said, "They're none of ours. They're foreigners."

The party arrived at the platform, and the crowd parted before them. "Witch," I heard a woman mumble. Others nodded in agreement. "Witch. Witch."

Mother was pulled up the stairs to the scaffold, where she was ordered to stand, facing Reverend Wilson and Pigghogg. "I know her," a woman said, pointing to one of the women who had supported Mother.

There were three…four women standing by the stairs. The beadle stood at the top, keeping them from ascending, which they attempted but were repulsed with his foot.

Wilson silenced the crowd and all eyes turned to him. Pigghogg stood on one side, the giant on the other, both of them joyful in their moment of glory.

Mother stood as well as she could, swaying back and forth. She was dressed in a somber black, and seemed shriveled into herself. A gust of wind rose from the ocean, swirling over the scaffold, and she reached for someone to steady her. There was no one. She fell to one knee, and still no one moved.

"Rise, woman, and hear your sentence," Wilson commanded. He waited while she slowly raised herself.

"In the absence of the governor, who has authorized me to speak for him and the court, I shall announce our decision." His voice rose as he addressed both Mother and the crowd. "The court has with due deliberation considered the evidence. We have asked our God for guidance, and he has given it. Though there can be no question that you, woman, have engaged with the Devil to do harm to our people; that you have denied your Creator who made you, as he made the first woman, Eve, who we are told in Scripture did turn away from her Maker and did eat of the apple; and though it is ordered that you be taken from us for your many sins, our God has asked that we be merciful." He walked to Mother's side, looking scornfully at her. "Hear me, Goodwife Mary Hoar, what the court in all its wisdom and mercy has decreed."

Mother paid him no attention, looking about her, as if searching for someone. I raised my hand slightly, but Thomas nudged me. "No," he whispered. "Not yet." She searched the crowd, finally finding the person she was looking for. I could see her eyes fix on the woman, but I couldn't yet tell who the woman was.

Wilson continued, as if speaking for God Almighty. "Woman, you will be allowed to repent of your grievous sins. If you kneel before us this day, before the magistrates and the visible saints among us; if you kneel before your God and freely confess your sins, confess to contracting with the Devil to do us harm; if you do this of your own free will, your life will be spared and you will be sentenced to prison for the rest of your days. But if you do not, if you persist in your malicious ways, you will be whipped at the post, thirty lashes, until you do confess. If you continue to be obstinate, refusing to confess, Goodwife Hoar, in the name of the court of the Massachusetts Bay Colony, I pronounce that your life will be forfeit, and you will be hanged until death."

The crowd was silent for a moment, taking in what their minister had said. Then quickly their voices became a Babel of tongues. I heard nothing they said. I could only look at Mother, who seemed not to even hear her sentence. She had already left for another world, beyond the talons of Reverend Wilson and the magistrates.

"Will you kneel, woman, and confess yourself?" Wilson paced back and forth in front of her, nodding his head. Pigghogg joined him, and the two of them circled like vultures watching the dying movements of a rabbit caught securely in a trap below.

Wilson stopped and confronted her. "How say you, woman?"

Mother was silent, her eyes still fixed on the woman as if only that woman kept her standing.

"You will not confess, then? This is your last chance."

She still said nothing, swaying back and forth, ready to collapse at any moment.

"It is done, then," Wilson snapped. He motioned to the giant. "Take her to the whipping post and strip her."

The crowd around the stairs parted as the constable and the beadle led mother to the stairs and began down. Mother fell forward into the arms of Stubbs, who held her straight. The man who had attacked her the night before now held her in his arms with the blessing of the court. I wanted to tear her from his grasp, but Thomas held my arm. "No," he said. "Wait." I strained but was unable to move away.

The crowd parted, moving back far enough so they could see, but not so close that Mother might touch them. We walked toward the whipping post, and then I saw her. The woman Mother had been watching. She stood at the post, surrounded by her men and women friends.

The giant stopped, surprised by their appearance. We all watched as Wilson approached and surveyed the scene. "Move aside," he thundered, "that the court may carry out the sentence."

No one moved.

Wilson approached the woman standing before the post. "Show yourself, woman," he called to the leader.

The woman pulled back her hood and we all could see her plainly. The slanting sun glanced off her face and for a moment I thought an angel had descended to earth. She was a beautiful woman, and she stood like a statue, unmoved, though the constable and the beadle towered over her.

Then I recognized her. It was Mistress Mary Dyer, the woman who had once befriended me, and was driven from the colony with Mistress Anne. She and her friends had become a wall protecting Mother from the wrath of the court and the people.

"Move her," Wilson shouted. "Who thwarts the will of the court thwarts God himself."

Just as the giant moved to cast her aside, she knelt before him, and raised her hands in prayer. Her friends did likewise. The crowd was hushed. For a moment no one knew what to do. Hundreds of men and women had been whipped at the post, without resistance, and here were citizens standing together to prevent it from happening. Even Wilson was momentarily confused.

But not for long. He regained his composure and moved to Mary, stopping directly in front of her. Now he also recognized her. He stared malevolently into her upturned face. "Mary Dyer, you have been banished from the colony, yet you come to us again to work your evil ways. Who brings you here but Satan?"

She smiled and spoke softly, "Our God brings us here and no one else."

"For what purpose but to do us harm?"

"We come to honor and remember Anne Hutchinson whom you so cruelly and unjustly banished."

Wilson snorted and turned to the crowd, which had crept closer to better hear Mistress Mary. "This woman, Mary Dyer, bore a monster and buried it in secret, opposing the law that binds and protects us all. The monster was a sign from God that her monstrous opinions would be punished by us in this life and by God in the next. For that, she was banished from the colony that we might all be saved from the infection she brought among us."

He signaled to the beadle. "Move her."

"Stop," Mary said. "What has this woman done to so offend you?"

"It is none of your business what she has done. You are no longer one of us."

"You do the work of the Devil if you whip her," Mary said, remaining composed. "As you did his work with Anne."

"Take her away," Wilson said, and moved back.

The beadle took Mary by the hands and pulled her from the whipping post. Another woman took her place. Wilson signaled for the giant to remove her as well. She was no sooner taken off when another took her place. Each of them knelt before her accusers, her hands raised in prayer. None of them resisted being removed, remaining to the side where they had been placed. Finally, when each woman and the two men had been removed, Wilson ordered the giant to tie Mother to the post.

Mother watched all of this with little sign she understood what was happening. The giant in one quick movement ripped Mother's clothes from her back and then began tying her to the post.

The crowd murmured excitedly. I turned away, unable to watch. Thomas held my arm more tightly, as if he knew what I thought of doing. He didn't expect what came next.

"Thomas Brattle," Wilson called. "Step forward."

Thomas relaxed his grip. "Sir?"

"Step forward," I said.

"Yes sir." He moved hesitantly to Wilson's side.

"Constable, the court has ruled that you are to be the first to instruct this woman and bring her to confess her sins."

"Me, sir?"

"It has been brought to our attention that you may have been somewhat remiss in your duties of late. That you have thought to interfere with the commands of the court."

"No, sir. I have never done so."

"Constable Stubbs tells us otherwise." He held up his hand. "But no matter. You have been chosen now to do God's will." He motioned for the whip, a stout, knotted rope, to be brought forward. It was Pigghogg who gave it to Thomas.

"Now, constable, show your mettle as you did with that foul creature we sent forth from the colony at the cart's tail." He stroked Thomas's arm. "Unless, of course, you have been seduced by others to do their will."

Thomas looked around him and saw only Pigghogg and a crowd of people who urged him on. "Witch. Witch," they taunted. He glanced at Mary and her friends and then turned away. They continued kneeling silently, praying to their God to save this stranger. If he was too busy to save Abigail, I thought, why would he save Mother?

I caught Thomas's eye and shook my head. If you touch that woman, Thomas, you will go to hell and burn forever, I said under my breath. If God is blind to what you do, I'll send you there myself, even if I must stand at your side.

Was there no one to help? I looked around the crowd and saw two men walking away on separate paths. One I recognized to be John Cotton, the minister who had once been a friend to Anne, and the other looked to be the magistrate who supported Mother in the court. Both were cowards, I thought, no better than Thomas had been and would be again.

Then a departing figure caught my eye, going the other direction, toward Roxbury. His musket pointed to the ground, as if it, too, would have no business at the whipping post. There could be no doubt who the figure was. Father was slithering off like the others, a base coward with no heart or stomach to help his wife.

I inched toward Mother, but the giant was quickly at my side. Pigghogg watched me closely, and I knew there was nothing I could do. We were all helpless.

Thomas was trapped. He would go to hell with the other cowards. His face drained as he struggled with his terrible duty. He slowly raised the whip high above his head, and then…he froze. His face changed into what seemed a raging, grotesque demon struggling to carry out its orders. He let out a terrible scream, twisted in the air as if some terrible force were attacking him, and then fell to the ground. He writhed about, striking about him with his arms and legs, all the while screaming "Stand away! Stand away!"

No one moved. Wilson stood over him, his mouth open in amazement.

Then Wilson realized what had happened and moved back. "It is Satan, or his familiar, come among us," he cried. "The woman has sent him. Stand aside." He knelt and held Thomas to the ground, but Thomas kept thrashing, striking out at anything in his path. "Thomas Brattle, hear me. Through my hands God will protect you. Believe in him. Believe in him and be strong."

Thomas kept thrashing about for the longest time, while Wilson was beginning to tire. "Help me," he called to the giant, who threw his body on Thomas, pinning him firmly to the ground. Wilson, on his knees, held Thomas's arms, calling out for God to come and strike Mother, to strike Satan, to deliver his people in their time of need.

God didn't answer his call.

But Mother was saved nonetheless. Wilson, like the others, was so terrified that Satan walked among them and would strike anyone dead who tried to beat Mother, that he backed off. He motioned to the giant to release Thomas, who had stopped writhing and was unconscious or perhaps dead.

I looked over at Mary and her friends. They were as astonished as the rest of us. They still held their hands high, praying to their God, but they didn't know what was happening.

Wilson ordered Mother to be returned to the prison until the court could consider what to do. Then he sent the crowd home.

"Should we bake urine cakes?" one lady asked. "Or put out horseshoes?"

"Do nothing but pray for your immortal souls," he snarled. "Go now."

He looked down at Thomas, but backed away, afraid to touch him. He walked to Mary and her friends. "You and that woman have brought this affliction on us. I order you to leave this colony before the day ends, or we will imprison you with her. If you do not leave, we will take sterner measures."

"We come in peace," Mary said. "To honor our friend."

"Hear me, Mary Dyer. Leave us today or you will feel our wrath. There will be no one to protect you."

He didn't wait for her response but turned and walked off. Pigghogg accompanied him, the two of them talking animatedly as they left. Thomas remained on the ground, unmoving.

The crowd dispersed quickly, the women hurrying to their homes, the men to their work. The constables and the beadle untied Mother from the post and prepared to return her to the prison. Before she was led off, Mother looked directly at me, but there was no recognition in her eyes. I strained to touch her, but the giant stood between us, leering at me. I hated to see him with Mother, but I needed to see Mary first. If everyone thought Satan protected her, Mother would be safe for the time being. She was led off between the men.

Thomas was still lying on the ground, unmoving. I didn't care about him. I wanted only to speak with Mary. When I approached her and her friends, they rose and greeted me warmly. I pushed back my hood. "Do you remember me?" I asked Mary.

She looked closely. "I do," she finally said. "You are the girl who once thought herself burdened by her name."

"Yes," I smiled.

"Do you still find your name so great a burden?"

"No," I said. "Truly I do not."

"Life has taught you well, then, as that poor woman was taught." She pointed to the figures moving slowly toward the prison. "Do you know her name, child?"

"She is my mother," I said, and broke into tears.

"Your mother? Oh, Lord above. Is there no end to this cruelty?" She pulled me to her and held me tightly. "Chastity, ah, that was your name. It comes back now. Forgive us, Chastity, for not saving your mother." She pushed me back gently, her hands on my shoulders. "We came back to remember Anne, not knowing of your mother's fate. We could do nothing. But be of good faith, child. We will, with God's help, do what we can. Won't we, friends?"

"Aye," they all said.

"There is nothing to do," I said.

"Never lose faith, Chastity. Our God is good and will smile upon us in his good time."

I shook my head. "I think not," I said. "Else he would have saved Abigail, who was whipped from the colony at a cart's tail."

"A cart's tail, you say." Mary looked at her friends, nodding. "We saw such a woman close to the border. We took her from the men who beat her, and sent them away. She was near to dying, and she may die yet, so great was her suffering. But she is with us now, and several women comfort her hourly and tend her wounds. God has put her in our hands to work his glory."

I was pleased that Abigail had survived and was being cared for. And I was most curious about where she was. "Where is it you live?" I said.

"Why, Rhode Island—where we live in peace and freedom and seek to do God's will."

"Rhode Island? You live there?"

"We do. Many of us have fled this colony."

"Is it near old England?" I asked.

They all laughed. "Not so far," Mary said. "Several days' walk and you'll be a free woman."

"Several days?" I couldn't believe it. Freedom could be found in a few days' walk. I promised I would walk those miles, and bring Mother with me.

But Mother was in prison, and the magistrates would be debating her fate. Next time they would show her no mercy, such as they thought they had just shown. They would hang her directly, Satan or not.

I explained how Mother had come to this place and how she had gone mad by allowing me to marry Pigghogg; I told of how she had been searched and found to have Satan's teat on her person and how she had been condemned for witchery at the court. Finally I told of how she attacked Pigghogg and Wilson with a knife, plunging it into the table at which they sat.

Mary shook her head sadly. "These men are no better than they were when my husband and I lived here. They think God speaks to them and they do his will, but they do evil instead and serve Satan and not our God. I fear they will not soon be swayed from the path they have chosen." She looked me over. "Chastity, you have walked a sad path yourself. I see it in your eyes. Tell me about this Pigghogg. He is your husband, you say?"

"Aye. In law he is. But in no other way." I told her then about my marriage, which she couldn't believe. The others all shook their heads, having never heard of such a thing. I told her everything about Pigghogg and his cruelty, but I thought it best not to mention James or Pigghogg's intentions for the barn. She listened to my story, shaking her head and murmuring quietly from time to time, "Oh, God in Heaven. Oh, God in Heaven."

When I finished she took my hands in hers. "Remember your faith, Chastity," she said.

"I have no faith," I said.

"Hush, child. You are being tried. We must leave this colony now, but your mother will be spared. You must trust in him."

Looking at her face, so beautiful, so rapt with love for her God, I could almost believe her.

"You will trust me, then?" she asked.

"I will try" was all I could say.

"Good," she smiled. "That's all we can ask."

She looked over at Thomas, who was beginning to stir. "Well, our smitten friend awakens. Let us see to him."

"Good friend," she said standing over him, "what afflicts you this morning?"

Thomas's eyes fluttered open to the vision of an angel, now kneeling at his side and caressing his forehead.

"Have I died, then?"

"Nay. You are still in this sad world," she said.

"Ah. I dreamed I was in another."

Thomas sat up and looked about him, staring at Mary and her friends. Then he saw me. "Aye, it is this world," he said and lay back down. "What have I done?" he groaned. "Oh, God, what terrible thing have I done?"

"For one, you have saved a woman from beating," Mary smiled.

He sat up again. "Is this true?"

"Aye. She has been led off with no stripes to show for it. I'm not sure whether it was God or Satan whom we should thank. I believe it was God."

Thomas looked blank. He didn't remember what had happened, but Mary convinced him that God had struck the magistrates and Wilson down in a blinding light, driving them from their purpose and saving Mother. I let her speak, but I knew that Mother was not saved and that God had not struck the magistrates. Mary was a good woman, and I had no wish to trouble her.

As I watched Mary giving hope to Thomas, I could not but remember that her friend Anne Hutchinson was driven from the colony in the bitter cold of winter by these same men. Where was her God when she was in sore need?

Mary and her friends prepared to leave for their home later in the day. "Keep your faith," she said, holding me to her. "God will speak to your heart as he has spoken to mine."

I didn't believe that, but I said nothing.

She touched my forehead one last time. "One day we will meet again and rejoice in our deliverance."

I took her hand and held it tightly. The tears poured forth. I didn't think I would see her again, and I had no faith in our deliverance.

CHAPTER 15

I ate alone that night and the following days. Pigghogg was busy with important matters out of town, Dorothy said, and would find his food elsewhere. I was pleased not to see him, but I had rather not see Dorothy either. James apparently accompanied his master, for he was nowhere to be seen. It was just Dorothy and me.

"Your master's in the barn, I suppose." I smiled maliciously one morning several days later.

"Why would he be in the barn?" she said, as she served breakfast.

"You would know better than I."

She glared at me. "I'll speak with Mister Pigghogg about you," she said. "He told me to report what you said and did in his absence."

"I don't care a fig for what you tell him," I said. And I didn't. I had passed the point of caring anymore about Pigghogg and what he'd do to me. I thought only of Mother and what he and the magistrates would do with her.

"Mind how you speak with me, Madam Pigghogg. I have your husband's ear, more than you, I'd venture to say."

"His ear, is it? Well, you can have his ear. And any other part of his body that you'd care to have. It's useless to me."

"You'll be sorry for this," she said, and she meant it with all her bitter heart.

"I'm already sorry to be part of this hellish place," I said, not thinking of what I was saying. "And I'll soon be rid of it," I added.

Dorothy was shocked. "Mister Pigghogg is your rightful husband," she bristled. "You have your duties."

"Yes, and so do you. Mind your own husband, and I'll mind mine."

She was stung by that, but I didn't care. Let them all go to Satan's kingdom, it would serve them right.

She stood next to me, dripping her bitterness as she often did. "Your mother will care," she said, and started to walk away.

"What? What is that you say? Dorothy, come back here!"

Dorothy hesitated and then returned. "Yes?"

It's strange, but I never thought of Dorothy and Mother at the same time. I assumed Dorothy knew no more than I did, but of course that was foolish. Dorothy went to town each day and had, as she said, Pigghogg's ear. She might be a source of information. "What do you know of her?" I asked with no sharpness in my voice.

"Of who?"

"Of Mother, of course. Don't be obstinate."

"What will you give me to know?" she said, smiling faintly.

"I'll give you nothing but my boot on your arse," I said, forgetting myself in her impudence.

"Then I know nothing," she said and tried to leave the room. I caught her arm and held it fast.

"What do you know of Mother?" I demanded.

"Let me go. I'll inform Hugh…I'll inform master what you said."

She tried to cover it up, but it was too late. She almost called Pigghogg by his first name, which I never did. I hardly knew he had a first name. Now I was sure there was something between them, and she knew far more than I had ever imagined. They were planning something, something to do with me, or maybe Mother, I didn't know.

"You know nothing," I said derisively. "What would you, a servant, know of anything?"

I freed her arm, and she moved quickly away, rubbing it and snapping. "Wouldn't you like to know?" she said and walked toward the kitchen. She paused in the doorway and turned, "I'd find a handkerchief if I were you," she flung at me and left the room.

Handkerchief? I didn't know at first what she meant. Later that morning, in thinking of Mother, it struck me. I raced downstairs to confront Dorothy, but she was gone, and the giant was on guard outside the door.

I climbed the stairs slowly, worried about what she said. Behind me the voices snickered. "You know, then, don't you?" one of them said. I whirled and faced the Pigghoggs. "Shut your filthy mouths," I shouted at them. "Or I'll rip you from the walls and burn you to ashes." "Try it," they said, "and you'll swing with your mother." I smashed my fist against Cornelius Pigghogg, rattling the picture so loudly that all the Pigghoggs shook on the walls. "Go to hell, all of you," I shouted, not caring who heard me. If I could put spells on them, I would. Unfortunately, I hadn't the powers that witches had, not being one myself.

I raced to my room and sat at the old dresser. So, she did know. And everyone else probably as well. The handkerchief would be to cover Mother's face when they hanged her, so she couldn't see her tormenters. Desire had told me that when we lay awake one night, talking of the old country and its cruel ways.

Dorothy probably also knew when it would be, but I wouldn't ask her. But then I thought. Maybe they didn't want to tell me. Maybe that was the plan: Pigghogg and Dorothy had hatched it among themselves. Mother would be hanged before the whole town, except for me, and everyone would think I was a hateful daughter, learning the dark arts myself so I could avenge her on the bodies of the townspeople. I was being kept away to protect the town from my anger, protect it from Satan himself who would find me and make me his disciple.

Such were my thoughts when I heard footsteps on the stairs, then a knock on my door. It was Dorothy, returned from her plotting. "You're wanted," she said. "Dress yourself properly."

"Properly for what?"

"I'm not to say."

"How can I know how to dress, then?"

"I think you know."

"Tell me, woman!" I shouted. "What am I dressing for?"

"Don't be superior with me," she sniffed. "You'll find your place soon enough. In an hour." She smiled and left the room.

I dressed quickly, sensing her meaning. Today would be the day. The magistrates had decided my mother would hang, and I would be permitted to witness it. Pigghogg's idea, no doubt, to torture me for being Mother's daughter and bringing suspicion on him and tarnishing his reputation. And for not agreeing to his unnatural demands in the barn.

The Pigghoggs gloated as I passed. I looked straight ahead, saying nothing, giving them no pleasure at my fears.

Dorothy answered the knock on the front door. It was the giant, the man I loathed now more than any other.

"Come with me," he ordered. "We have business to attend to."

I said nothing, but joined him at the door. We made our way toward town, neither of us speaking. I silently cursed the man, cursed him to the everlasting fires. But I wouldn't give him the satisfaction of hearing my curses. I walked with him through the streets, muddy now from last night's cold rain. I held my head high, looking neither right nor left.

Out of the corner of my eyes I could see the people leaving their houses, eager as always for more excitement. I paid them no attention, but silently cursed them. Let the whole town be consumed in the flames, I thought. And me with it. It matters not to anyone living or dead. And dead is where we'll all be soon enough.

I could hear the drum rolls beginning, and saw people rushing forward, afraid they would miss whatever would be revealed on this cold and bitter autumn day. Rat-a-tat, rat-a-tat, the drums called, beating their ominous refrain. Step lively now, they said. Step lively.

I could see Wilson on the scaffold. And Pigghogg standing next to the governor, dressed in his finest waistcoat and matching cape. Wilson, dressed in black, strutted back and forth, casting eager glances down Prison Lane and snapping his cape from side to side. His face shone with an inhuman pleasure: this was to be his finest hour, and he wished everyone to know his part in carrying out God's will.

The crowd, buzzing with anticipation, parted grudgingly when they saw the giant and me. He pushed through them so I could stand near the platform, looking up at the men standing high above me. I closed my eyes, not wanting them to see my tears.

Behind me I could hear several women talking quietly. The tree was prepared, they had seen it on the Common, not far from here. The scaffold was only for show, for ceremony, for announcing what the penalty would be. It was better that way, announcing the verdict close to the meeting house where they worshipped their God on the Sabbath.

I opened my eyes and saw that everyone was looking intently down Prison Lane, waiting. The drums increased their beat, and my head throbbed with pain. It would soon be over. Very soon. I longed to be gone, to be under the blankets in bed, burying myself in darkness. Or maybe in the bay, the cold waters washing over me, carrying me into their darkness. What did it matter?

We waited…and waited. No one appeared.

The wind whipped around us, and we drew closer for warmth. Where was Mother? And the procession?

Then I thought, oh God, she hasn't survived the night. She would be spared the gallows after all. Her death would be a blessing. I was ready to give thanks for her deliverance.

The crowd began rumbling, and I saw two men approaching, the beadle and a constable, with no one between them. They had left her body in the prison, guarded by someone, probably Thomas since I hadn't seen him anywhere around. She was dead, and I would finally be allowed to touch her, my dear mother, gone now from this world of pain and sorrow. Gone, I hoped, to a better place.

The beadle and the constable climbed the stairs, slowly. I thought it strange they showed no excitement now that they were rid of the witch who had so afflicted them. In fact, their faces seemed troubled. That was it. Troubled.

The beadle spoke quietly to Wilson, who ordered him to speak that all might hear.

"She is gone, sir. Gone." He trembled, looking away from Wilson.

As I thought, she had died and escaped their infernal torture.

"Gone? You mean died? God in his wisdom has taken her from us? Glory be to God."

I closed my eyes again and prayed for Mother, that she find a better place in Heaven.

I could hear nothing and opened my eyes again. The beadle looked about him, unable to face Wilson, who took his arm roughly. "She is dead, then? Is that the news you bring us?"

The beadle shook his head and stepped back, imploring the constable to say something.

"What? She's not dead?"

"She may be dead, sir."

"May be? Either she is or she isn't? Which is it?"

"I know not, sir."

Wilson seized the beadle's arm. "Man, speak clearly. Where is the condemned witch?"

He shook his head again.

Wilson turned to the constable. "Constable?"

He also shook his head.

Wilson was furious and could hardly speak. "She's disappeared? Is that what happened?" he sputtered. He shook the beadle roughly. "Speak, man, or I'll whip you myself."

"We arrived there, sir, as you ordered. A short time ago. To transport her. And…and she was nowhere to be seen. Isn't that right, Roger?" he asked the constable, who nodded agreement.

"Nowhere to be seen? Where was the guard? Where was Thomas?"

"He had been hurt, sir. In a struggle. But he had seized the man. And tied him."

"Man? What man? Speak up!"

"He comes now, sir."

We all turned to Prison Lane again, and saw Thomas leading a man by a rope. As they came closer, the crowd gasped. My knees gave way and I fell.

It was Father.

The giant pulled me to my feet, but I pushed his hands away and watched in horror as Father, his head bowed and hands tied in front of him, stood before Wilson. Pigghogg grunted, and the governor moved forward, alarmed at the unexpected development.

"Goodman Hoar, what is the meaning of this?" Wilson asked.

Father shook his head.

He turned to Thomas. "You, Thomas, what is this man doing here? Where is his wife?"

Thomas rubbed his head. "My head aches, sir."

"I don't care about your head. Answer my question."

"His wife has gone, sir."

"Gone? How?"

"Well, sir, I stepped outside early this morning, to relieve myself in the privy. It was still dark, I couldn't see my nose in front of my face. Someone seized me. I heard voices. Then I was hit. On the head. When I woke up, the woman was leaving, surrounded by others on horses."

"And what of him?" He pointed at Father.

"He came to visit his wife."

Wilson seized his arm. "He was not visiting his wife. At night. He helped her escape, isn't that so?"

"I don't know, sir. I was dizzy. But I caught him before he could leave. I think him innocent."

"He is *not* innocent, constable. Nor are you if you're lying."

"It is the truth, sir. He came to visit his wife."

Wilson turned to Father. "Well, we have ways to determine the truth. With your permission, Governor."

Governor Winthrop nodded agreement, though he seemed uneasy.

Then Pigghogg stepped forward. "They cannot be far. Let the constables summon the men on horses to track them down." He turned to the governor, who nodded agreement. He motioned to the giant, who left my side and began rounding up the men.

Pigghogg approached Thomas. "What direction did they go?"

"I'm not sure, sir. I think west."

"Strip the man and tie him to the post," Wilson ordered. "We'll find out what happened. And what direction they went."

I saw the quickest of glances between Thomas and Father, but Thomas moved quickly, taking Father to the post, where he untied his hands, removed his shirt, and then tied him to the post. Father offered no resistance.

Pigghogg had retrieved the whipping rope, stained now with the blood of so many others, and went to the post where Father stood, his head down, a pitiful creature for all to behold. It was Pigghogg who would punish him for whatever crimes he had just committed. But not for the crime of selling his soul and marrying me to that hateful man. Father would not be standing here today if he had shown more courage when it mattered.

Thomas moved away and took his place at my side now that the giant was busy appointing men to lead him on the search for Mother. Wherever you are, Mother, I thought, pray make haste. These beasts will kill you in their anger.

Many of the men had left with the giant, but those remaining, and their women, crowded near the whipping post. The wind was swirling around, cold in its fury, and I could see Father shivering.

Pigghogg bent over and whispered something in Father's ear. Then he raised the whip, high over his head, and brought it down on Father's back. It was a terrible blow, and Father sank beneath it. Pigghogg raised it again, and again the whip flashed down, snapping on his back, which had turned red. One more time, in fury, he brought it down. Father sank to his knees, groaning quietly.

Wilson held his hand up. "Let us see if he has softened in his resolve. What can you tell us now, Goodman Hoar?"

Father said nothing.

"You will not tell us where she is, then? Or what direction she rides?"

He shook his head.

Wilson addressed the governor. "The man stands mute. He is, no doubt, in league with the witch. They mean to join their master in the forest and return to torment us. What is your counsel?"

"Complete the punishment," the governor said curtly and walked away.

"Carry on, then," Wilson said to Pigghogg. "Let him feel the wrath we accord those who mean us harm."

I could endure no more. I pulled my cape about me and turned toward home. Pigghogg was about to raise the whip again when he saw me. "Hold, wife. This is for your instruction."

I didn't turn back. I needed no more instruction from any of these men. I could hear him calling to Thomas. "Follow her to the house. I'll deal with her later."

I could hear the whip falling again and Father crying out. He hadn't seen me watching his humiliation, but he knew I was there. Pigghogg had told him, the more to punish him I suppose. He would stop at nothing to humiliate any one of our family.

I walked as fast as I could, hoping that the wind would stop his pitiful cries. They lingered on. I held my hands to my ears and walked faster.

Just short of the house, Thomas caught me. "Mistress Chastity, hear me."

"I don't wish to hear you," I said. "Have you not brought enough misery to my family?"

"Chastity, please. Listen to me."

"Well…" I turned to him. "Be quick. And don't be so familiar."

"Yes, ma'am. Thank you."

"Well…?"

"Ma'am. It's a long story. But the short of it is, your Mother is safe. She goes south."

"You said west before."

"I know. But she goes south. Accompanied by friends."

"She's a condemned witch and has no friends."

"She rides a great horse, held from falling by a powerful man. Behind ride the women on their own horses. One of them, as she was leaving, spoke to me. 'The Lord has kept his promise,' she said. 'Tell her that.' She meant you, ma'am. She meant you."

"Promise. I know no promise. Did you recognize her?"

"I've seen her before. She came here a few days ago. And spoke with you."

"And she rides south you say? Not west?"

"Yes, ma'am. To Rhode Island. They'll never catch her."

"Ah. Rhode Island." I knew then who it was.

I fell to my knees and thanked whatever power had freed my mother. The wind whipped me about the face, as if mocking my pretensions.

"And Father?" I said, still on my knees. "What part does he play in this? And you?"

He looked about. "I cannot say, ma'am. It's too dangerous. But without him, she wouldn't be free. He was a brave man."

I stood and faced him.

"Is this the truth, so help you God? Do not lie, Thomas, if you value your life."

"It is the truth, ma'am. Your father saved her. And God watched over all of us."

I was overcome with emotion. I went to Thomas and took him in my arms and kissed him on the cheek. "Thank you, Thomas, for your kindness."

I moved away and looked about me. Fortunately, no one had seen us.

I thought of Father, a weak man who had sold his soul and me to Pigghogg to save his inn. But he had also found the strength, though almost too late, to free Mother from her prison. I could not forgive him for his weakness and all that had happened since my marriage. But it was wrong for Pigghogg and Wilson and the magistrates to bring him to his knees, crying in pain and in humiliation, before the town. For doing what any man would do to free his wife.

My rage boiled up, and I hit Thomas with my fist. He staggered back.

"Ma'am. I tell the truth. Please."

I stopped. "I'm sorry. I was thinking of my husband. I hate the man, Thomas. Hate him more than Satan himself. I would cut him into little pieces and feed him to the pigs if it was in my power." I stepped back and called to the silent heavens. "If you can save my mother, save me. And my father. Save us all. But not my husband. Kill my husband and send him to hell."

"Mistress Chastity, please. You should not speak this way."

"I say it again, strike my husband down and send him to hell."

I saw the anguish on Thomas's face. I took his hand. "If God is deaf to my cry, then you are not," I said to him. "You have heard me."

I turned and marched into the house and closed the door behind me. I needed to be ready for the monster.

CHAPTER 16

The Pigghoggs were gleeful when I passed them on the stairs. "It's your turn now," they said. "You've got it coming, willful woman that you are," Cornelius sneered. "Stripes for the wicked woman," Dorcas added. "A long time in coming I'd say."

I went to my room to consider my situation. I wanted to be with Mother, but I had no knowledge of how to get there and no way of doing it. Besides, our house was guarded during the day, and perhaps at night as well. And Father was still in Boston. He had, Thomas told me, something to do with Mother's escape. Perhaps, if I could contact him, he could help me as well. And save his soul in so doing.

But how to contact him? And if I did…? I stopped, remembering that Pigghogg had savagely beaten him. He was a prisoner of the court, of Wilson and Pigghogg and the rest of them—even the townspeople, who would give him no sympathy since he had deprived them of their pleasure in seeing a witch hanging on the Common. But then, of course, they could sate their appetites by hanging him, if the whipping hadn't already killed him.

I would need to find out, and there was now only one person I could count on: Thomas Brattle, my sometime guardian, except that he, too, would be under suspicion after his fainting fit at Mother's feet at the whipping post. Hadn't the officials thought Mother had bewitched him and given him and herself over to Satan's power?

I heard the front door open and Pigghogg's voice. "Where is she?" he shouted to Dorothy or James or whoever met him. I couldn't hear the reply, but his footsteps were quickly on the stairs. I would have locked the door, but

Pigghogg had long ago decided that his wife's door should have no lock, to give him access at his every whim.

I had no weapon either, nothing to defend myself. I stood and waited, helpless as Mother and Father had been, insects in a spider's web.

Pigghogg entered with his whip in hand. His face was flushed, burning with anger. I sought to appease him. "My husband, what troubles you so that you cannot wait until night to seek your pleasure?"

He said nothing and moved toward me threateningly.

I thought quickly. "Is it the barn you seek?"

That stopped him. He had not expected any thought of the barn. Nor had I until just this moment. Now I had created a new problem for myself, one that I had dreaded worse than the whip.

"The barn? You wish the barn?"

"I only ask what you seek."

"I seek to punish you." He held the whip up, ready to bring it down on my shoulders.

"For what, my husband? Do I not bring you pleasure at night, as you desired?"

"Bah. That is no pleasure."

"You seem to enjoy yourself."

"It is nothing but what a husband deserves."

"You deserve much, my husband."

He brought the whip down across my shoulders. I stepped back, stung with pain.

"I deserve your support, woman," he snarled. "You mock me at every turn. You support your mother, a confirmed witch—and your father, who aids her escape. Because of you, the townspeople turn against me."

"Because of me? Only me?"

He brought the whip down again, this time striking my arms, which I had raised to protect myself. "They suspect you for a witch. I am coming to think you are."

"I am no witch, sir. Nor is my mother."

"A filthy witch. When we find your mother, we will hang her from the highest tree, together with your father. And then, after you've witnessed their punishment, we'll hang you with them. The three of you together. To purge the colony of your filth."

He turned to me, menacingly, his face contorted with outrage. "Now strip. I'm going to give a lesson you'll not soon forget." He raised the whip. "Now!"

I don't know what happened to me. Suddenly, I was blinded by my own rage. At what he had done to me since the day I married him. The beatings. The threat of the barn and its bestiality. At what he had done to Mother, driving her mad, searching her naked person for the Devil's teat, and for allowing, encouraging for all I knew, that monster constable to assault her in the prison. And then, if that weren't enough to satisfy his unholy desires, to beat Father senseless at the whipping post.

"Strip," he said again. "Or I'll do it myself." He moved closer.

"No," I said. "No."

That surprised him. "What?"

"I said no. I'll not strip for you. Now or ever again."

He was blind with rage. "You will strip if I demand it." He brought down the whip again, but this time I backed away just in time. The whip fell across the back of a chair.

He moved toward me again, seizing my arm, which I had raised to defend myself. Then he dropped the whip and took my other arm, bending it back so hard I couldn't stand the pain. He pushed me against the wall. "You will strip as I commanded." His face was against mine. His breath made me sick. Everything about him made me want to vomit. All the ugliness in the world had sunk into his body and filled it to overflowing.

He squeezed harder on my arm, bending it behind me so that the pain was intolerable. I could bear no more. I was growing dizzy and almost sunk to my knees.

In desperation I said, "Wait."

"Yes?"

"I'll do it."

He relaxed his grip. "You'll strip?" he gloated. "And then to the barn?"

"Not the barn."

"The barn or else." I could see his mind working. "Or else we bring your father to the whipping post again. To instruct you both."

Oh, God, now it was Father. There would be no end to Pigghogg's cruelty, not as long as he lived. As long as one member of my family lived.

It came to me in my desperation and I blurted out, "I'll tell the court. I'll tell everyone."

"That your husband punishes you as he is required to do?"

I paused, and then took the leap. "I'll tell them you're not a man."

He seized me again. "What is your meaning?"

"I think you know my meaning."

He glared at me, unsure of what to do. "Idle and baseless threats will not save you, or your father."

I held firm. "It is no idle or baseless threat."

"Baseless I say."

"I think not. At night. For your pleasure."

"A husband's right."

I knew it was dangerous. That it put my father at risk. And myself. He could kill us both, and no one would much care. He might even find Mother and hang her as he had threatened. But I was too angry to care. I attacked him. "A man's right," I said. "And you are no man. A woman knows these things. I'll tell everyone."

He hesitated, not knowing how much I knew or how serious my threat. But I could tell he was worried.

His eyes narrowed. "Do not threaten me, Chastity. I warn you. I will bring your father to his knees in such pain that he has never known. And you as well."

I took a chance. "Touch my father or me again, and I'll tell the world."

He looked me over, scornfully. "You'll do nothing, Chastity. Because you are nothing. You and your mother and father. None of you. Nothing. Nothing. Nothing."

He picked up his whip and raised it above me. I didn't back away, and I didn't raise my arms. I stood waiting for the blow. But none came. He turned and left the room. I was safe. For now.

So it was done. I had hit him at his weakest point: his manhood. He had backed off, surprised by the blow, but how long would it last? Would my threat make our lives worse? Should I have said nothing, hoping that time would favor us? I didn't know. But I had done it, and there was no turning back now. I would have to live with the consequences. And so would Father, not knowing that this time his daughter had compromised his life as he had years before compromised hers.

I remained in my room for the rest of the day, not even coming down for dinner. I didn't want to see Pigghogg again. Or the sneering Dorothy, who must by now know my situation. I didn't even want to see James or hold him close. It stank too much of Pigghogg and his ugly desires.

Late in the evening I heard muffled voices, but not coming in my direction. I opened the door a crack and saw, at the end of the hall, Pigghogg standing in front of Dorothy's bedroom. She welcomed him in. I was about to close the door when James appeared from his own room. He quietly opened Dorothy's door and closed it behind him. Pigghogg would be finding his pleasures elsewhere, at least for this night. I could only hope that it would continue.

I ate alone the next day and the following. Dorothy said nothing to me, and I saw no one else. A silence, heavier than a winter snow, fell over the house, smothering any hope for release. The giant remained in the yard, mutely guarding any escape. It had grown colder now, and he huddled near the shed, out of the wind. One time I noticed he had built a small fire to warm himself on his lonely and futile vigil.

I was desperate to know if Mother had indeed escaped, and how she fared. And Father, what of him? Had Pigghogg, afraid to attack me because of my threats, taken his revenge on Father's back? Would the court condemn him, as it had Mother, for witchcraft? Or for aiding a witch to escape? And what were Pigghogg's plans for me? If he worried that I might expose him, he might think it time to eliminate the threat. He might petition to divorce me, which I welcomed. He might do worse. I thought of Hannah. That was enough. I felt a black despair sweep over me. I had to move before it was too late.

I had to escape. If I couldn't get to Rhode Island and Mother, I could at least find Father or learn what was happening.

It was then I hit on my plan, my only chance to learn anything. It would be, even if successful, a dangerous and bitter plan, but I could see no other choice.

One afternoon when Dorothy was gone and James was in the barn working on something, I went out the back door. The giant was huddled by a small fire near the shed, warming some coffee. He jumped up when he saw me. "Where you going?"

"Nowhere. I saw you by the fire, and thought to warm myself. The fire's low inside, and Dorothy is lax in her duties." I moved in closer. "Would you mind?"

He looked about him. "What does Pigghogg...Mister Pigghogg say?"

I saw an opening in his response. He was a servant to Pigghogg and the colony, but likely had no more love for either than I did. "He doesn't say anything. I hardly see him."

He grunted a response, but I didn't know what to make of it.

"I suppose he speaks more to you than to his wife."

"He don't speak to me neither," he said, not looking up from his fire.

"Well, at least you're paid well for it. That's more than I can say."

That struck a chord. "He don't pay me what I'm worth. The court neither." He attacked his little fire, stirring it to heat.

"Hmm. Your coffee looks good. Could I sample a bit?"

"I got no extra cups."

"Well, it so happens I came prepared." I pulled out a small pewter cup from my coat pocket. "Do you mind?"

He shook his head, and I dipped my cup into the pot. I sampled his brew, which I thought the most bitter I had ever tasted. "Hmm. Good," I said. "I suppose your wife prepares it."

"I got no wife," he said. "She run off to another colony. I'll whip her myself if I ever catch her."

I took another sip, the smallest I could manage. "I'm sorry to hear it."

He grunted, sullen in his anger.

"Well, you make a good coffee. For a man."

He said nothing and just stared glumly into the fire.

"It must be lonely."

He shook his head. "She left me with the brats. My sister looks after them."

"Ah. It might still be lonely."

He didn't want to talk about it. But I thought I had found his weakness. I needed to take the chance. When he squatted by his fire again, I said, "You could use better pay, then?"

He looked up. "Couldn't we all? Except you and Mister Pigghogg. You got more than you need whiles the rest of us is starvin'."

"Well, suppose you were to have more money."

"No use supposin'. I ain't got it and I ain't going to."

I leapt into the dark waters, hoping I could swim. "Suppose I found you more money?"

That caught his interest. "How you proposin' to do that?"

"I have my own money. I've saved it, for a good purpose."

"What're you gettin' at?"

"I might offer you some."

Now he was suspicious. "What for? You tryin' to get me in trouble?"

"Not at all. It's simple enough. I think you're not paid enough. I know what that feels like. My parents were often poor."

"You're hidin' something. What is it?"

"Well, it's like this. I give you some money, say ten shillings, and..." I was afraid to go on. If he reported me to Pigghogg, it would be grounds for serious action against me. But I needed to get away. "I give you the money, and you close your eyes when I leave."

"And where will I be when Mister Pigghogg finds you're gone?"

"Oh, I'm not going for good. Though I'd like to. Much as you would yourself, if you had more money. No, I'm just going to town. A short visit with friends. I'll be back, my husband won't know a thing, and you'll be ten shillings the richer for it. What do you say?"

I held my breath while he considered it. I could see in his eyes the hunger for the money, but I could also see the concern he would be caught and whipped at the post himself. And if he reported me, I would be at the post myself. I knew he would turn my offer down.

He looked around him. "Let me see the money."

"I'll show it when I'm ready to go."

"How can I trust you?"

"How can I trust *you*? We need to trust each other. I have what you need, and you have what I need. My husband won't know. He doesn't deserve to know."

"It smells like bad fish."

"Most things in this town do. But a little more money will ease the stench. Make it a little sweeter. For both of us."

I squatted by him, close to the fire. "This is surely good coffee. I'd never run off if my husband made coffee this good."

"How do I know you're not running off? I can't chance it."

"I've got no place to go. Besides, I'm a married woman. I'd be whipped at the post if I tried to leave."

"Hmm." He still wasn't convinced, but the lure of the money was greatly tempting him.

"All right. It's done." He took my arm and squeezed it. "But I'm tellin' you, you try to escape, and I'll come after you myself."

"I understand."

"You better."

"So, when would be a good time?"

"I'm on tomorrow night. About eight. You be here with the money."

"I'll be here." I touched his arm. "Thanks for the coffee."

As I left for the house, I glanced toward the barn. Standing in the door watching me was a man. I gasped and slowed down. It was James. How long had he been there watching? Would he suspect something and inform Pigghogg? I thought of speaking to him, but decided against it. I would need to chance it that he suspected nothing, and that I had given him enough pleasure that he wouldn't report me for no more than talking with my guard.

The next day went slowly. I went to breakfast when Pigghogg would normally be there, hoping that my presence would suggest life was normal again.

But Pigghogg wasn't there, and Dorothy served me silently. I tried to make conversation. "Where's my husband?" I asked. It occurred to me he might be hiding close by, hoping to overhear what I said to her.

"None of your business," she said.

I hated her tone, her thinking she was so superior. "I am his wife. I deserve to know."

"Ha. You're no wife to anyone. You're lucky I feed you."

I wanted to hit her, to wipe that superior smile off her face, but I resisted. I remembered that I saw Pigghogg entering her room with James. There was no telling what they were doing or planning. So, I had to be careful with her. "Well, I suppose town business is keeping him busy."

"You'll know it soon enough," she said and left the room.

Damn the woman. She always knew more than I did. And it was me she knew more about.

Pigghogg was not at dinner either. I became suspicious he was lurking outside the house, just waiting for me to leave. The giant had talked with him and told him my plans. He would seize me when I got to the shed and I would be lost. The two of them would drag me to the barn and assault me, with no one to come to my aid. Then I would be taken to court and found guilty and punished.

I looked out my bedroom window and saw nothing. It was a cold and bitter night, and I was a fool to even think of leaving. Where would I go and who would I see?

I wavered and then went to my closet where I had hidden the money. It would be worse not to go, not knowing what had happened to Father. And what might happen to me.

I crept down the stairs, looking the other way when I reached the Pigghoggs. They were sleeping, but a creak in the stairs awakened them. I hurried past before they knew who was passing them in the dark.

Outside, the dim moon outlined the shed, deep in shadows, and I walked toward it, seeing nothing. He had deceived me after all. I needed to get back inside.

"Over here," a voice called.

I looked to a tree, where I could just see a man standing. It was the giant. But was Pigghogg with him?

I went to him, knowing that Pigghogg was behind the tree.

"You got the money?"

If I produced it and Pigghogg saw me, it was all over.

I brought out the money, and waited for Pigghogg to leap from behind the tree.

He took the money. "Good. You better be back now. Two hours. No more."

"I will."

I pulled my coat about me and made my way toward town. It was bitter cold, and the streets were deserted. I could see flickering lights in several homes. Happy people with their families, huddled together around fireplaces, keeping warm. I remembered the night we buried Mary's child with only the light of Reverend Cotton's lantern to guide us. Tonight I had only the dim moon.

But where was I going? I could find my way to the gaol, if Father was still there, but it would be guarded and I risked being caught. And I might find out nothing for my pains.

Why hadn't I thought about this before? I was wandering in the cold darkness, alone, no home to find and no home to return to. No one wanted me. I had nowhere to go.

I was about to return to Pigghogg and the giant, when I thought of Thomas. He had told me once he lived down by the dock near the marshes, it was easy to find he said, if you didn't slip first into the marshes or the bay.

I turned to the docks at the end of King Street. The wind was picking up, and I nearly turned back. How could I find his house in the dark? I had seen it once in the day, but that was long ago. I stumbled in a rut and nearly fell. I could feel the water close by—the bay, the marsh, and I heard the creaking wharves. I dared go no farther.

Then behind me I heard footsteps. I stepped off the road and waited for Pigghogg, who must have quietly followed me the whole way. The man approached, then went by, swinging the lantern.

I saw who it was. "Thomas! Thomas!"

He whirled and held his lantern up. "Who calls?"

"It's me. Chastity." I went to him.

"Mistress Chastity?" He was dumbfounded at seeing me.

"Is this your house?"

"It is. I'm just returning from the prison."

"Oh, Thomas, could I speak with you?"

"Of course. But, it's cold."

"Could I, could we go in? Just for a short while."

He didn't say anything at first. Then he shook his head. "Mistress Chastity, you know it's not allowed. An unchaperoned woman. At night."

"Thomas, please. It's urgent. I'm in dire trouble."

He hesitated, then opened his door, and I followed him in. He was clearly uncomfortable. "Forgive me, ma'am. I have only one chair."

"I'll sit on the floor by the fire."

"Well, all right. Let me bring it to life."

I sat and watched him at stirring the embers. He tossed on a small log, then a bigger one. Bring it to life, I thought. Bring it to life. It was more than the fire he was bringing to life. But I didn't know that yet.

When he was finished, he sat near me, facing the fire. "I often go to bed when I come home…" He stopped, embarrassed. "That is, it's dark and I have no reason for a fire. It's warmer in bed." Now he was even more embarrassed. "I'm sorry, ma'am. I'm not used to company."

"Nor am I, Thomas. I'm married, but in name only." Then it was my turn to be embarrassed. "That is, I'm often alone. Pigghogg is busy with his business in town."

"Yes, ma'am. He seems very busy."

"Please, don't call me ma'am. It makes me uncomfortable. I've never felt a ma'am. Or been one." I smiled at him. "Just call me Chastity."

"Yes, ma'am…Chastity."

The fire was leaping into life, sending sparks into the darkness. Strangely, though I was in the greatest danger of my life, I felt more comfortable, more at home than I had ever felt. "The fire warms my soul," I said.

He said nothing, and we stared at the fire, warming ourselves.

Finally, he spoke, "You said dire trouble brought you here."

"Yes. I'm afraid. Terribly afraid."

So I told him about Pigghogg and his threats. How he beat me most every night, how I had refused him the last day and how he had threatened to bring me to court and find me guilty of not submitting to my husband, as the law required. Of being a witch and practicing witchery with my mother. But I threatened him in return and he backed off. For how long I didn't know.

Thomas was silent for a moment. Then he asked, "How did you threaten him?"

I hadn't wanted to say anything. But he had asked, and I could keep it to myself no longer. "He's not a man," I blurted out.

"Not a man? What does that mean?"

I was terribly embarrassed. I had never talked this way to a man. Maybe to Desire and to Mother, but not to a man. A man that I hardly even knew. "Not a man. As a husband should be to his wife."

"Not a man? He doesn't support you?"

"Thomas! Will you force me to say it?"

"I'm sorry."

How could he be so muddled? "Thomas, he's not a man! He is lacking in performance. At night. In bed." I was angry with him for his slowness. "There, you've forced me to say it. Are you pleased?"

He looked away, embarrassed. "Forgive me, Chastity. I've never been a husband. I was betrothed once. Long ago. But she died, of the fever."

I felt foolish in chastising him. How would he be expected to know of the unnatural Pigghogg and his appetites? He would never believe Pigghogg's intentions for the barn, and I decided not to tell him. I had disturbed him enough already.

"How have you managed to stay unmarried, Thomas? The court frowns on unmarried men."

"Aye. But I've found no woman who'd have me. Constables do not make desirable husbands I think."

"Nonsense. Every woman would have you if they knew you. Even if you are a constable and your duty is guarding women." Then I remembered. "And whipping them," I said softly.

He turned away, saying nothing.

I knew I had hurt him. It was an unkind thing to say. But he had done it, had whipped Abigail mercilessly, as he'd been ordered by the men whose cruelties plagued my life.

"I'm sorry about that," he said softly. "I could not see my way to escape."

He looked at me, and I thought I saw tears in is eyes. "Will God forgive me, Chastity? Does he see my heart? Does he know I meant well."

"I cannot speak for God, Thomas. Nor do I wish to."

"No, I suppose not." He considered the matter. "Then can you forgive me, Chastity? You sought to help her when I was a coward."

I looked into the fire, thinking about what he had done and what I had done when I hid my face so Abigail wouldn't see me. I had silently betrayed her as well. "I forgive, you, Thomas. May God forgive us both."

"Thank you." He turned to the fire again. "You know," he said, after a time, "I tried to make amends. With your mother."

"Yes. What happened? Everyone thought you possessed."

"I don't know. I told myself that never again would I whip a woman. I said it over and over. Even here, in this house, I spoke to the fire, to the chair, to the walls, I said I will not do it. Let me take the woman's place, let them lash me until I collapse, but I will beat no woman. I was thinking that even when Reverend Wilson called me. I was fighting with myself when I took the whip. I raised it and saw you standing close, and I saw your mother and then, I know not what. It all went black. Until I woke up with the woman kneeling over me. I thought an angel had saved me."

He looked at me. "Chastity, you do believe me, don't you? I would not have harmed her. I swear to you. I would not have harmed her." Now there were tears in his eyes.

"I believe you, Thomas. An angel saved us all that day."

He frowned at that. "Do you mock me, Chastity?"

"No, Thomas. I thought her an angel myself. A good and glorious angel."

"Yes." He seemed pleased. "You know, she freed your mother from prison."

"Ah. I've been wondering. Do you dare tell me now?"

He became frightened, as if he heard Pigghogg outside the window. Maybe he was for all I knew. "You'll not tell your husband? Or Reverend Wilson?"

"I tell you truly, Thomas, I would tell those two men nothing, even on the gallows."

He looked deeply into the fire, as if he could see the scene rising before him in the smoke. "Your father did not come to visit, as I claimed. He came with your friend, the angel we spoke of, and her friends. They all came to free your mother. I released her from her cell, as they requested. They worried about me, that I'd be found guilty of freeing a condemned witch, so they wanted me to go with them. I told them it was not my wish to leave, that this was my home, no matter how bad it was. I told them they should hit me on the head so that it would look as if I'd struggled. Then your father said he'd be hunted down and hanged, that he had no stomach for leaving with them, even with your mother, and that he'd stay behind so I could arrest him and be free of suspicion myself." Thomas smiled at the thought of it. "That's how it was, Chastity. Your father is a brave and good man. And your friend is an angel."

Now it was my turn to cry. I thought of father, on his knees at the whipping post, the blood running down his back. He had surrendered his life for Mother. God had nothing to do with it. It was Father. And Mary. Both of them had saved Mother, with Mary riding her to freedom in Rhode Island, far from this hateful colony.

"Thank you for telling me, Thomas. It was a good and brave thing you did." I reached over and touched his arm. The fire crackled and sputtered and leaped into the air. We both had tears in our eyes.

"You should have left with them, Thomas. All of you."

"No. My home is here."

"This is no home, Thomas. What is here to keep you?"

He looked away and sighed. The shadows from the fire danced on his cheeks and on the tears which were flowing freely. "You, Mistress Chastity," he finally said. "You keep me here."

I didn't know his meaning. "I keep you here? You are my guard, Thomas. I think it's you that keep me here."

He continued to look in the fire, afraid to look at me. "Thomas, what is your meaning?" I didn't know. No one had ever spoken to me in such a way.

He struggled with his words, but he finally put them together. "Mistress Chastity…Chastity, I mean. I've watched you since that day in court when your mother was tried. I knew you were married. And it was wrong to think of you in any way but a married woman—married to an important magistrate. It was not proper that I think of you at all, me, a common man of little worth." Now he finally turned to me. "But I did nonetheless. I did think of you. I thought you the most beautiful woman I'd ever seen. I think it still."

I was stunned by his declaration. I didn't know whether to laugh or cry. I didn't know what to say or do. From deep within me, from my cold heart, frozen so long in the bitter cold of the Pigghogg prison, the tears poured out.

"I should not have spoken," he said. "It was wrong of me. God will not forgive it."

I moved to him and touched his face. "God will forgive it, or he is heartless. Thank you, good Thomas. Your words brought me more joy than I've ever felt." I tried to stop crying but the more I tried, the more I cried. Was I crying or laughing? I couldn't tell. All I know is I felt, for the moment, like I had found a new life. That I was born again, ready to face Pigghogg and Wilson and the whole colony if needed.

Thomas put his arm around me and held me to him. We sat that way for several minutes, enjoying the warmth, each of the other. There was only the fire and the warmth of the other's body. It was enough, I thought, to last me all my days.

Suddenly, a cracking sound outside broke the stillness. We sat upright, expectant. Had Pigghogg found us? Was this the end? Thomas rose and went quietly to the door and opened it. "Ah, it's only a branch from the old tree," he said. He came back to me, worried. "I fear it for a sign," he said.

"A sign that nature breaks for my happiness," I said, but I didn't believe it. I remembered Pigghogg and his fury at my obstinacy. And father, still in prison. I had, for the moment, forgotten him.

"Thomas, is Father, is he…?"

"As well as can be expected. Mister Pigghogg would have him beaten and tried for witchcraft, but Mister Thorton, the magistrate who spoke at your mother's trial, defends him. He has supporters, I'm told. For now, I think your father's safe. But Pigghogg is dangerous. He'll not be thwarted."

"Good. Please, Thomas, send me a message if anything should happen."

I moved to the door, still holding his hand. "I must go now. I told the giant I'd return in two hours."

"He knows you're here? Your guard?"

"He knows only that I went to visit friends. I paid him well."

"Chastity. You must be careful. He may report you to your husband, and then…"

"I think he loves money more than Pigghogg. But I'll be careful."

Thomas was silent for moment. He held both my hands. "I cannot bear you to be with your husband."

"Nothing can be done about that, Thomas. I married him, and I must endure him. Knowing you care for me will soften the pain."

"I would soften it," he said grimly. He seemed far away. "I've heard your cry," he said and opened the door for me.

I didn't know what he meant.

I quickly retraced my steps, seeing no one until I reached the house. I signaled to the giant I'd returned.

"You're late," he growled. "You've put me in danger."

I stood close to him, hating him for what he'd done to Abigail and Mother, but knowing I needed him if I were ever to escape again. "I'll raise your pay," I said, smiling, touching him lightly on the arm.

"Next time it's more than pay I want," he leered at me. I didn't stop to consider what he meant, but entered the house and crept past the sleeping Pigghoggs, finding my room in the blackest of the night.

The dark was no longer quite so fearful for me. Sometimes, I thought, when one expected nothing, there would instead be light and fire.

It was enough to warm me to sleep.

CHAPTER 17

When I awoke the next morning I felt the world had changed. I could see from the window the trees hanging low, covered now in a blanket of white. The snow had come in the night, some time after I had returned home. The dark trees and ground were innocent again, clothed in white garments for the long winter facing us. I thought of Thomas sitting with me before the fire, and the warmth of his body as he held me and spoke of his care for me.

I held the picture in mind for as long as I could, but then, seeing James walking to the barn, lost it to the real world. I was still in danger: James may well have told his master about my talk with the giant. It was a trap, and I had fallen into it. I remembered the muffled noises I heard on the path the previous night, stealthy footsteps on my return from town. Pigghogg had sent James to follow me, or perhaps had followed me himself.

I didn't want to go down for breakfast, fearing Pigghogg, but I dared not make him suspicious in case he didn't know of my meeting with Thomas. So I dressed and went downstairs. The Pigghoggs were just awakening, and said nothing. They merely smiled. They knew something was afoot. I nearly went back, but then I heard Pigghogg talking with someone. I moved quietly to the wall just behind him and listened. It was what I feared. Pigghogg was talking with James. They talked quietly, so I couldn't hear them at first. When I heard my name, I decided it best to enter the room and forestall any plans they were hatching.

They stopped when they saw me. James nodded and left the room. I took my place at the end of the table and waited. I didn't have long to wait.

"I'm told you've been outside," Pigghogg said, scowling.

"You've been told correctly." I didn't know where this was leading, but I had a good idea.

"In the cold."

"It was. Quite cold. I warmed myself at the guard's fire."

"You were seen."

"Seen? Is that so strange? Anyone with eyes would have seen me outside my own house."

He examined me carefully. "Why would you talk to the guard? In the cold?"

"I had no one to talk to. It was cold in the house. No one had built the fire, so I joined the guard at his."

He grunted. "I'll talk with him later today."

"Yes. You should. He makes good coffee, for a single man."

I hadn't meant to say that. It just slipped out, and Pigghogg leapt like a cat. "Single man...?"

"I mean he was alone. In the cold."

I couldn't tell what Pigghogg was thinking. But I convinced myself that he knew only that I had talked with the guard. He didn't know any more. But the guard might tell him everything, hoping to raise his salary, thinking that Pigghogg would pay him more than I could. But he would also need to assume Pigghogg would be grateful for the news, not angry. I knew from experience it was foolish to assume Pigghogg would be grateful about anything.

I watched him begin eating, seeming to have forgotten the conversation. But I knew it would be more dangerous now, if I should want to escape again to see Thomas or my father. Pigghogg could never be trusted. He was just as dangerous when he seemed to be absorbed with eating or drinking or just walking around the house.

Then, nonchalantly, as if it hadn't even been on his mind, he said, "You will be in town this afternoon."

He caught me by surprise. "In town? Whatever for?"

"A surprise."

"I'd rather not go. I don't like surprises."

"You will go as I've ordered."

"I won't. I care nothing for the town."

"Ah, but you do. This concerns you."

"Nothing in the town concerns me."

He sat back and smiled. "As you wish. You may remain."

"Good." I began eating, thinking that was the end of it. With Pigghogg, only death would be an end of anything. And death is exactly what he had in mind.

"Of course, you deprive yourself of seeing your father."

"Father? What of Father?"

"You'll need to come to town to find that out."

I knew he was planning something evil. His tone of voice gave him away, as it always did. It was like the voice he had at night, sitting by the bed when James had his way with me.

"You don't frighten me," I said as bravely as I could. "If you touch Father, I'll tell all I know."

"Oh, I won't touch your father, Chastity. Trust me. I will not lay a hand on him."

"Because if you do…"

"I won't need to."

"I make no idle threat."

"I won't need to," he smiled, "because others will."

"Others?"

"It's quite simple. The court has noted that there is much dissention in the colony. Many portents that Satan is among us. So we have decided it imperative to find your mother and bring her to justice. As long as she is free, she remains a threat to the colony." He leaned forward, pointing his finger at me. "Your father knows where she is, but unfortunately he remains obstinate. So, we have decided that you will help him to remember his duty to the colony. This is your opportunity to show that you mean us no harm."

"I care nothing for the colony. I care only for my parents." And Thomas, I thought to myself.

"Be careful, Chastity. This is your final opportunity. If you refuse, I cannot hold back the tide any longer. It will sweep over you and your parents, and we will be rid of you forever."

"I will tell everyone what I know. As I promised."

"No one will believe you. The daughter of a witch. And the traitorous man who protects her."

"They will believe me. I'm sure of it."

"The choice is yours. You either return to town and assist your father in his duty, or you remain here, isolated, condemned by all. You will be next on the scaffold, alone, forsaken by everyone." He drank again, swilling the drink in his ugly mouth. "Think well, Chastity. Your fate rests on your decision."

He said no more. I picked at my food but had no appetite. I left the table before he was finished. He looked up at me, pure hatred in his eyes. I knew then what his purpose was: to kill us all, Mother, Father and me. And then, as he had done with Hannah, find himself a new wife.

The Pigghoggs knew my time had come, and stared icily ahead when I passed them on the stairs. They would soon be rid of me and would have a new and more promising mistress of the house. I said nothing to them, and repaired quickly to my room to think about my decision.

Looking out the window I saw the giant taking up his post. I remembered what he said the night before. Next time he would want more than pay. I stifled a scream. Suddenly, I knew what he meant. More than pay. Oh, God, what could I do?

It didn't take long for me to decide. If I remained at the house, I would be trapped. The giant would take no more bribes, unless I submitted myself to his carnal lust. And Pigghogg could say what he would about me, to the court and to the townspeople. They would believe what they heard.

I would have to go to town and take my chances.

So it was decided. I went downstairs to tell Pigghogg of my decision.

"A wise choice," he smiled. "Your escort will be here shortly."

"Who might that be?"

"Who fitter than the man you loathe?"

That would be you, I thought.

"Your guard will be Thomas Brattle. Be good to him, and it may go easier for you."

"What does that mean?"

"You will be so instructed at the scaffold."

I dressed in my warmest clothes. I brought out the warm black cape Mother had once given me, and waited for Thomas and my fate. Dorothy appeared, and then James. The two of them had also been given permission to leave for town. It would be a celebration they would not want to miss—or, as it turned out, none in the town would miss.

Thomas appeared at the door, and I left with him. I didn't take his arm, and he didn't offer it. We walked along in silence, the snow crunching beneath our feet. As before, townspeople heading to the marketplace stayed some distance from us, fearing contagion.

Thomas and I were alone in the world.

"Thomas, what is it?" I whispered. "What will happen?"

"I cannot speak of it."

"Thomas, please. If you know. Let me prepare myself."

"Mistress, it is too black to endure."

"Thomas, if you know, I must know. We are together now. Against them all." I moved to him, lightly touching his swinging arm with mine. "If you care for me…"

"I do. You know I do."

"Then tell me."

I could see the frightened look on his face. "It's the end," he said. "For both of us."

"The end? What does that mean?"

"I will try to protect you. But I don't think it possible."

"Thomas, tell me." Now I was really alarmed.

"Your father will be made to confess."

"But he won't."

"He will, Chastity. Because you will force him."

"Me? I won't do it."

"And if you refuse, then I am to take your place."

Then it sank in, the utter villainy of the man. There was no evil in the world he was not capable of inflicting. If Satan was among us, as everyone thought, then Pigghogg was his right arm.

"But why you, Thomas?"

"There is some suspicion of me as well."

"Oh, Thomas, I'm so sorry. I bring this on you."

He looked over at me. "No, Chastity, you bring nothing on me."

"Forgive me, Thomas."

He put his finger to his lips. "Hush now. Let us each do what we must do, and pray that our God give us strength."

I didn't know what that was, and had no confidence that God would give me strength.

We approached the scaffold, teeming with people, their breaths rising slowly in the cold air. There was no sun this time, and the darkening sky would soon bring the fury of a winter storm.

Everyone was already present. Reverend Wilson was in charge, acting for the governor and the court. Pigghogg stood close by, with several other magistrates and ministers. They all awaited the prisoner, who was just now coming down Prison Lane, brought by the other constable and the beadle.

Father was led up the stairs to face his accusers.

Wilson addressed him. "Goodman Hoar, do you know why you're here?"

Father shook his head.

"You are here because you are a threat to the colony. Our God has favored his people, bringing us to this new land that we praise and magnify his glory. But we have failed our good Lord; we have allowed contagion to rage unchecked in the colony—first with the reprobate and seditious Anne Hutchinson and her friend, Mary Dyer, and then with the blasphemous Abigail Murdock, all of whom we have driven from our midst that they afflict us no more. But now a new sickness is upon us, brought by your wife, an accused witch found guilty in our highest court. She has escaped, with your assistance, and not been found. Your duty is clear. You must reveal where she is and what she does. We are gathered here this morning, watched over by the good Lord above, and in Christ's name, to offer you the opportunity to save your soul and live with us in peace. What say you to this charge?"

Father shook his head. "I know not where she is. Nor would I tell you if I did."

"Then you force us to take sterner measures. Do you know what these are?"

Father shook his head again.

"The whipping post will instruct you in your duties. You've experienced it before, but it failed its office. This time, however, it will be a better teacher. Do you know what that means?"

Father shook his head again.

"Let me instruct you." His eyes shone with excitement as he told Father what I already suspected. "This time it will be your daughter who teaches you your duty. Thirty lashes with the whip. Until you confess."

The crowd was silent now, and I could see Father look up at the words. He had not seen me yet, and perhaps thought it a bluff.

Wilson went on. "And if she refuses, persisting in her willful disobedience to her husband and to the court, constable Brattle will perform the office. Your daughter will be at his side, that she observe every stripe upon your bare and bloody back." He turned and spoke to the crowd. "God requires no less of his people. Let you remain steadfast in your faith."

Father glanced away and saw me standing at the scaffold. Now he knew it was no bluff. Now he knew the black hole we had all fallen into, coming to this new land. The men he faced would stop at nothing to find a witch and save themselves from God's wrath.

"Once more," Wilson asked, "will you confess?"

Confess it, Father, I thought. Mother is safe now in another colony, beyond the reach of these men. No harm will come from telling them. But, of course, he didn't know she was safe. Nor did I. Perhaps, no place in the world was safe from these men who smelled witches at every door.

I could see the pain on Father's face. He would endure the lashes from these hateful men, as long as he lived, but from his daughter was another matter.

Father only said, "I know not where she is."

Wilson motioned to the beadle to lead Father to the whipping post. At his side, Pigghogg signaled for Thomas and me to join him. I moved close against Thomas, so that we were touching arms, and the two of us walked through the parting crowds, which spoke now in hushed whispers that could hardly be heard above the cold wind rising from off the sea.

Father was stripped and tied to the post. This time he wouldn't survive the lashes, and I would be his killer. Pigghogg gave me the whip and stepped back. Thomas stood near me, blinking, terrified, frozen to his spot. God help me, I didn't know what to do. "Begin," Wilson said. "Unless you wish to observe the constable."

Just then, Father whispered to me. I barely heard him. "Chastity…" I moved closer, holding the whip tightly.

"Yes."

"Closer." I moved in closer, almost touching him.

"Do it, child."

"Do it? I can't."

"Do it. That is my wish."

"No, I won't."

I could see tears in his eyes. "Please, daughter. It's my wish. My punishment for…"

Pigghogg stepped between us and roughly took my hand. "Enough. Begin the punishment."

Father wanted me to punish him. Not for his hiding Mother, but for forcing me to marry Pigghogg and bringing us all to this hateful place. There was a time, once, long ago, when I would have relished the task. Looking at Father now, so bent and weak, I could feel nothing but pity. The welts from his last whipping had not yet healed.

I raised the whip and brought it down on his shoulders as softly as I could. Father tensed but said nothing.

Pigghogg was angry. "Harder, woman. The Devil laughs at such weakness."

I brought it down again, just as softly. Father tensed again. This time it brought forth blood.

I was dizzy and weak. I could do this no longer. I looked pleadingly at Thomas, who didn't move.

Pigghogg stepped to me. "Like this." He seized my arm and raised the whip, this time guiding it down with as much force as he could. Father moaned quietly, but said nothing.

Pigghogg bent over Father. "Once more, where is she?"

Father shook his head. He was in terrible pain and would soon collapse.

Pigghogg seized the whip from me and brought it down himself, this time with a terrible force. Father sank to his knees. Again he brought it down, and Father fell forward, hanging from the rope attached to the post.

Pigghogg gave the whip to Thomas. "If you can do no better, we'll have you both at the post. Begin."

Thomas took the whip and looked at me. I nodded. Do what you must, Thomas. Do what you must.

I slipped to my knees as he raised his whip.

This time no fit saved him. He brought the whip down on Father's back. Father was unconscious now, hanging from the post, the blood pouring from his wounds.

My eyes closed and my head was swimming. I slipped to the ground, next to Father and Thomas. I waited for the next lash.

None came. I heard voices and looked up. I couldn't believe what I saw. A woman stood between Father and the three men, holding up her hands.

"Enough," she said. "My husband will not approve."

I could barely see her face beneath her hood. But I recognized her. It was the governor's wife. Margaret Winthrop. The woman who had smiled at me when I was but a child. The woman who seemed sympathetic to Anne and Mary, though they bore no sympathy for her husband.

Pigghogg and Wilson were shocked. Thomas lowered his whip, waiting to see what would happen. She didn't move, and the men merely stared at this black-hooded apparition. It was as if God had struck them dumb. No woman before had ever interfered in the men's work, and now that one had, they had no guidance. And it was not just any woman; it was the governor's wife, respected throughout the town and colony.

"Ma'am," Wilson finally spoke. "We are doing the colony's work. As God requires us."

"I do not know God's will, Reverend Wilson," she said. "But I find it difficult to believe he would punish this man in front of his daughter."

Wilson looked about him, as if he wasn't quite sure that the townspeople supported him. "Ma'am, with respect, I am the one trained and authorized to know his will."

Mistress Winthrop never wavered. "I don't dispute that, Reverend Wilson. I'm merely asking that you wait for my husband's return from business in the colony."

Wilson and Pigghogg were both angry at being thwarted, but they didn't dare oppose the governor's wife. Besides, the crowd, seeing my father unconscious before them, had their fill of blood. They were murmuring, showing their displeasure.

Wilson and Pigghogg conferred. Finally Pigghogg spoke for the court. "We will honor your wishes, madam. But there is danger in waiting. The Devil delights in procrastination. We will postpone the punishment. Until your husband returns.

Madam Winthrop lowered her hands. "He will be pleased, I'm sure."

"How long before his return?" Pigghogg demanded.

"Two days. Perhaps three."

"In two days then. The punishment is postponed."

The beadle untied father, who fell to the ground. I went to him and touched his face. He was hardly breathing.

Thomas called for a small cart, into which he and the beadle gently lay Father. Thomas briefly glanced at me, telling me something with his eyes. I didn't know what, but I could see that he was more serious than I'd ever seen him.

James and Dorothy escorted me home, the savage wind raging about our heads, straining to blow us from the earth. Neither of them said a word. What was there to say? The governor would return in two or three days, and it all would begin again, unless Father died in prison. I almost hoped he would.

The day went quickly. No one spoke in the house, and I stayed in my room. The giant stood guard by the shed, looking up at my window from time to time. In my despair, I thought to give in to his lust, to debase myself with him, and then, when he closed his eyes, escape, running as far from this place as I could. Perhaps, with help, I could find Mother and Rhode Island.

The second day arrived, and I went down for breakfast. The Pigghogg family were strangely silent. Pigghogg was not at breakfast, so I ate alone. Then I dressed and waited for my escort, assuming he would come for me at nine, the usual time for these affairs.

None came. I didn't see Dorothy or James or even the giant, so I left the house myself, walking alone to the scaffold. It was a raw, biting day, threatening more snow. I was forced to walk slowly through the heavy snow, which had been piling up during the night.

At the scaffold it was also quiet. Wilson stood there somberly, looking about him, as if searching for someone. The governor stood behind him, dressed in his finest clothes. His boots sparkled in the dim sun low in the winter heavens, and his wife stood below, wrapped warmly in her black cloak and hood. She looked over at me and smiled, slightly raising her hand. I smiled back. At least there was one friend I could count on, though she had no lasting power to save anyone, not even herself.

Father had not yet been brought to the scaffold. But that wasn't the problem. He was usually brought last, after the magistrates and Wilson had assembled.

Then I realized what was wrong, and who Wilson was searching for. It was Pigghogg. It was unlike him not to be the first arrival at occasions such as this. Had he found another woman to join him in the barn? Another man to beat senseless along the way? Had he drunk too much the night before and was still in bed, asleep, perhaps unconscious. I prayed it to be so.

We waited in a strange silence. Even the wind had died down, and we huddled together in the cold, stiff air. Wilson began pacing back and forth, first going to the governor and speaking with him, and then to other magistrates. He avoided Mister Thorton, who stood with his arms folded close to Mistress Winthrop.

The silence was broken by a loud screeching, and we looked up to see a huge, black bird circling us, as if searching for carrion in the marketplace below. The bird kept circling, lower and lower, until it was almost in reach. We could see its eyes, gleaming in its black head. Seeing no carrion worth its time, it soared into the somber sky and was soon gone. We were all frightened at the omen.

The silence descended again.

Wilson, dressed all in black, came to the side of the platform and leaned down over me. I thought he was another black bird, seeking its carrion feast. "Where is your husband?" he hissed.

I shook my head. "I don't know."

He turned to Thomas. "Seek him out. Quickly. Before we freeze to death."

Thomas seemed almost pleased with the assignment. At least that's what it looked like as he descended the stairs.

He didn't get far. Another high-pitched shriek, this time not from a bird, came from a distance. We looked down the street and saw a woman running toward us, screaming louder than the bird. It was Dorothy, running through the snow as quickly as she could.

We all waited, wondering what had so disturbed her.

"Come quickly. Quickly," she cried.

"Why do you disturb us, woman?" Wilson shouted at her.

"It's Mister Pigghogg, sir."

Wilson approached the stairs. "Where is he?"

Dorothy couldn't speak. She fell to the ground, exhausted, crying.

Wilson was at her quickly. "Where is he, woman? Speak up."

"He needs you. Quickly," she gasped.

Wilson was so angry he was ready to strike her. He took her hand and pulled her to her feet. "Stop your jabbering, woman, and tell us where he is."

She sobbed words that no one could understand.

"Woman, has the Devil taken your tongue? Speak clearly!"

Dorothy tried to catch her breath. "He's…he's…oh my God."

Wilson shook her violently. "Woman! Speak or I'll whip you!"

She took a deep breath. "Behind the house."

"What?"

"I was coming here…I heard a noise…from behind the house. I went back, but no one was there. The guard had left. There was only snow." She looked about for help. No one could help her. No one had been there.

Wilson shook her again. "Yes. He was behind the house. Where behind the house?"

She swallowed hard and said: "In the privy, sir."

He struck her in the face. "For your insolence. Now where was he?"

Dorothy rubbed her face. "It's the truth, sir. He's in the privy. He fell in. I couldn't…I came as quick as I could."

"Fell in?" It took a moment for her words to sink in. Then there was a mad rush toward our house. Even the governor and his wife joined the crowd, curious as the rest of us.

Thomas joined me as we walked swiftly toward the house.

I could hear voices on both sides. And laughter.

"Thomas, what is the meaning of this?"

He shook his head. "I wouldn't know," he smiled. I wondered at his smile.

When we arrived at the house, several men had entered the privy and were extending a rope through the opening. But it was no use. He was too heavy to be brought up.

One of the leaders called out. "I need a volunteer. To go down and fetch him."

No one answered. Wilson stepped forward and grabbed the giant, who was enjoying the spectacle. "You. Go down and be quick about it."

Laughter erupted all about us, which made Wilson all the more furious. "A shat-on Pigghogg," I heard from behind me. Wilson couldn't see who it was and so turned to lead the giant to the privy. He resisted. "I'll have none of the shithouse," he said. "It's not my job."

"Fetch him, or you'll go to the post yourself."

"No, I'll not."

"Fetch him or you'll lose your position. And I'll see to it you'll never have another."

The giant hesitated, but then agreed to let the other men lower him to Pigghogg.

When Pigghogg was finally brought to the surface, he collapsed in the snow, groaning and driving his head into the snow. The giant walked off, cursing his luck and picking up the new snow to wipe himself clean.

All about me were laughter and crude remarks. It was a better spectacle than the whipping post.

The governor and his wife left quickly, not wishing to be associated with these unseemly events. After seeing that Pigghogg was taken inside and administered to, Wilson also left.

When we were alone, I grabbed Thomas's arm. I didn't know whether to laugh or cry. All I knew was I had been delivered. I didn't know by whom.

CHAPTER 18

No Pigghogg or James invaded my room that night, and I slept a dreamless sleep, the first in a long while. I woke up the next morning to a bright sun, reflecting off the new-fallen snow on the roofs of the shed and barn—and even on the privy, its doors closed now as if they'd never been opened. The fresh snow covered the ground as far as one could see, leaving almost no evidence of yesterday's commotion in the yard. I saw a lone boot sticking forlornly from the snow near the privy. Perhaps it was the giant's or even Pigghogg's, a grim reminder of all that had happened.

The Pigghogg portraits stared mutely as I went to breakfast—milk and eggs and biscuits, which I made myself and then ate alone in blessed silence, punctuated only by Pigghogg's continual coughing. Dorothy attended to Pigghogg, who called for her throughout the morning. I didn't see him, and didn't want to.

A doctor was summoned in the afternoon and remained with him for some time. As he was preparing to leave, I inquired of Pigghogg's condition. "He's very bad," the doctor said. "Pneumonia, fever." He looked at me seriously. "But we must do what we can. You should prepare this medicine for him, and give it to him a few drops at a time. Not too much, mind you. Too much is as bad as too little."

"I'll do what I can."

"Well, then you must find balm leaves and stalks, rosemary, tarragon, red fennel leaves, hyssop, savory—that should do for a start. Mix them well in an earthen pot with a sufficient quantity of white wine. Again, not too much or too little." He smiled proudly. "It's a potent medicine and has worked well for me over the years. But," he shook his head sadly, "it's not encouraging. I fear

his condition may be out of our hands now. Prayer may be the only medicine."
He took my hands. "We must pray to God for your husband's deliverance."

I nodded agreement. "Yes. We must do that. Thank you, doctor."

I decided, when he left, to leave Pigghogg to God's deliverance.

Pigghogg coughed and groaned throughout the day and night. I could see
Dorothy passing in and out of room, several times accompanied by James. I
could hardly tolerate the sound, and placed a pillow over my head at night to
shut it out.

The next morning at breakfast, as I ate alone, there was a knock at the door.
I opened it to find Reverend Wilson stomping the snow off his boots.

"Good morning, Reverend Wilson," I said, bowing slightly.

"I've come to see your husband."

"And not me?"

He approached me angrily. "Madam, I hope, God willing, never to see you
again."

"The feeling is mutual," I said, for I hated the man almost as much as I
hated Pigghogg.

He looked at me more coldly than I had ever seen in a man's eyes. "And if
we discover your hand in what happened to your husband, you may be sure
your neck will feel our wrath."

I believe he could have choked me there if Pigghogg hadn't cried out, "Save
me, oh God, save me."

Wilson pushed me aside and raced up the stairs. I could hear nothing but
screaming coming from the room for the longest time, and was about to step
outside to escape the noise when Wilson came down the stairs, grim-faced.

"He accuses you," he said.

"Me? Of what?"

"Of killing him."

"I thought it more the privy's work," I said, straining not to laugh.

"What happened here is unnatural, the work of Satan. The court will investigate."

"Investigate the privy then. What could be more fitting for you and the
court?" I shouldn't have said that, but I hated the man so fiercely I couldn't
help myself.

Wilson was quick to remind me, "Remember, woman, we still have your
father."

In my anger, I had forgotten.

"And we will soon have you." He pushed past me and walked down the snow-deep street, speaking to none of the townspeople who addressed him.

Several more magistrates visited and left. Then late in the afternoon, I opened the door and faced Mister Thorton, the magistrate who had helped me. He was alone.

"Sir, step in. Please."

"How is your husband?" he inquired gently.

"I fear he's dying," I said. "And will soon go to a better world."

"Ah. Better than privies," he said quietly, a slight smile crossing his face.

"Yes, sir."

"Let us hope," he said.

"Yes. Let us hope."

"Well, I should pay my respect."

"That way." I pointed to the stairs.

When he returned shortly, he paused at the door.

"How is he?" I asked.

"His language would make the Devil blush. He seems to think you had something to do with this. Did you?"

"No, sir. I have nothing to do with privies. That is, I have nothing to do with Pigghogg...well, what I mean to say..."

"I understand," he smiled. "You are innocent." Then he looked more seriously at me. "You should know, however, that others think differently. Take care not to offend them."

"That is difficult not to do. Reverend Wilson—"

"Just so. Reverend Wilson is much exercised."

"He is often much exercised."

He nodded. "Yes. Well, I'll do what I can. But I am often alone."

"Yes, sir. I appreciate that. All that you've done." I held out my hand and he took it. "I'm much alone myself," I said.

"Well, then, perhaps my wife and I will have you for dinner. When matters are resolved." He thought about it for a moment. "But then, perhaps that's not the best of ideas."

"No, sir. It might not be." I knew what he was thinking. I was the daughter of a condemned witch. To be associated with me was dangerous. He couldn't risk his reputation.

"Well, then, goodbye."

"Goodbye," I said. "And thank you. You're a good man."

He sighed. "I try to be. It's not easy, you know. Harder, in fact, each day."

With that he turned and trudged off slowly through the snow, walking in the footsteps of Reverend Wilson before him. I wished that Wilson could have walked in his.

Early the next morning, when it was still dark and cold, I heard Dorothy screaming. I ran out of my room.

"He's dead," she cried.

James came from his room, and the two of them closed Pigghogg's door behind them.

I never saw him again.

It snowed again on the day Pigghogg was buried. As was custom, there was no service, and six strong men carried the coffin to the small burial ground where the gravedigger had prepared the grave. Reverend Wilson and Reverend Cotton followed the coffin into the graveyard, where Reverend Cotton had helped us bury Mary's child. How distant all of that seemed, and I noted that Reverend Cotton's hair had turned white. He walked stooped, as if his back had been bent by the troubles of his life in the new world. I wondered if he remembered that night when we huddled together to bury the child. Or what he had said, on another cold day, when Anne and Mary had been driven from the colony.

Soon, it was all over. Several people said kind words to me, but there was no celebration afterwards at the meeting house or in any of the townspeople's homes. I had not thought to have one in mine, nor had any others been so moved.

When I returned home, I removed the Pigghogg portraits from the wall and buried them under some dirty boots in the closet. They spoke no more, and I never saw them again.

So ended that part of my life, in the wind and snow of the sad little Boston graveyard.

I hoped the next part would be better.

CHAPTER 19

I was now a free woman—or as free as one could be in the colony at that time. I could rise when I wished, make whatever food pleased me, and go to town whenever I desired. Dorothy and James refused to have any more to do with me, and I wished to have no more to do with them. Of course, they expected the house to be theirs, rewards for their long service to Pigghogg. They were quickly awakened to his true nature. When the will was read, there was no mention of them. They received neither money nor the house and other distant property. They didn't even receive their freedom. It turned out that Pigghogg had a nephew in Connecticut, one Mathew Pigghogg, and the two servants were bound over to him to serve out their time.

There was, of course, no mention of me.

One morning shortly after, I heard voices outside the window. I rose to see Dorothy and James packing their worldly belongings in a small cart. I wrapped myself in a robe and went downstairs to see them off. Dorothy was climbing onto the cart.

"You left the door open," I called.

She looked straight ahead, saying nothing in her proud defiance.

"Goodbye, James," I said, touching my hand to my mouth. "I've enjoyed your company."

He looked briefly at me, showing no expression. The cart jumped forward, and they were soon out of sight. I had wanted to ask him if he was my lover on those heated nights in bed, but I never had the chance. They were gone, out of my life, so my first lover was forever a mystery.

I was alone now and free, for the first time in my life.

But Father was in prison, and Mother was gone. I needed to find them both.

The very next day, when I was preparing to go to town, Thomas knocked on my door.

"Thomas. It's good to see you. You've been neglecting me."

"I cannot be seen with you, Chastity. The magistrates are suspicious."

"Then how is it you're here?"

"I've been sent. To leave a message."

"Well, what is it?"

"You are to report to town. You'll be met there."

"Where, Thomas? Where in town?"

He wanted not to tell me. "The prison."

"The prison? Is this John Wilson's work?"

"I'm not sure. But you are to be there as quickly as possible."

"All right." I found my coat and closed the door behind me. It was a good feeling closing that door and walking freely into town. "How pleasant not to see that wretched constable guarding me," I said, wondering what happened to him.

"You'll see him no more. He left in the night, and no one's seen him since. His sister has the children."

"Ah. Meager pay and a cold privy did him in."

Thomas laughed, but then turned serious. "They investigated the privy, you know."

"But found no Pigghogg."

"They found evidence."

"Of what? That Pigghogg had fouled his own nest?"

"Sawdust."

"Sawdust? Is there meaning in that?"

"They believe someone weakened the boards."

"Was Pigghogg not fat enough to fall through without help?"

"They think not."

"Ah. And what do you think?"

He puts his fingers to his lips. "I think we should not speak of it. Let the Lord's will be done."

He said no more about the privy, and I asked no more. Nor did I use it again, preferring a neighbor's kind offer.

As we approached the town, I grew wary. Could this be Wilson's idea? Would he have me seized and thrown in gaol, together with my father?

I was thinking that when Mr. Thorton approached. He greeted us warmly and guided us down Prison Lane, stopping at the prison. "Well, Chastity, I have news for you. Your father is free to leave. There are no charges."

"No charges?" I couldn't believe him.

"None that could be proved anyway."

"He's free? He can leave?"

"He is indeed."

I seized his hand. "And Reverend Wilson, he's not waiting inside? This is acceptable with him?"

"No, it's not acceptable with him. But Reverend Wilson does not rule this town, though he often thinks he does."

I was overcome with emotion. "I thank you, sir. It is not so difficult, then, to do good in this world?"

"It is very difficult. More so than you'll ever know." He smiled and squeezed my hand. "I must be off now. To my official duties, which, I assure you, are not so pleasant as this." With that he waved and was gone to whatever duties called him.

Thomas pushed open the heavy oaken door, and we passed inside. It was cold and dark, with only a small lantern for light. Thomas opened the door to Father's cell, and I saw him, huddled in the corner, no bigger than a small animal.

"Father." I ran to him and knelt, taking him in my arms. He seemed like a small child. "Father. Father."

"Chastity."

"You're free, Father. Free to go."

"Free? No, I'll never be free."

"But you are. The magistrate just told me. You're free. There are no charges."

He wouldn't believe me, even when Thomas and I brought him out the door into the clear morning air. "You see, Father, you're free. As that bird overhead."

He raised his eyes. "I see no bird."

"Nor do I anymore," I laughed. "He's flown away, gone to his home. Just where we will go."

He shook his head and nearly collapsed on the street. Several curious people watched us as we made our way, holding Father between us, to the marketplace. We passed the whipping post and the pillory, but took little notice of them. There would be time enough to consider what part they would play in our future lives.

Thomas helped me bring Father into the house and to a bed where he could rest. He could sleep now in the house where he had sent me, his daughter, in marriage, to save his inn and pay his debts. Fortunately, the debts were paid, and Pigghogg was at rest in the graveyard.

I cared for Father each day, preparing his meals as I had done in the inn. I went to the marketplace and purchased supplies, using money that Pigghogg had hidden in a dresser drawer and some that I had saved, no longer needing it to bribe the giant. Meat and poultry and fish peddlers sold me their products, gladly taking my money, but they were reserved, saying little. I was still under suspicion, for there were still many unexplained, unnatural events disturbing the townspeople.

I had heard for some time about a monstrous black dog running wild through the area, terrorizing the people and then disappearing into the swamps and marshes when men hunted it with their guns. In one case the dog was thought to have seized a baby and carried it off to its home, where it suckled the child and raised it with its own brood. It could only be the work of the Devil, many said, seeking more familiars to do his work.

I had never thought much about the dog, but one day when purchasing fish in town, I heard a screaming coming from the docks. We all looked in that direction and saw a large black dog bounding up the hill, snapping and growling at the people in its way. Several men were following it with their muskets, but dared not fire lest they hit an innocent bystander. The dog raced toward us, sending women and children, and even some men into panic. I didn't move, afraid to attract its attention. The dog leaped around the marketplace, attacking first one person, then another. Then it saw me, standing alone. It bounded toward me. I didn't move but held out my hand. The dog slowed down and walked to me, its red tongue hanging out. I tried to act calmly and reached down to touch its head. The dog became gentle and nuzzled my hand.

Suddenly, there was a shot, and the dog fell dead at my feet. One of its pursuers had killed it, narrowly missing me. I was furious at the man and asked if he had no better things to do than kill a dog running for its life. "It's the Devil's dog," he said. "Nonsense," I said. "It was in fear for its life."

It was soon known throughout the town that Satan's beast knew its mistress, the only one who tamed its wrath.

From then on, I heard hushed voices speaking of the many strange events in the town and surrounding villages. One man told of a snake crawling into a

Sabbath meeting, frightening the women and children until a man stomped it to death, but not before it hissed and prophesied the end of the world.

One old lady told another just behind me of a spider found swimming in her husband's ale. "What is the meaning?" her friend asked. "The spider gave birth to babies," she replied, "and they did crawl from the ale and attack my husband, giving him a terrible fright. He is a Christian man, you know. The Devil would frighten Christian men."

I knew the woman's husband from my days at the inn. "You would see spiders yourself," I told her, if you downed your ale like water." She walked away, anxious not to be thought too familiar with common sense.

The stories went on and on: The rats from a ship in the harbor pursued a sailor onto the docks and ate him whole. A crow's dung fell on a woman with her child, killing the woman and marking the child with scars about his face. A baby in its cradle, but six weeks old, began speaking to its parents, telling them the sky would open and flames would set their barn on fire. That story had a ring of truth, for one night after a fierce storm their barn did catch fire and burn to the ground, killing their cow and horse.

Another woman complained to a companion that her pigs had escaped and were found the next day being too familiar with her neighbors' goats. "When I went to Goody Easty's house, she was reading from a book," the woman said. "Indeed," I said, turning to the women. "Reading is the enemy of silliness." They turned away, mumbling that Satan gave the gift of reading so as to gather more followers for his work among us.

It was not long before I met Reverend Wilson walking toward Prison Lane. I had not seen him for some time but could not avoid walking past him. "Good morning, Reverend Wilson," I said. He stopped. "I hear much about you," he said.

"You hear much about everyone," I replied.

"None that tame the Devil's dog."

"Or those that shoot it," I said.

"You are suspected."

"That is no news. I am always suspected. What is it now? That Goody Stoddard's cow had three eyes and two noses and I was the cause?"

He spoke calmly and deliberately. "That you killed your husband. Or arranged it."

I was surprised at the charge, though I shouldn't have been. Thomas had given me some warning.

"I believe it was the privy that killed my husband."

"So we understand," he smiled and turned away. "You'll hear more from us," he said in parting.

That worried me. Thomas had said something about sawdust and the privy. Wilson would never relent until he proved my guilt and had me in his grasp. Mother and Father, too, if he could find the means.

I decided we needed to leave Boston—to find Mother in Rhode Island, where we could breathe freely.

I returned home to find Father kneeling at the fireplace, warming himself.

He rose and gave me a note.

"What's this?"

"A boy just dropped it off. It's for you."

"For me? Who would send me notes?"

He shrugged. "The boy didn't say. He just said it's for you."

I opened the note and read the small, clearly written script. I sank to my knees. "Oh, God. Oh, God."

"What is it, Chastity?" Father knelt next to me.

"It's from Mary. In Rhode Island." I read it to him:

"Chastity, dear friend, I write to tell you that your Mother died yesterday quietly in her sleep. May God grant her the peace in Heaven she never found on earth. God bless you, Chastity. Love, Mary Dyer.'"

Father lowered his head to the floor, and let out a cry from deep within him, as if he had harbored that pain for years, as if he could hold it in no longer. It was a cry for his wife whom he had loved dearly but oft unwisely. It was a cry for his many mistakes, for trying to thwart Mother when she wished to attend to Hannah's dying, and for marrying me off to Pigghogg, losing me for what must have seemed forever. It was a cry for Mother's madness and my despair. A cry for the stripes on his back, which still burned hot, though I tended them daily. It was, finally, a cry for his life, shattered now, broken beyond repair, all lost.

It was a cry for both of us, bereft now of wife and mother.

We wandered about the house for the rest of the day, boats broken free of their mooring. Ghosts seeking the warmth which had once given them life and had now departed.

At dinner that evening, Father and I sat across from each other. We left Pigghogg's chair vacant, as we had done each night since Father had returned.

"Father?"

"Hmm?"

"Father, we must leave. This house is no longer mine."

"It's an evil house."

"Where shall we go?"

He said nothing at first. Then his face lit with the first smile I had seen since his return. "The inn."

"The inn?" I had not even thought of the inn for weeks. I had no idea what had become of it in Father's absence. "Yes," I said. "A fine idea."

That evening I left Father and made my way in the cold darkness to Thomas's house. I walked swiftly, carrying a small lantern, unmindful of the danger in being seen. I had too much on my mind to be concerned with busybodies.

Thomas slowly opened the door and held his lantern up to my face. "Chastity?" He looked worried.

"You expected Reverend Wilson?"

He shook his head and quickly ushered me in, closing the door behind us. "Chastity, it's dangerous."

"I had to come, Thomas."

He could see in my face that something was wrong. "Is your father…?"

"Father's fine."

"Oh. I was worried."

"Oh, Thomas…Thomas."

"Chastity, what is it?"

"It's Mother. Mother died. Mary wrote it in a note."

He drew me to him. "I'm sorry. She was a good woman."

"She was. She was." I let him hold me. And then my own cry, which I had held within me so long, burst out. I hit him on the chest. "It was Pigghogg, that filthy swine. And Wilson, black-coated monster. They killed her. They killed her, Thomas. They might as well have taken a knife to her as what they did. I hate them with all my soul."

Thomas held me tightly, saying nothing. "I hate them. I hate them," I cried.

I felt my knees give way, and I sank to the floor. Thomas held me as I slipped. "Chastity, he's gone. Pigghogg's gone."

"Damn his soul to hell."

Thomas knelt beside me. "God forgive me."

I'd gone mad with anger. "I curse him too. He allowed it."

"Hush, Chastity. That is wrong to say. God forgive you."

"No…no…no." I lay on the floor, striking it with my fist. "I'll never forgive. Never."

Thomas lay beside me, his arm over my shoulders. Gradually, without realizing it, my anger cooled. I saw Thomas's kind face, stained by his own tears, and I wiped them away. I put my arm around him and snuggled into his arms.

The low fire crackled and cast its shadows across the floor, licking our feet and hands. I relaxed, the anger draining into the ground, and lost myself in Thomas, in his gentle and strong arms. My mind fell asleep, and my body awakened.

That night Thomas and I became lovers.

I opened my eyes later to his caress. "Thomas?"

"Hmm?"

"You said God forgive me. Meaning you. Why did you say that?"

"No reason, Chastity."

"What had you to do with him? With Pigghogg and the privy."

"Nothing, Chastity. Speak of it no more."

I smiled. "Would that Reverend Wilson join him."

He tried not to smile. "I think one is enough for now."

"Yes."

I would have lain in his arms all night, but footsteps passing in the dark alerted Thomas. He sat up.

"Chastity, you must go."

"Why cannot I stay as your wife?"

He looked at me sternly. "Because you are not my wife. And if you are discovered, it will go hard on both of us."

"The magistrates would forbid love?"

"Aye, they would. But they would call it another name. Fornication."

"The word struck me as if I were slapped in the face. "Ah. I see." I felt a coldness creeping over me again. "Well, then I'll leave."

I gave him a quick kiss.

"I'm sorry for your mother, Chastity. Please tell your father."

"I will. Goodbye, Thomas." I started out the door and then remembered. "We're leaving shortly."

"Leaving?"

"To Roxbury and the inn. Father suggested it."

"I'll not see you then?"

"You said yourself it's dangerous. And fornication."

"But I meant…"

"Whatever you meant, we're leaving. Tomorrow or the next day. It's not so far, after all."

I touched his hand again and left in the darkness, this time without the lantern's light.

It didn't matter, though. I knew there were shadows not far from the door. We had been seen. What that meant, I didn't know.

CHAPTER 20

On a cold, windless day in the new year we moved our things back to the inn. No one saw us off, except a few children playing in the snow. One lone dog, far smaller than the monster black dog shot in the marketplace, gave a few half-hearted barks, but even he had better things to do than mark our departure.

The monster dog, however, was not quite gone, for it had become a ghost dog roaming the surrounding woods with a pack of wolves, revenging itself on those that had hunted and killed it. I wished that it would attack Reverend Wilson and the magistrates who had hunted Mother, finally killing her in a distant colony.

The inn's name, A MAN'S CASTLE, had been removed, but other than that the inn was much like I had remembered it. Good riddance to the sign, I thought; we can do better. And we did. A few days later Father proposed that we name it MARY'S CASTLE, for Mother and for the woman who brought her to freedom in Rhode Island. I instantly agreed, and Father went to work on the sign. When it was finished and Father was about to hang it, he said, "Take the other end. I need help." So we hung the sign together, one on each end, and as we stood there, admiring his work, I could see his tears through my own.

Desire had left a note for Father on a long table. It simply said she was leaving for a better place. No telling where that was or how she found it. I silently wished her well, not knowing if it was but a dream she was pursuing. I had thought Rhode Island a better place, but now I didn't know. It hadn't kept Mother alive, and perhaps it would not keep others alive either. Perhaps there was no better place, except for Heaven, but even that seemed dark and doleful when spoken of by the learned ministers from the pulpits.

Not long after, Father posted a sign announcing we were open for business. He posted several other announcements, as he had always done before, but I noted he posted nothing about punishments in the pillory or at the post.

It was not long before travelers and local people began stopping at the inn, for drink or food or lodging for the night. In fact, Father said that business was better than it had ever been. He marveled at his good fortune, after so much bad. I didn't tell him I thought the people were drawn to the inn, as they were to punishments in the pillory or at the whipping post, because they were curious, desperate for excitement in their bleak, drab lives. And if there were no punishment on the days they craved it, well, one who had escaped the gallows would suffice just fine.

No one had yet actually been hanged, though several, like Mother and Father, had come close, so the townspeople had to wait for that. I knew that it would not be long before these hateful men found someone to satisfy their needs.

Spring came early that year, as if Nature had been made to wait too long to dress in its bright seasonal finery. The little stream in front of the inn filled up to overflowing, so Father took great delight in lowering the drawbridge each morning, part of the ceremony he adopted with the reopening of the inn. He and I would stand at attention, the rising sun warming the earth and the wind whispering in the trees, as he lowered the bridge. Then he would give a little salute to the sign, caressing it gently as he passed inside. It touched my heart to see him remembering Mother as he did, for she was much in my heart as well.

When I saw him caressing the sign, I would think of Thomas, who finally visited me one afternoon when he had finished his duties. He appeared at the kitchen without warning.

"Chastity," he called, as I was preparing a stew.

"Oh. Hello, Thomas," I said and kept working.

He seemed hurt. "I've had more enthusiastic greetings from prisoners in the gaol."

"I'm sorry, Thomas. But I have work." I kept preparing the food.

"Perhaps you're too busy for me."

"Well, yes, I am. Just now. But I might have time in mid-morning tomorrow. And sometimes later in the evening, though travelers often find they need a meal and drink before retiring."

"I see."

"It's just Father and I, Thomas. We'll be hiring another girl soon, but for now it's just us. I have little time."

He stood there, watching me. "How are you, then?"

"Good. The work is good for me. And Father as well. It keeps our minds off…other things."

He nodded. "I understand."

"And how have you been?" I asked, putting more ingredients in the stew and stirring them.

"Good. I'm busy as well. We have several prisoners."

"Ah. Reverend Wilson and the magistrates are busy as well."

"Yes." He watched me for a spell, saying nothing. Then he said, "We were seen, you know."

"Seen?" Then I remembered. "Oh, yes. Yes. I thought as much."

"You don't seem concerned."

I wasn't a bit concerned. "I have better things to think about, Thomas. Such as this stew and the evening meals."

"Then you won't care they're gathering evidence. About the privy, too. Mr. Pigghogg's nephew is helping them."

Perhaps it was the name. I hadn't heard it for several months, and had put it out of my mind. Perhaps it was being interrupted in making the stew, which Father would need very shortly. Whatever it was, I said sharply, "I don't care a damn for what his nephew does. Don't ever mention that name to me again. I curse it and whoever speaks it." I was instantly sorry and tried to take back my words, but it was too late.

He looked at me sadly and shook his head. "Well, if it's like that, I'll be going."

"I'm sorry, Thomas, for what I said. Could I see you tomorrow morning perhaps?"

"I'm working then. We have much to do with the court."

"Well, then, soon, I hope."

"Yes, soon."

He nodded to Father who was just coming in for the stew. I could see him looking about the inn, thinking of my life here and what it would mean to me and perhaps to him. Then he left.

Something had happened between us. It might have been what I said that day in the kitchen, but it might have been when he called our loving—fornication. The word sounded so heartless and cold. It was like he had erected a wall between us without meaning to. And I had done the same when I cursed the

Pigghogg name and whoever uttered it. I don't know what happened, but it was a great sadness to me. I did see Thomas from time to time when I went to Boston on various errands but it was never the same. The wall remained. Then one day I saw him with a young lady, her arm through his, and that was the end of it.

Or almost the end. He was not yet out of my life. As long as Wilson was alive, there would one day be trouble. I knew that as I knew my own name, Chastity Hoar, which I took proudly now that I was rid forever of the other name.

The year passed swiftly and then another. We hired a new girl, not from the Clap family, as I had never forgiven Goody Clap for testifying against Mother. Then we hired a second girl, so we now had two girls and me helping Father with the inn. That eased his life a bit, so he could spend more time talking with the guests, which he enjoyed, except when they would mention something about Boston and his time there. Then he would grow quiet and leave the guest as soon as he could. Sometimes he would even go to his room and not return until the guest had left.

Father fixed up a room in the attic, which the girls used, and I could often hear them talking and laughing well into the night, much as Desire and I had done. I kept to my room, despite some of the unpleasant memories which it held. If I looked, I could barely make out where the hole in the closet door had been, but I soon forgot even that reminder of my marriage.

From time to time, Father would note that a guest had called for me and not the other girls. I had taken no notice until he called it to my attention. "Be careful," he warned. "I'll not have that again."

Nor will I, I thought. But several times a man would catch my fancy. I might have heard in his voice an echo of Thomas, or perhaps I saw something in his eyes. Sometimes he would be handsome, sometimes rather ill-favored. It didn't matter. He would catch my eye and I would feel the attraction.

These men I would invite to my room, long after Father and the girls had retired, and I would enjoy their company. Sometimes they were married to shrewish wives and told me their sad stories. Sometimes they were searching for the right woman, and thought I might be that woman. But either I was not the right woman or they were not the right man, and I would often not see them again. Still, there were two or three that came by regularly, passing through on their travels to and from Boston, and I came to greatly enjoy their visits.

I married none of them, for which Father was greatly relieved. I had been married once, and that was quite enough for me. There are some things for which once-in-a-lifetime is enough to satisfy one's curiosity, and marriage was one of them.

Many years later, when Father didn't attend our little ceremony of lowering the drawbridge and saluting the sign, I went to his room and knocked. There was no answer. I knocked again, and then, hearing nothing, I entered. Father was lying on the bed, as if asleep, the most peaceful look on his face. I held his hand in mine, cold now, and prayed he and Mother had found a better place than they had discovered in this new world.

I removed the locket from around my neck, the one Abigail had given me long ago. I believe it contained Mother's hair, which she had given Abigail in the prison. I closed it in Father's hand.

As I looked at Father, I asked his forgiveness for cursing him as I did when he married me to a man I loathed. Mother had told me that Father loved me, and I believe he did, despite what he had done to save his inn. I had made too many mistakes myself to hold him to his.

The reading of the will produced some consternation, for Father had bequeathed some money to a friend. What the will said was, "I hereby leave five pounds to Mary Dyer, a good woman and a friend when one was needed." I kept the five pounds for the time I'd see Mary again, if that day should ever come.

The inn was left to me, his only daughter who, the will said, he "loved more dearly than any other but my dear wife."

We buried Father in the graveyard in Roxbury, many miles from Mother. I trusted they were together in spirit, though I had lost much faith in people being together in this life or the next.

And so my life went on, month after month, year after year, regular as the seasons. The young girls I hired married and left, and I hired more. Each year they seemed younger and more full of hope, and each year they left to better their lives. I loved them all and wished them well. Several of them brought their children by the inn for me to see, and I became a grandmother to some, though I had none of my own.

It seemed my life had calmed, and would go on that way until I died, peaceful as the bay on a warm summer day. And so it might have in a better world.

But I was living in this one, in the Massachusetts Bay Colony, and so, many years later, when I was an older woman, the storm broke.

The force behind that storm was no secret.

CHAPTER 21

I visited Boston many times over the years, and gradually most of the towns-people forgot who I was and what had happened to me. A few remembered, and I could see them draw their children aside, telling them to avoid me, much as Mother had warned me about being seen too close to Mary and Anne.

Sometimes I would see Reverend Wilson, who still lived and scowled whenever I passed him. He had the ear of the new governor, John Endicott, a man worthy to follow in the dark footsteps of the honored John Winthrop.

After so much time had passed, I actually enjoyed seeing the minister, for it gave me an opportunity to tweak him. "Good day, reverend, I'd say you're growing white. It will not be long now."

Sometimes he'd say nothing. Other times, he'd announce they were watching me. They'd heard stories about the inn—dark stories of intrigue and evil.

I paid little attention to those stories. They were told by the men, not the women. The women told other stories: of men who voted when their wives could not, though the laws applied to both men and women; of men who owned the property and their wives, and controlled the women's lives in all things, except in childbirth, and even then they condemned the midwives for being too much with the women in their travail.

So of course there were stories about me. No other women owned an inn or even much property in all of Boston or surrounding towns. It made the men furious they could not control such women, and they searched everywhere for the slightest fault or provocation to fine these women or, much worse, hang them. They had, in fact, hanged a woman relative of Governor Winthrop, for doing no more than arguing her rights. An uncivil tongue they called it, and hanged her for a witch.

I mocked John Wilson whenever I could, for he could do nothing to me without evidence. I was careful that he find no evidence.

I was not careful enough, though it would have made no difference. What happened, happened. It was destined to happen.

It began one autumn night after I had retired to my bedroom. There was a gentle knock on the door. "Come in," I said, assuming it to be one of the girls.

"Chastity."

Recognizing the voice, I turned to the woman, but didn't at first recognize her.

"You don't remember me?"

"Oh, Lord." I hadn't seen her for twenty years, but it was the same beautiful woman, her eyes shining still. "Mary Dyer," I said, and rushed to her. "Oh, Mary, how good to see you."

"Chastity, my friend. God has kept thee safe."

"Well, I am safe. Whether it was God or luck, I couldn't say."

She smiled. "It was God, I'm sure."

I wouldn't argue with her, the woman who had meant so much to me. "Sit down, please. We have much to speak of."

"I cannot stay long. My friends await me. But I did want to see you one last time."

"Last time?"

"I mean again…before…well, before I leave."

She sat on a chair, and I sat on the bed, across from her. She never took her eyes from me, always searching for something. She told me of Mother, of how she had improved somewhat in her final days and of how she had spoken my name just before she died. It almost seemed, Mary said, as if Mother could see me in the room with her. They gave her a simple funeral, and William, her husband, had assisted the gravedigger to ensure that it was done proper for a fine woman. He had spoken the words himself at the burial, and she had added her own. I thanked her for the news.

I told her of Father and his peaceful death, and then remembered the five pounds he had promised her in the will. I found the money in the drawer and asked her to take it, but she refused. "I have no need of it where I'm going," she said, so I returned it to the drawer.

When I sat again, she reached over and took my hands. "Chastity, I have much to tell thee and little time to tell it."

"Please tell me everything," I said.

"I have been in England for many years now. There I met a man like I've never known. I have a new religion now, much unlike the one practiced here in Massachusetts. I'm called a Quaker, and I've become an elder, charged with spreading the seed."

I knew nothing about Quakers, though I had heard the word mentioned in my trips to Boston. I thought they were more Devil worshippers and so paid them no attention. Mary explained their religion to me quickly: how the Quakers believed that men and women were equal in the eyes of God, and both were called to serve him. How God spoke not through the ministers like John Cotton or John Wilson, but to their hearts, which he warmed with a ravishing joy.

Looking into her shining face, I thought it was indeed a ravishing joy that had overcome her.

"You learned this in England?"

"I did. From a wonderful man. God has spoken to him, and now he speaks to the rest of us.

"Was it your husband?"

She laughed at that. "No, William is a good man, but he's more interested in business matters. I was alone in England. William cared for the children."

"The children? You have children?" I don't know why it surprised me, but it did.

"Yes. Yes. Lovely children. Six of them."

"Were you gone for long?"

"Yes. Five years. Five wonderful years. My heart has never been so warmed and full."

I couldn't believe what she said. I had no children myself, but I missed my grandchildren the girls brought to see me when they could. "You left your husband and your children, for five years?"

"I did. I missed them. But my heart was full."

I couldn't speak. It seemed unnatural. How could a mother leave her children for five years? And her husband as well. My mother was gone only a short time, and I had missed her daily with a pain in my heart. I missed her still and would miss her always.

What was it about these people and their religion that caused such unnatural acts? I didn't know and never had the chance to ask.

"Kneel with me," she said.

I hesitated, but then did as she asked. "Thou would make a good Quaker," she said. "I can see it in thine eyes."

Then she prayed to her God to open my heart and shine his love into mine that I would know the same joy she and others had felt. I felt nothing, but did not tell her so. She wouldn't have believed it anyway.

She squeezed my hands and smiled at me from another world than mine. It was the smile of an angel, as I had thought her so long ago. I could hardly endure its force.

"Well, I must go now," she said, rising from the floor. "One day thy heart will warm as mine has, and thou will join us to spread the word."

I didn't quite know what she meant. I had my life, and she had hers. Mine was running the inn, preparing the food and drink for those in need. Hers was—I didn't know. Only that it was not mine and likely never to be.

I accompanied her to the door. "Do you wish food or drink?" I asked.

"No. I thank thee. The Lord provides my sustenance."

Then she was gone into the night.

I thought she was going home to Rhode Island, where she could live freely as we could not in Massachusetts. It wasn't until many days later I heard the news. I don't know how I could have missed what had happened. Perhaps it's because I posted no notices of punishments on the walls, just as Father had refused to do when he was in charge of announcements.

Mary had not gone back to Rhode Island. She had gone instead to Boston to face Governor Endicott, the court, and the Devil's own man, John Wilson. They had hanged, on the Common, two of her friends, both Quakers, and were about to hang Mary as well. Just when they placed the rope around her neck and were about to push her off the ladder, a reprieve came and she was released. No one knew what happened to her.

My heart beat wildly when I heard the news. Now, beatings and the pillory were not enough. I heard they were even cutting off the ears of Quakers and those who prayed in a different way. And now it was hanging. Murdering those who believed differently.

I was furious, and the next visit to Boston I vowed to tell Wilson what I thought of him. I passed him near the scaffold.

"You are a Devil," I called to him at some distance, loud enough that many heard me and looked our way.

He stopped and waited for me to approach him. He was as eager as I for the confrontation.

"I think you would be wise to guard your tongue, woman, or you will find yourself joining your friends."

"What friends?" I said. "Tell me that I may join them."

"You will join them in the graveyard, then. They have been hanged."

I thought he meant Mary, that they changed their minds and hanged her secretly. "Mary?"

His eyes gleamed. "Yes, Mary. We thought her to be your friend, and now you admit it."

"It is no secret. What have you done with her?"

"We have banished her from the colony. If she returns, she will be hanged. Along with all those who persist in their wicked beliefs."

Several townspeople had circled around us, two vipers locked in mortal combat.

"Devil," I hissed at him. "Devil."

"Daughter of Eve," he hissed back. "We will cast you out as well."

I turned and left the scene, unable to control myself and fearing that I might strike the monster, giving him the evidence he sought to arrest me.

Back at the inn, I went to my room to calm myself. At least Mary was safe. She was in Rhode Island, her life spared, and she could live out her life in peace, far from these Boston devils. She could be with her husband and children, and live as people were meant to live.

At least, that was my dream.

The following year I was reminded of where I lived.

CHAPTER 22

All spring the following year we heard the wolves howling in the woods around the town. Several wolf drives were conducted, the men circling the wolves and killing them when they were surrounded in a tight circle. But it made no difference. The wolves were replaced by more wolves, and the howling would continue. The guests complained about the hospitality, but there was nothing we could do but stop our ears and wait to learn the meaning.

In May of that year the portent became clear. On a clear, sunny day with no hint of danger, two men came to the inn. "Are you Chastity Hoar?" one of them demanded. "I am called that," I said, wondering at their rude greeting. "Then you are ordered by the court to come with us." "I will not. I have guests to feed," I said and turned away. It made no difference to the men how many guests I had or that I was not dressed for travel. They seized me, holding firmly to each arm, and prepared to take me off. My hired girls came to me. "What should we do?" one of them asked, helpless as a rabbit in a snare. "What you always do," I said. "I'll return shortly."

"I can walk without your assistance," I said, pulling my arms free of the men's grasp as we walked towards Boston.

"All right then," the leader said. "But walk properly. We have orders."

"What orders?"

"We cannot speak."

A curious crowd came out of their houses and joined the procession. We walked through Boston until reaching the scaffold. More townspeople were already gathered, waiting for us.

I was led up the old stairs, warped and broken now after generations of feet had trod them. It occurred to me that I was following in the footsteps of my parents and hundreds of others too numerous to know.

Standing on the scaffold, as if time had stopped, was John Wilson, ugly as a black toad. Thomas, still a constable, was standing next to him, looking very uneasy. Wilson stepped forward. "So, your time has come at last. As it was meant to be."

I said nothing. Fear and hatred churned my stomach.

He led me to the pillory. "Bend your head," he commanded.

"I'll not bend it to such as you," I said.

"Constable, bend it for her."

Thomas hesitated before advancing. He was a man the toad would never be, and I hoped he would show his mettle.

"Well, what are you waiting for?" The toad could never restrain himself when it came to punishing women. It was more satisfying than praying to God, who seemed to answer only with plagues of locusts or raging pestilences.

"Sir, I'd rather not, if you please," Thomas said, looking wistfully at me.

Ah, good for you, Thomas.

"Rather not? Rather not?" the toad croaked and moved toward me. Not too close, of course. I might infect him.

"The court will hear of this."

"Sir, I've heard she's been good to women in need."

What did the Reverend Wilson care about being good to women in need? He was tyrant to his own wife, Elizabeth. She could hardly tolerate the man. She came to the new world only to ease his shame for not making the first voyage with him.

Wilson stood before me and thought to stare me in the eyes, but turned away when I smiled at him. Yes, I knew him well, as I have known many men. He was excited, throbbing with pleasure. He had to look away rather than face me.

"You have no cap," he muttered.

"Indeed," I said. "It's too hot a day for caps." Then I remembered how I had been dragged from my home to this foul place. "Your men with their dung-stench hands permitted no time." "Your loose tongue, as ever, is an abomination in the eyes of the Lord," he cried. "Did not the apostle Paul say that if a woman be not covered, let her also be shorn? Did not the court think that a bare head is no better than a bare breast?"

"I had not heard that," I said, smiling. "Do you wish me to bare my breast then?"

Thomas looked away, unable to still a chuckle. In truth, he knew the tenderness of my bare breast.

In a fury the Reverend Wilson reached for my head, to bend it to the wood. But as he hadn't yet enclosed my hands, I reached out for his arm and held it firm. I was stronger than he was, and he knew it. I had worked my whole life, lifting barrels or vats or tree stumps, while he had done nothing but send empty words into the air. I tightened my grip, knowing that later it would be sure to bring me more pain. I couldn't help it, though. I hated the man. I could have pushed my favorite bodkin into his black eyes and screwed it in.

So there we stood, he on one side of the pillory, shaking with rage, and me on the other, squeezing his arm and spitting my own venom.

"Constable, bend her proud head!" he cried. "Or the court..." This time he didn't need to say more. Thomas knew what would happen to him if he didn't obey. Twenty lashes at the whipping post, at the least. So he approached close, pleading with his eyes for me to comply.

He put his hand gently on my head and looked into my eyes. I didn't want to cause him any more pain, so I pursed my lips, as if to gently kiss him, and bent my head. For him, Thomas Brattle, not for the toad, whose arm I released.

Wilson jumped back and reached for the heavy wooden top of the pillory, swinging it over my head and hands. He carefully locked it into place. I was his now, or so he thought.

He turned to Thomas and barked, "Get me a cleft stick. The slut needs a sharper lesson."

Thomas looked pleadingly at me and turned away to find a teaching stick, as the magistrates called it.

I hated the pillory as I hated the men who put me in it. Nothing but that cold wood would ever force my head to bow before men such as the Reverend John Wilson. It bent my head, but not my spirit.

"So, woman, what do you say now?"

I said nothing, unwilling to give him any satisfaction. I closed my eyes so I would see nothing.

"Your tongue is learning its place, I dare say. The teaching stick will reinforce the lesson."

I could hear him walking back and forth in front of me, savoring the sight.

"You know why you're here?" he asked.

I didn't want to answer him, but I couldn't help myself. "Because it pleasures you," I said. "Because you're shriveled as my corn in drought. Because it makes you feel a man, such as you never feel except that you're bringing pain to women."

He seized my nose and wrenched it, sending pain through my whole face. "Take care, woman," he said. "We've slit the nostrils of better women than you."

I shuddered and said nothing. I knew what he and his kind were capable of.

"And for those who will not listen to the words of the Lord, those who will not use the ears the good Lord has given them, the court has ordered that these gifts are forfeit. I believe you know what that means."

Of course I knew what that meant. Hadn't I heard from travelers of what they'd done to those who broke their laws?

The reverend looked as if he were savoring a rich pie or tasty venison. "We are forced to crop one ear and throw it to the pigs. Then if they persist in not hearing, in resisting the authority of the magistrates, we crop the other one and feed it also to the pigs. The pigs, I'm told, are not particular in their food."

The stench of his hand as it held my nose was more than I could bear. I needed to watch my words, but I also wanted to send the man to the everlasting hell he preached on every Sabbath.

"Pig," I spit at him. "Filthy pig."

He twisted my nose again. I would have bit him, but the wood held my head and hands in place. I closed my eyes and tried to think of better things.

He released my nose and rubbed his hand on his coat. "The stench of Satan," he said. "Worse than your mouth."

He looked around for Thomas, who was still searching for a proper stick. Keep looking, Thomas, I thought. I'll have no part of the cleft stick if I can help it.

The Reverend Wilson stood back and folded his hands, as if in prayer. "You know why you're here?" he asked again.

I said nothing.

He smiled and glanced down Prison Lane. "You know who's in gaol now?" he asked.

I pretended not to hear him. Of course I didn't know who was in gaol, and I didn't want to know. Probably some poor woman who was found begging in the streets to fill her children's hungry mouths. Or working her garden on the Sabbath that her children not starve in the coming winter.

"It's a friend of yours, I believe."

"It must be a good woman, then," I said.

"More like Satan's disciple," he snarled. "A viper's contagion, meaning to sicken and wound God's chosen people."

"Who is this woman?" I asked. "I mean to meet her and give her thanks."

"You'll meet her in hell, then. Because that's where she'll be tomorrow morning at nine o'clock."

Now I was curious. Who was this woman? What had she done to so anger the magistrates? Had she killed her child as one poor, sick woman had done some years ago? Had she shot her husband in his maleness after he raped her every night? Were they charging witch as they had with the good Mistress Hibbins, hanged because she had more wit than her accusers?

"Who is it, then? And what is her crime?"

He was enjoying the suspense, knowing that he was now in full control. Finally, he said, "She's known as Mary Dyer in this world. She'll be Queen of Hell in the next."

Mary Dyer! I strained my head and hands against the wood. I would have laid him open as I did my pigs each autumn.

He smiled when he saw my anguish. "Ah, so that did get your attention. We thought it might."

Mistress Mary. Mistress Mary. She was living free in Rhode Island. Why had she returned after they had threatened hanging if she did?

"And her crime?" I asked.

"Blasphemy. Sedition. She works to end God's kingdom on earth. But as you see, God's kingdom prevails, and Mary Dyer will soon quake before her master in hell."

"You are not fit to touch her gown," I said.

"I wouldn't touch that vileness," he said. Then he looked at me with such a blackness that I almost turned away. "But we're told that in the past *you* have found delight in touching that filth. Touching and holding it to you," he said, turning away as if he couldn't bear the sight. "You with the filthy name," he added.

He came to me again, stopping so close I could smell his breath. "You will accompany us tomorrow to watch your friend receive her just punishment for coming among us when she was ordered not to. She spreads contagion wherever she walks. We mean to stop it and restore the colony to health."

"Tomorrow?" I gasped. "Tomorrow?"

"It is so ordered. The gallows are a stern teacher, but such as you will learn in no other." He smiled, devil that he was. "It will not be long and you will join your friend."

I hardly heard him, the threat he was making, I was so pained to hear of Mary. I said nothing.

"Yes, yes, I believe your tongue is silenced now even without the teaching stick." He looked toward the marketplace, where Thomas was shuffling along, in no hurry to do his duty. I almost felt sorry for him.

"Come along, man," the toad called to him. "I have work to do."

Thomas arrived with the stick into which he had carved a slit.

"Give it here, man," he commanded. "You give the snail a bad name."

At that, he seized the stick and approached me.

"Open your mouth, woman."

I clenched my teeth.

"I said open your mouth!" He was burning with fury. "Or we will force it open with a hot iron."

I relented and opened my mouth, and he prepared to fix the cleft stick to my tongue.

In his haste and pleasure he forgot what he was doing and who he was doing it to. I snapped my mouth closed on his fingers.

"Ahh!' he screamed. "Whore! Stinking whore!"

I pressed down on his fingers, though their taste was foul.

"Constable, pry her mouth open! Break it if you must!"

Thomas approached slowly, appealing to me with his eyes. All right, Thomas, I thought, you owe me something. I opened my mouth and released the reverend, who backed away as from a poisonous snake. He held his fingers behind him.

"Fix the stick, constable," he said, "or you'll be at the whipping post tomorrow with her."

Thomas looked at me, and I looked at him, the man who had pressed me to him that lusty night so long ago. I smiled and opened my mouth.

Thomas could hardly look at me as he fixed the stick to my tongue, then turned away.

Oh, God in Heaven, the pain seared my mouth. I closed my eyes, trying not to weep in front of that monster of a man. I would show him no weakness, not even if he hanged me next to Mary on the following morning.

When I opened my eyes again, Thomas had left for other duties. Only Wilson watched me, delighting in my pain.

"Justice will now come to pass," he said, holding one hand behind him. "Tomorrow you will witness your friend and mentor on the gallows as we break her stubborn neck. Then it will be your turn. Think on it, woman, where your evil ways have led you. To the gaping pit of hell. We know your mother died in Rhode Island, witch that she was. And your father escaped us also, but not his death. But now we have you. You will not be so fortunate." He seized my nose again with his other hand, and I snapped at him but missed. "Until we meet again," he said and strutted off the scaffold.

I was left alone under the hot spring sun, my tongue burning as if on fire. Many people had come close to observe, but backed away, as if shamed by my example. I saw several women I knew with their children. They put their hands over their children's eyes so as to shield them from such a poor example. Then they turned away, shielding themselves as well.

I realized then that I needed to walk my own path, without assistance, to whatever place it might lead me. I trembled to think of where that might be. All I knew was that on the morrow I would see my dear friend Mary on the gallows.

I closed my eyes again and tried to shut out the fearsome pain.

CHAPTER 23

I spent the day in the pillory, enduring such pain as I have never felt. About mid-day, when there were few curious bystanders, an older woman came to the edge of the scaffold and peered up at me. "Are you Goodwoman Hoar?" she said. "The one who is friend to Mary Dyer."

"I nodded that I was. The woman seemed familiar, but I couldn't place her.

She boldly ascended the stairs and approached me. She removed the cleft stick and touched me gently on the cheek. "One good turn deserves another."

My tongue still burned, though the stick was gone. I thought it would burn forever.

"I would remove this work of the Devil if I could," she said, her fist tapping the solid wood post over my head, "but I have not the force to do so."

Who was this woman who dared to mount the scaffold and talk with me?

She looked around her. "How well I know this place—and the instrument that holds thee, as it held me when I was younger."

Then I recognized her. "Abigail. It's you."

"Aye, it is. Come back to return the favor."

"How did you know?"

"Hush." She looked about her. "I'm one with Mary now. I'm a Quaker. I come to comfort her in her final hours."

She looked about her. "It's dangerous. If they catch me…"

"Save yourself," I said.

She touched my face again. "Thinking of me again, as always," she smiled. "I think thou should become a Quaker."

"That is for better women than me," I said.

"I think not. But I must go."

She went quickly down the stairs and was soon lost in the marketplace.

Later in the day, Thomas unlocked the lock which held the post over my head. I could hardly lift my head to face him, and my tongue was still sore.

"Where's the cleft stick?" he asked.

"Gone," I said. "No thanks to you."

"Chastity..."

"All right, all right. I know. You had your orders. And of course you were bound to obey them."

"Aye," he said sadly. "With more courage I might have—well, it's no matter now. We've walked our separate ways."

I nodded, thinking of the paths we'd walked. He was married now, probably with children, and I was a woman alone, with surrogate grandchildren who came when their mothers could spare the time. I was feeling sorry for myself when I remembered Mary.

"Thomas. How is she?"

"Who?"

"Mary Dyer. She's in gaol now?"

"Aye. She prays alone. The windows are boarded up so that her followers cannot speak with her."

"Could I...?"

"No Chastity. I'm sorry."

"The rules, I suppose."

"Aye. The rules."

Thomas led me to the prison where I'd never visited, though it had been so much a part of my life. I was put in a cell at the other end of the prison and never saw or heard Mary. Another constable remained just outside my door. I slept fitfully, thinking of what would happen the next morning.

Early the next day a constable took me from my cell and led me to the Common, about a short distance away. The streets were lined with people, and I looked about me for a friendly face. I saw none. The people were looking beyond me, expecting the woman who would soon follow me on this path to the gallows.

Then, on the Common, with Thomas at my side, we waited for Mary. Neither of us spoke, wrapped up as we were with our thoughts on the meaning of this day.

It was not long before we heard the drummers, beating their rattling tune as they marched along side a small band of soldiers guarding their prisoner. The soldiers pushed back the crowds straining to touch Mary's gown as she walked past. One man, I could see, ran out and knelt at her feet, looking up at her. Mary reached down to touch his hand, but the soldiers knocked him to the ground before she reached him.

I could hear people shouting to her: "Go back, Mary. Go back to Rhode Island and save yourself."

She looked neither right nor left but straight ahead. She clasped her hands, and I could see she was speaking softly. Not to us, I think, but to her God. As she passed me by, I said quietly, "Mary, don't die. Please don't die."

Thomas nudged me not to speak, but I didn't care what anyone thought. "Please, Mary, don't give them your life."

I don't know if she heard me or someone else, but she spoke to those of us close by: "Nay, I cannot go back to Rhode Island, for in obedience to the will of the Lord I came, and in his will I abide faithful to death."

She saw none of us. Her eyes were fixed on Heaven now.

Reverend Wilson stepped forward on the scaffold to greet her. "Mary Dyer," he said, speaking as much to the crowd as to her: "You have been here before and received the sentence of banishment upon pain of death. You have broken the law in coming upon us again. It is therefore you who are guilty and not we in your punishment."

"Nay," she said, "I came that you might repeal the unrighteous and unjust laws made against the innocent servants of the Lord. Therefore, my blood will be upon your hands."

She then turned to the crowd and raised her hands to them. "I ask the Lord to forgive those who in their ignorance do this thing. I came to do the will of my Father, and in obedience to this will I stand even to death."

"Repent, Mary Dyer," Wilson said. "You are deluded by the Devil."

"Nay, I will not repent, for I follow the will of the Lord."

I heard a familiar voice call out, "Did you say you have been in Paradise?" I think it was Abigail, but I didn't turn to look. I could not take my eyes off Mary.

"Yea, I have been in Paradise several days now, and I am about to enter eternal happiness."

Wilson would have no more of this. He signaled to the captain of the guard to move her away.

The captain directed her to the ladder against a great tree. He adjusted the noose around her neck. Wilson went to her with his handkerchief and placed it over her face. I looked one last time at that lovely face, suffused now with what she had called a ravishing joy. I had never seen such a look on anyone's face.

"Save her," I said silently to her God. "Save your disciple."

Mary climbed the ladder, and with no further ceremony the captain pushed it away. The crowd gasped in horror at the sight of her broken body swinging in the soft spring breeze.

Someone shouted, "She hangs like a flag," and another responded, "Aye, she hangs like a flag for others to take example from."

No one moved for the longest time. Wilson ordered the guards and drummers to leave, but even they hesitated. Mary's body held us all.

Wilson climbed down from the scaffold and sought me out.

"Are you properly instructed in how we deal with lawbreakers?"

"I curse your proper instruction," I said and spit on him.

"Then you will join your friend in hell," he snarled and walked away. "Return her to the prison," he said to Thomas. "The court will decide later today when she hangs."

"What is my crime?" I cried, but he paid no attention. He was busy sending the crowd back to their homes. Many resisted, wishing to stay until their saint was removed and buried.

We walked slowly back to the prison. "Will they hang me, Thomas? What have I done?"

"If Wilson has his way, they will."

"I've done nothing."

"In their eyes you have. For one thing, you're a friend to Mary Dyer. They think you a Quaker."

"I am no Quaker, Thomas. I could not do what she has done. Think of it. She left her husband and children where they safely lived and came to Boston where she knew she'd die. She died for a God too busy to hear her plea. What kind of God is that?"

"She wanted to die," Thomas said softly.

"If that is being a Quaker, I am no Quaker," I said angrily.

"No. I believe you're not," he said simply. "I truly believe you're not."

We walked farther, saying little. I couldn't get Mary out of my mind. Why had she done a thing so foolish? What had driven her from the safety of Rhode Island to the Boston gallows, when she knew exactly what would happen to her? Oh, Mary, Mary, what kind of God have you found in England and brought to this country? He let you die, hanging from that rope, with Wilson and the others gloating over you. Why, Mary, why?

Suddenly, I turned to Thomas and shouted, "I don't want to die, Thomas. Do you hear me? I don't want to die. I'm not like her. I want to live. I reject their God. I reject John Wilson's God. I reject all gods. They are cruel and heartless."

He put his hands to his lips. "Give them no more evidence of your beliefs, Chastity, or you will surely die."

I went quietly to my cell in the prison, as he suggested.

"When will I hear, Thomas?"

"I think tomorrow. Or the next day."

I pleaded with him as he was about to leave. "Thomas, please. I don't want to die. I'm not like them."

"Hush, Chastity. Have faith."

"I have no faith. In anyone. Least of all in God," I shouted at him as he left my cell. Thomas had better things to do, more rules to follow. What did he care of me?

I spent the day alone, except for another constable assigned to guard my cell. He glanced in at me from time to time, but said nothing. I was given stale bread and a thin soup, but I turned it back. I wanted none of their food. I wanted my own, at the inn, where the girls would be needing me.

Late that night I heard muffled voices outside the gaol. I sat up quickly, my heart beating loudly. Had Wilson come to hang me in the night, when no evidence was needed? I prepared to fight him with all my power. I would never let that man touch me again.

It was dark and I could see nothing. Then a lantern. The voices and the lantern were coming closer. They stopped in front of my cell, and I prepared to hit Wilson with what little strength I had. I would send him to hell if I could.

It was Thomas, not Wilson. "Thomas?"

"Quiet." He unlocked my cell. "Quickly now. Run."

"Run?"

"You're free, Chastity. Quickly, now. Run for your life."

I couldn't believe him. It was a trick. Wilson and his men were waiting outside for my escape, so they could kill me and wash their hands.

"I'll not run. It's a trick to kill me."

"They'll kill you if you don't run. Now go!" He dragged me from the cell and pushed me toward the door.

"Thomas, if this is a trick…"

"Run, I say. Stop talking."

I went to the door and opened it. There was nothing but blackness outside. "Run," he said again, "before I'm discovered."

I took his hands in mine. "Do you break the rules, then?"

"I do. Now run. I don't want to see you again."

I turned and walked swiftly through the night. Here and there I saw lanterns bobbing along, men and women out for a walk on this warm spring night.

I didn't stop until I reached the inn. All was quiet. The guests and the girls had retired for the night. I found a lantern and went quietly upstairs, all the way to the attic, and opened the door.

The girls were still awake, talking among themselves.

"Madam," they said. "It's you."

"Aye. It's me. Or what's left of me."

I climbed into bed with them, and they snuggled against me as if they were my children and I their mother.

"What happened to you?" they wondered. "We were so worried about you."

We talked long into the night. Tomorrow would come soon enough for making plans.

CHAPTER 24

I awoke the next morning with my two girls resting against me, sleeping like babies without a care in the world. I smiled at their innocence, but I knew it could not last for long. The magistrates, the ministers, the men of the colony would soon find them, and their innocence would be gone, like the rainbow we had seen just a few days earlier over the western hills. I would like to have seized that rainbow and held it to me to give us hope. If I were God, that is just what I would have done. I would have given my people rainbows that they could hold and know that better things would lie ahead.

Mary had found herself a rainbow, a special warmth in her heart for a God who loved her as she loved him. What did it get her, though, but separation from her husband and children, and now the gallows? There was no rainbow that cloudless spring day, no warmth in my heart, though the day was warm. I felt only a bitter coldness and saw only a pitiless sun with no hint of clouds or rain or rainbows. I carried with me the pain of the pillory and the horror of the gallows, nothing more. If Mary found more, she was a better woman than I was. I knew that to be so.

Meanwhile I had my children, my two girls to care for. The Reverend Wilson would soon be seeking me in the prison and finding me flown. I wondered how Thomas would explain my absence and even how he had managed my escape. It would go hard on him this time, and I gave him silent thanks for my delivery. He was a good and brave man after all.

Early in the morning Abigail came by on her way back to Rhode Island. "There is freedom there," she said. "Quakers, Catholics, Jews, even the Indians—all of us worship as we please. Our life is harsh, but we are allowed to freely worship. Come with us, Chastity. Thou would make a good Quaker, as I said before."

I asked the girls if they wished to leave. "If you go," they said without hesitation.

I thought about it for a time. Abigail was my friend, and I longed to be with her. But she was, like Mary, driven by something I couldn't understand. Whatever it was, it took Mary from her family, leaving them bereft of wife and mother as she went to her death in Boston.

So, finally, I said, "No, Abigail, I thank you for the offer. This is my home, and this is where I'll stay."

"God give thee peace in thy heart then," she said, "and keep thee from harm." She came over and kissed me on the cheek.

"Goodbye, Chastity. We may not meet again in this world. But in the next…" She didn't finish her thought.

We waved goodbye and went back to work. We had no time for John Wilson and the magistrates. Our guests needed food and drink, and that is what we did. That was our work in this life, and we would do it as long as we could. John Wilson would need to wait.

We talked no more of Wilson, and neither he nor his constables ever came for us. Gradually, we forgot him. I paid no more visits to Boston and forbade the girls from ever going there as well. I heard that Wilson had become deathly sick, a fever having struck him down not long after Mary's hanging. A young woman, who professed herself a Quaker, told me when passing through that it was God's judgment on him for his many cruelties. Perhaps it was, but the punishment was so long delayed that it seemed no punishment at all. Too many innocent men and women had died waiting for deliverance. Where was that punishment when they needed it? If God so loved his children, as Mary claimed, he should have saved them from the unspeakable cruelty they faced. Mother and Father, Mary and her Quaker friends, Abigail, all of them.

Well, it wasn't long before my girls found young men who fancied them, and they both left me for western lands. They sent letters now and then, telling me of their joyful lives. I hoped it was so.

Some years later I heard that John Wilson had died. There was a great outpouring of grief at his burial. It brought me no joy that he was finally gone and could harm no more women. I had no more joy or sorrow to waste on him.

I hired two more girls, bouncy, happy children, to help me with the work. It was harder for me now, but I managed, as I always had, on my own.

I would bow my head no more to any man or god. And I didn't—ever again.

AFTERWORD

Smoke and flames burst from the schoolhouse, sending over a dozen desperate young girls out of the burning building. Outside and seemingly safe, they were met by the religious police, who forced them back into the raging inferno. The girls, fourteen of them, perished in the flames. The question arose quickly: what in their behavior so troubled the police? The answer came just as quickly: in their haste to escape the fire, the girls had neglected to put on their scarves and were thus immodestly showing their hair.

This horrifying episode didn't occur in the distant and barbarous Middle Ages. It happened a few years ago, and it's only one of many such incidents occurring daily in countries around the world.

This episode was in Saudi Arabia, but it might have been in Afghanistan, except in that country under the very strict Taliban rule, the girls wouldn't have been allowed to attend school—or anything else for that matter. Many of them, in fact, would have already been married in a country where a recent report estimated that almost sixty percent of the girls younger than sixteen are already married, some of them being as young as seven or eight years of age. These girls might have been married off by their parents in arranged marriages, or they might have been abducted and forced into marriage, or a sexual relationship, by men thirty or forty years their seniors. They would then become virtual prisoners inside their houses, unable to visit their parents and friends and subjected to whatever pain and abuse their masters might subject them to.

That abuse might come from any male and for any infraction of sharia, the strict religious code enforced in Islamic countries. If these girls, or older women, married or not, might decide to paint their fingernails, for example, they risked having their nails forcibly pulled out as punishment; if they lived in Iran, they would be subjected to seventy-four strokes of the lash, the precise amount the Iranian constitution requires for such infractions. If any of these girls or women tried to escape from their prisons to visit their families, they would be rejected and sent back to more abuse from their owners, which might be anything from having acid poured on them to severe flogging.

And if, by chance, these young women were observed being innocently friendly to another man—or worse, accused of committing adultery—their fate would be clearly defined in religious law: they would be buried up to their chests and then stoned to death, the stones according to law being of the right size—that is, not so big as to cause immediate death, but not so small as to not inflict death over a certain length of time. (Men committing adultery would be buried only up to their waist, thus making it easier to escape, in which case the charges would be dropped.)

If these women should have protested their arranged marriage and chosen their own husband, or if they were not virgins when they married, even if they had been gang raped, they risked being murdered by their own relatives, perhaps a father or brother, in an honor killing designed to protect the family's good name.

These examples of almost unbelievable human cruelty occur in theocracies around the world—societies in which religious authorities write the law, determine its application, and ultimately inflict the punishment for its violation. Pick up a daily newspaper or weekly newsmagazine and you will be assaulted with stories of theocracies in action. It is not pleasant reading.

Not long ago, an Afghan man who had converted to Christianity sixteen years earlier was sentenced to death for apostasy from the Muslim faith. No one in his country—not the government, not the citizens, not even his own family—protested the punishment, which strict interpretation of Islamic law requires. The man, fortunately, was able to flee his country and was granted asylum in Italy.

Americans reading today of such cruelty may have convinced themselves that these barbarisms occur only in other lands far distant from ours. These readers might also convince themselves that such behavior has never occurred in this country since its beginning in the early seventeenth century, because, after all, we've never been a theocracy.

But these Americans would be wrong, very wrong, because the treatment of women in fundamentalist Islamic countries today is not so different from what the average woman faced in the Massachusetts Bay Colony, a very Christian theocracy uniting church and state in an unholy alliance that made life for women similar to that in Iran, Saudi Arabia, or Afghanistan when the Taliban were in power.

It was, after all, in a Christian theocracy that twelve women and seven men were hanged—one man being pressed to death—in Salem, Massachusetts, in 1692, their crimes no more than being suspected of witchcraft.

Those troubled today with the required punishment of the Afghan convert should remember that in the seventeenth-century Massachusetts colony, men and women were branded, their tongues bored with hot irons, and their ears cut off for differing religious views. In a few cases, they were actually hanged for the same kind of apostasy that the Afghan man faced. Their crimes, in these cases, consisted of calling themselves Quakers and thus believing and worshipping differently from the Puritan Congregational authorities.

Now it should be said in fairness to our New England ancestors that the early colonies such as Massachusetts Bay were not, strictly speaking, theocracies. The General Court in Massachusetts, which acted as both a legislative and a judicial body, was composed of laymen, not clerics. Still, the clerics advised the laymen (including both the governor and deputy governor) on making the laws, which generally conformed to their literalist reading of the Bible. If the Bible said "Suffer not a witch to live," then killing the alleged witches was clearly mandated by the law.

The men ruling the colony were Puritans and very religious men, Calvinist in thought, who wished to purify the English Anglican Church from which they had recently escaped. They desired freedom to worship as they pleased, but that never meant granting their own citizens the same freedom. The Puritans' God was a wrathful Old Testament God, easily angered, and while he granted them safe passage to the New World to build their city on the hill in Boston, he would just as easily strike them down if they disobeyed his commandments.

So while Massachusetts, strictly speaking, was not a theocracy, church and state were in reality only nominally separated. And it was the women who most felt the burden of living in the male-dominated theocracy, just as they do in modern theocracies. Though Puritan women fared much better than, for example, Afghan women, being seen equal with men as children of God, they nevertheless were severely restricted in many ways. They were, after all, descendents of the first mother, Eve, who in her weakness had determined the fate of all succeeding women. These Puritan women could not vote or serve on the courts, no matter how knowledgeable or bright they might be, though their teen-age sons, by virtue of their maleness and perhaps little else, could and did vote for their representatives on the various courts. (It was almost three hundred years before American women would win those same rights.)

Though Puritan women had much greater freedom to travel without their husbands or other males, they still had to cover their hair, the symbol of their seductiveness (think of the Afghan women shrouded from head to foot in their burkas). And though the Puritan women had more freedom in finding a husband, they still could not defy their fathers in their selection, because it was his duty as head and protector of the family to at least approve, if not select, the husband.

Most seriously, though, if they should commit adultery (proscribed in Scripture), they were committing a capital offense. Though the law was seldom enforced, and though it was carried out by hanging rather than being buried and stoned, that fact would have been small comfort to those found guilty and hanged. Here again, though, there was a double standard. It made no difference if the married woman's adultery was with a married or single man; the punishment in either case was death. But a married man having sexual intercourse with an unmarried woman was guilty of fornication, a lesser offense punished by a fine or whipping.

There is much to despair about in our early history, since the treatment of women, to say nothing of the institution of slavery, was often just as shameful as anything found recently in Islamic countries. We should be wary, however, to think that those days are dead and buried. A number of observers today, noting the powerful influence of fundamentalist Christianity on national and local governance, believe that we are moving steadily in the direction of another Christian theocracy, and that all that protects us is the Constitution, with its clear separation of church and state, and over two hundred years of living in a liberal democracy.

Chastity Hoar, the fictional narrator of this memoir of her life in the early seventeenth-century Bay Colony, knows nothing of Islamic fundamentalism and its treatment of women. But she knows all too much about Christian fundamentalism, because not a day goes by that she and her family don't experience it firsthand. What she faces not only could have happened, it did happen to countless men and women. Trial testimonies from the time show the women suffering from the kinds of abuses that Muslim women face today, and though that pain, on the whole, was not nearly as bad as what Muslim women under the Taliban faced (and still face), it was bad enough that it should cause a bit of humility as we remember the early days of our country.

Chastity meets many women in Boston; most of them are fictional, but living the lives that real Boston women faced every day. Some of the women that she meets, however—Anne Hutchinson and Mary Dyer, for example—were actual women whose lives were much as she describes them.

A word might be said about John Wilson, the pastor of Boston's First Church in Chastity's story. Hawthorne in *The Scarlet Letter* shows him to be a kind and compassionate man. That is Hawthorne's view, and there is, very likely, some truth to that picture. But any man who exalts in women's miscarriages and deaths, as he did, along with his fellow clerics—all of them claiming that the miscarriages and deaths were God's punishments meted out for the women's erroneous and deformed opinions—is quite capable of being the man who in Chastity's story becomes her chief antagonist.

Life in any century is never entirely bleak. Every generation and every people produce individuals whose courage and lives provide beacons of hope for their people and future generations. Anne Hutchinson and Mary Dyer were just such individuals, and their statues at the Boston statehouse today are testaments to their courageous lives.

My fictional Chastity Hoar, from a much meaner background, has virtually none of the resources or support those two women had in facing life in that male-dominated colony. But I would like to think that Chastity, in her own humble but feisty way, still provides a beacon to those around her. Perhaps she might receive, from those reading her story, her own kind of statue on whatever pedestals we erect in our minds for such individuals.

George Evans
Forest Grove, Oregon
June 2006